"You Yankee Cad!"

"How dare you besmirch Southern womanhood with your Northern indecency? How dare you sully my daughter? Do you have anything to say for yourself, you Yankee swine?"

"Y-yes, sir!" Tyler stammered. "I only took off my suit-coat and lent it to Sarah last night because she was cold. I didn't mean a thing by it, sir."

"What are you talking about?" Beauregard yelled. "It's what you did to Vallen that concerns me, you good-for-nothing Yank!"

Vallen threw herself into her father's arms, looking up at him with a helpless expression. "Oh, Papa, I don't know if I can face marrying him."

"What?" Tyler yelped.

"'Course you'll marry him," Beau snapped. Turning to Tyler, he said, "Get dressed, Mr. Adams. I'll expect you downstairs in fifteen minutes to discuss the wedding."

Dear Reader,

Evelyn A. Crowe's legion of fans will be delighted to learn that she has penned our Women Who Dare title for November. In *Reunited,* gutsy investigative reporter Sydney Tanner learns way more than she bargained for about rising young congressman J. D. Fowler. Generational family feuds, a long-ago murder and a touch of blackmail are only a few of the surprises in store for Sydney—and you—as the significance of the heroine's discoveries begins to shape this riveting tale.

Popular Superromance author Sharon Brondos has contributed our final Woman Who Dare title for 1993. In *Doc Wyoming,* taciturn sheriff Hal Blane wants nothing to do with a citified female doctor. But Dixie Sheldon becomes involved with Blane's infamous family in spite of herself, and her "sentence" in Wyoming is commuted to a romance of the American West.

More Women Who Dare titles will be coming your way in 1994. Patricia Chandler and Tracy Hughes have two great, daring stories lined up for you in the spring. And watch for titles by Vicki Lewis Thompson, Margaret Chittenden and Margot Dalton this month and next as we begin to draw the curtain on '93!

Marsha Zinberg,
Senior Editor

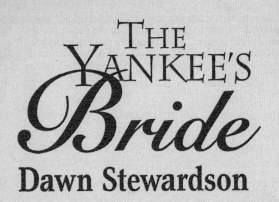

THE YANKEE'S Bride

Dawn Stewardson

Harlequin Books

TORONTO • NEW YORK • LONDON
AMSTERDAM • PARIS • SYDNEY • HAMBURG
STOCKHOLM • ATHENS • TOKYO • MILAN
MADRID • WARSAW • BUDAPEST • AUCKLAND

ISBN 0-373-70571-9

THE YANKEE'S BRIDE

Copyright © 1993 by Dawn Stewardson.

ABOUT THE AUTHOR

Dawn's time-travel Superromance novels have proven to be a hit with readers. Her first, *Blue Moon,* won a Special Achievement award from *Romantic Times* magazine and her second, *Moon Shadow,* won the Golden Leaf award from the Romance Writers of America. *The Yankee's Bride,* the third book in the series, is a rollicking adventure in the past that readers will be sure to enjoy.

Dawn lives in Toronto with her husband, John, two dogs and a cat.

Books by Dawn Stewardson

HARLEQUIN SUPERROMANCE

Don't miss any of our special offers. Write to us at the following address for information on our newest releases.

Harlequin Reader Service
P.O. Box 1397, Buffalo, NY 14240
Canadian address: P.O. Box 603,
Fort Erie, Ont. L2A 5X3

To the readers of *Blue Moon* and *Moon Shadow*
who asked for more.
To Brenda Chin,
for all her work on this manuscript.
And to John, always.

CHAPTER ONE

"THAT'S IT," Clayton said, gesturing toward the side of the road.

"*What's* it?" Tyler demanded. The headlights were picking up nothing but a dark ruin, shrouded by the blackness of a sultry Georgia night.

"Over there...see?"

Tyler pulled Clayton's Ferrari to a halt, wishing to hell he was back in Manhattan with a cold beer.

There were few things in the world he loved more than a good game of poker. But Clayton Willis was drunk. And if he figured there was a poker game going on in that ruin, he was also a few cotton bales short of a load. A meeting of a witches' coven, maybe, but not a poker game. Hopping that plane tonight hadn't been a good move.

Clayton might have been his client for several years, but aside from the odd meeting in New York, they'd simply conducted business over the phone. From the looks of things, though, Clayton was one weird guy.

Tyler had barely made it from Savannah International Airport to the plantation before Clayton had started in about this game.

"How about," he'd asked Tyler, "we drop in on a real Old Southern-style poker game. I know where there's one every Friday night. And it would prime us for *my* game, tomorrow.''

Well, it had seemed like a great idea at the time. That is, until Clayton had hauled the Civil War-era suits out of his closet and handed Tyler a stack of ancient State of Georgia money.

That was when Tyler should have put an abrupt stop to Clayton's game. Dressing up in strange clothes to play poker for funny money definitely wasn't his scene.

And if it turned out Clayton and his friends had more in mind than just dress-up...well, he'd make it damned clear he wasn't into any of that kinky stuff. Bad enough it was early August and he looked like he was ready for Halloween.

He spotted a widening on the shoulder and pulled the Ferrari to a halt.

''That ruin useta be another plantation house,'' Clayton offered, pulling a flashlight from the glove compartment. ''Got burned down during the war. Winter of 1864 to '65, when Savannah fell to Sherman. Come on.''

''Clayton,'' Tyler said. But Clayton was already out of the car and unsteadily making his way across the rough ground.

''Dammit,'' Tyler muttered, reluctantly opening his own door to follow his inebriated host. Clayton might be an important client, but that didn't give him the right to dress him up like an escapee from the set of *Gone With the Wind* and drag him out into the middle of nowhere.

Tyler trudged after Clayton, sweat pouring down his back and collecting under the band of his stupid top hat. New York had been hot, but Georgia was so muggy it was tough to breathe. Exactly the kind of night a guy wanted to be wandering around in a wool suit with an old-fashioned jacket that reached his knees.

Clayton waved the flashlight around unsteadily as the two of them picked their way around the side of the burned-out house and stopped at what would have been the back porch. Now it was nothing but a few scorched and weathered pieces of board.

"Okay," Clayton said. He aimed the light at a charred wooden door lying flat amidst the rubble. "All we have to do is lift that. It leads to the root cellar."

Tyler considered asking why the hell they cared about the root cellar, but decided not to. He'd probably get out of here faster if he just went along with this. And since Clayton wasn't making any move toward the door, Tyler went over and wrestled it open.

Sure enough, the flashlight revealed rickety stairs leading down into the ground.

"What now?" Tyler said.

"Now we go down, of course."

"Of course," Tyler said. "How stupid of me." He started down the ancient stairs after his host.

Clayton made it about halfway down before he missed a step. With a thud, he landed on the dirt floor. The flashlight smacked against the ground and promptly went out.

"Damn," Clayton said. "Oh, well. Doesn't matter, anyway. Close the door, will you?"

Tyler had to think about that for a minute. He was only prepared to humor Clayton so far, and they'd just about reached the limit.

Against his better judgment, he finally stretched up and pulled the door down, plunging them into absolute darkness. "Now what?" he demanded, carefully feeling his way down the stairs.

"Now we wait," Clayton said.

Dammit, that *was* the limit. "Wait for what? What the hell are we doing here?"

"Shh...we'll be at the poker game in no time."

Tyler stood gazing into black space. If he could *see* Clayton, he just might wring his neck. This was the most insane thing that had—

Suddenly, Tyler felt something seize him. Although nothing was physically touching him, he felt like he was being shaken from head to toe. It was like a psychic jolt passing through his body, and it scared the hell out of him.

"Okay, that's it," Clayton announced calmly. "We can go up again."

Tyler didn't say a word, just climbed back to the top of the shaky stairs, shoved the door open, stepped out into the steamy night...and got the shock of his life.

The burned-out ruin had suddenly become a mansion, with pale light glimmering from some of the windows. And he was standing on its perfectly maintained back porch.

In disbelief, he turned to Clayton, who was unsteadily climbing out of the cellar.

Clayton put a finger to his lips and shook his head. "Later," he whispered, brushing dirt from his suit. "First we have to sneak inside." He started quietly along the porch toward the kitchen door.

For a moment Tyler just stood there, his mind racing. Clayton was playing an enormous practical joke.

That had to be it. The crazy clothes, the trip to the ruin—maybe even his drunkenness was all an act.

And somehow the root cellar had moved, transporting them to wherever they were now. But why hadn't he felt any motion?

"Come on," Clayton hissed from the door.

Silently, Tyler followed him into the mansion and through to the front foyer, not quite believing the differences a few minutes had made. The stairs ran up the side wall, rather than from the center of the foyer like the ones at Clayton's plantation house. And the decor of this place was old-fashioned. Looking up, he noticed that even the damned lights weren't electric. There were candles where the light bulbs should have been.

Clayton paused at the sweeping staircase, carefully smoothed back his blond hair, then hollered, "Joseph?"

Moments later, a middle-aged black man came barreling down from the second floor, dressed in a white shirt and knee-length breeches with long dark socks and shoes.

"Welcome back, Master Willis," he said from halfway down the staircase. "Didn't hear no carriage or I'd a come runnin'. Don't know how you does it. I don't never hear no carriage when you come from the train station."

"That's all right, Joseph," Clayton said. "Just hitch up one of the horses. Mr. Adams here and I are going to Booker's Knoll for a little poker."

"Yes, sir, Master Willis." Joseph dashed out the front door.

"Booker's Knoll?" Tyler said to Clayton. "But that's the name of *your* plantation."

"Uh-huh. At least, in 1993 it's my plantation. Right now, though, it's still owned by the man who built it—Beauregard Booker."

"Right now?" Tyler echoed.

"Uh-huh. Right now in 1850."

"WE'RE ALMOST THERE," Clayton said above the clatter of the horses' hooves.

Tyler nodded, gazing past the front of the buggy at the bay mare. She was trotting evenly along—nothing unusual in *her* world. But in his...

Clayton had sobered up some, yet the story he'd just told Tyler *had* to be the product of a drunken fantasy. People couldn't actually travel through time.

But if that wasn't what they'd just done, then Clayton was perpetrating the most elaborate hoax in history.

"Let me make sure I've got this straight," Tyler tried. "You're saying you've been doing this for years? And you still don't understand how it works?"

"Right. When I first discovered the root cellar, I thought I was hallucinating. But, somehow, that cellar can move people through 143 years. The first time, I left 1989 and found myself in 1846. Now it's 1993 back there and 1850 here."

"But that servant, Joseph..."

"Slave. This is 1850 Georgia. Joseph is one of Beauregard Booker's slaves."

"Okay...slave. But he called you Master Willis and acted as if you belonged. How can he think you live here when you actually live in 1993?"

"Well, it's kind of complicated."

"That's an understatement," Tyler muttered.

Clayton grinned, then went on. "See, the ruin used to be the plantation house next to Booker's Knoll. Then Beauregard Booker bought the property. He intended to give it to his eldest daughter, Ella-Jane, when she married but . . . well, that's another story."

Something in Clayton's tone told Tyler it was a story he didn't want to get into.

"At any rate," Clayton continued, "the house was furnished but unoccupied. So, when I discovered that I could travel back and forth through time, I rented it from Beau. Told him I was a traveling man needing a residence near Savannah. And I've just been coming and going ever since."

"And no one's gotten suspicious?"

"Well, Joseph knows something's up, but he's smart enough not to ask any questions. If Beau hadn't made him caretaker, Joseph would still be living in the slave quarters."

Clayton flicked the reins and turned off the dirt road onto a tree-lined drive.

The moon had risen, bathing the plantation house before them in silver. It sat on an enormous sweep of lawn, looking like a Grecian temple exiled to southern Georgia.

Tyler stared at it, his heart pounding. There really *was* a twilight zone. Straight ahead was the same mansion he'd arrived at earlier tonight—by cab, from Savannah International.

The landscaping had been different then. And now, soft light was glowing from the house, not harsh electric light. But it was the same place. The same place in a different time.

No one could perpetrate a hoax of this magnitude, no matter how wealthy he was. So Tyler was stuck with the only other possible explanation. Unbelievable as it seemed, he was actually in 1850.

Looking ahead, Tyler saw three young women sitting on the pillared veranda, watching the buggy approach. He looked at Clayton for an explanation.

"Beauregard's a widower with three daughters," Clayton said. "The younger two live here with him. The eldest visits a lot, but she lives in Savannah now. She's married to a rich old git by the name of Ewell Endicott."

Tyler nodded. Seeing them sitting there in the moonlight made him realize just how real the situation was.

He'd been trying to convince himself that Joseph could have been a figment of his imagination, but he doubted his imagination was good enough to have dreamed up three women who looked like these ones.

They were all pretty, but one of them was positively ethereal. She was sitting directly in front of a window, the soft light from within creating an aura around her. She looked like an angel in a long white dress.

Her silky dark hair was piled up on her head, and her pale, creamy skin glowed. She had, he realized as the carriage drew closer yet, the most luscious lips he'd ever seen.

Clayton reined the bay to a halt in front of the house and swung down to the ground.

Tyler followed suit, hoping he looked like he knew what he was doing. The only horse-drawn carriage he'd ever ridden in was a hansom in Central Park.

Clayton removed his top hat as they reached the veranda. Tyler immediately did the same, starting to feel as if he'd joined a game of monkey-see, monkey-do.

"Clayton," one of the women said softly. "Papa will be so pleased to see you." She rose from her wicker chair and walked toward them, holding her long skirt up a little so it didn't trail. When she reached Clayton, she took both his hands in hers for a second.

Tyler thought he saw Clayton stiffen.

"Ella-Jane," he said. He sounded reasonably sober but not the least bit at ease. "I guess your husband is inside playing poker."

Ella-Jane nodded.

"Well, I'd like to present a friend who's visiting from New York. Mr. Tyler Adams. Tyler, this is Mrs. Ewell Endicott."

"Ella-Jane," she said quietly to Tyler.

He nodded politely.

"And her sisters," Clayton added, gesturing toward the women who had remained seated. "Miss Vallen . . . and Miss Sarah."

Sarah. The angelic one's name was Sarah. Tyler smiled at them both, trying not to focus too much on Sarah, but it was impossible. Up close, he could see her eyes were the deep, dark brown of melted chocolate.

It wasn't until she shyly lowered her long lashes that he realized he'd been staring.

"Why, Clayton Willis," the other sister, Vallen, said, rising and walking over. "You should have come earlier. For dinner. We would have been delighted to offer your friend some Southern hospitality."

Vallen was speaking to Clayton but looking, Tyler realized, directly at him. Catching his eyes, she gave him a smile that made the word *barracuda* pop into his mind.

No, he must have just imagined that come-hither look. As far as he knew, Southern women in 1850 had been the epitome of prim and proper gentility.

He glanced at Clayton, who was eyeing Vallen curiously.

"Your *fiancé* not here tonight, Vallen?" Clayton asked.

Tyler was certain he hadn't imagined the glare she shot at Clayton in response.

"Thought Fitzhugh always made the Friday games," Clayton pressed.

"He happens to be busy tonight," Vallen snapped. Then, focusing on Tyler once more, she manufactured another smile. "But you must find the evening stifling, Mr. Adams, coming from up North and all. Would you like some refreshment? Cold lemonade, perhaps? Or iced wintergreen tea?"

Tyler glanced at Clayton again, feeling more uncomfortable by the second. Suddenly, they were blessedly interrupted by a deep booming voice.

"Lord Almighty! If it isn't my wandering neighbor come to join us."

A bear of a middle-aged man stood in the doorway, grinning at Clayton. He had a mane of white hair, a full white beard, and was wearing a white suit. He put Tyler in mind of a larger and younger version of Colonel Sanders, of Kentucky Fried Chicken fame.

"I was *hoping* you'd have a poker game going, Beau," Clayton said as they shook hands.

"Hell, it's Friday, isn't it?" Beau said. "And we can always use fresh money. Fitzhugh didn't make it tonight. There's only Ewell here, and a fellow from out West.

Clayton introduced Tyler, and Beauregard's grin grew wider. "Can always use Yankee money, too, son. Come in, come in. We just barely got the game underway."

Tyler followed Clayton and Beauregard to the doorway, then paused. Looking into the foyer gave him an eerie sensation.

The decor was different, but he'd stood in this very mansion in 1993. He recognized the sweeping central staircase and the stone fireplace that dominated the wall on his left. And beneath a large oriental carpet was the same dark polished wooden floor. The Civil War obviously hadn't devastated Booker's Knoll the way it had the neighboring plantation house.

He glanced back across the veranda and caught Sarah watching him. The guilty blush that crossed her face fascinated him. It almost made him want to pass on the poker game.

Startled, Sarah looked away, but she wasn't fast enough. That Yankee had spotted her staring at him, and she could feel her cheeks burning.

Whatever had come over her? She wasn't normally the least bit bold. But then again, Tyler Adams was, without a doubt, the most gorgeous man she'd ever seen—Yankee or not.

He had broad shoulders, an even nose and strong, white teeth. His eyes were the same beautiful slate blue as his cravat, and he was *so* tall—taller even than Papa. Perhaps even a tad taller than Clayton Willis.

She forced her thoughts from Tyler Adams and glanced worriedly at Ella-Jane. Sure enough, she had that sad look in her eyes that she always got when she saw Clayton. At the moment, though, it was tempered by flickering annoyance.

"Vallen," she was saying sternly, "why were you making a spectacle of yourself over Mr. Adams?"

Vallen turned on Ella-Jane with a look of wide-eyed innocence. "I wasn't doing any such thing. I just couldn't help thinking that whatever they feed their men up North, we should be feeding ours down here. Ella-Jane, come walk with me for a minute. I've got a little idea in my head that I need to talk to you about."

"Sarah?" Ella-Jane said, smiling over. "Do you feel like a walk?"

"No, no," Vallen snapped. "Just you, Ella-Jane. Sarah wouldn't understand."

"Vallen . . ." Ella-Jane said disapprovingly, the way she always did when Vallen was being thoughtless.

"It's fine," Sarah said quickly. "I'd like to sit awhile longer, anyway."

She watched her sisters head off across the lawn, without any hurt feelings. At twenty-three, she was three years younger than Vallen and four younger than Ella-Jane. The two eldest had grown up together, while she'd been the tagalong baby. So she was used to them thinking of her as the little sister who didn't understand everything the way they did.

Not that she believed it was true. She'd graduated from the Chatham Academy, and she knew more than they gave her credit for. But whatever Vallen was up to, it was usually better not to get involved. And whatever this particular scheme was about...Sarah gazed uneasily after Ella-Jane and Vallen.

Ella-Jane had been perfectly right. Vallen *had* made a spectacle of herself over Mr. Adams. Sarah hadn't missed those coquettish glances.

And from what Vallen had said, it wasn't difficult to surmise that whatever idea she had in her head involved their Yankee guest.

Sarah looked through the window into the gaming room, her eyes immediately finding Tyler Adams. He was already seated at the poker table, concentrating on his cards. A lock of his straight brown hair had fallen across his forehead in a most dashing way.

She'd heard about men who made a woman's heart go pitter-pat, but she'd never before met one who'd made *hers* do anything thing out of the ordinary. So it was a little disconcerting when her heart had begun fluttering the minute she laid eyes on Tyler Adams.

Not that she had any real interest in him. After all, he was a Yankee, the furthest thing possible from a Southern gentleman.

No, she wasn't interested. She just didn't like the thought of her sister setting her sights on Mr. Adams.

Vallen had no place setting her sights on *any* man. She already *had* a fiancé. Heavens, her wedding was only two weeks off, so some of the out-of-town guests were already on their way to Savannah.

Of course, Vallen didn't like her fiancé very much. She'd only agreed to marry Fitzhugh Farnsworth to pacify Papa. But she *had* agreed.

And that was the way things happened sometimes—just as it had happened with Ella-Jane. She hadn't wanted to marry crotchety old Ewell Endicott, but Papa had finally insisted.

Vallen was different from Ella-Jane, though. Vallen was far more stubborn. She wasn't accustomed to doing anything she didn't want to do. And she *didn't* want to marry Fitzhugh Farnsworth two weeks from now. She'd probably rather marry just about anyone else.

Sarah glanced at Tyler Adams once more, feeling strangely unsettled. Then, in the window, she noticed the reflection of her sisters coming back to the house. They were walking slowly across the lawn, immersed in conversation.

"I don't like it," Ella-Jane murmured, her voice drifting through the still night air.

"But you *must* understand," Vallen said. "Having had to marry Ewell, you've got to understand why I want to do it."

"I do…and I sympathize with you. I wouldn't want to marry Fitzhugh, either. But you've seen what Clayton's been doing to himself. Every time he comes to play poker he's half inebriated. It was obvious he'd already been drinking tonight. And I just don't want any part of—"

"But it's perfect, Ella-Jane. The perfect plan. And it would only take a few extra drinks."

"Well . . ." Ella-Jane said reluctantly.

"It's settled then. Come on. We'll go right in and tell Louis that Papa said he should be serving Mr. Willis his drinks faster."

Vallen and Ella-Jane swept across the veranda and into the house.

Sarah couldn't hold back a tiny sigh of relief. She wasn't sure why it made her feel better, but she was glad to hear that whatever Vallen was plotting didn't involve Tyler Adams, after all.

CHAPTER TWO

TYLER FOLDED, glad he was only playing with a stack of Clayton's funny money—currency issued almost a hundred and fifty years ago by the Merchants Planters Bank, State of Georgia.

He didn't normally lose at poker, but he just hadn't been able to keep his mind on the game tonight.

Stepping into the past must have caused that. Or maybe it was the distraction of these characters he was playing with.

His poker buddies at home were all regular guys. But Beauregard Booker and Ella-Jane's husband, Ewell Endicott, were a couple of *irregulars*.

Beauregard clearly was an autocratic law unto himself at Booker's Knoll. The backslapping type who smiled a lot, yet somehow let you know you'd regret crossing him.

In contrast, his son-in-law, Ewell Endicott, seemed to have a permanent scowl. He was an old stork of a man who'd spent the entire evening frowning over his beaky nose at his cards.

Tall, skinny and extremely pale, Ewell couldn't be more than a few years younger than Beauregard. A rich old git, Clayton had said earlier.

But how Ewell Endicott, no matter how wealthy he was, had managed to snag a young wife as pretty as

Ella-Jane was a question to ask Clayton later. One of about a million questions.

The final player was a fellow who'd apparently just shown up at the plantation earlier in the day. John McCully was about Clayton's age, a few years older than Tyler. And, as Beauregard had put it, John was *almost kin.*

No one had met him before. But the story was that Ella-Jane's best childhood friend had married a McCully from Nevada. And John was that man's cousin.

Beyond that, John McCully was a mystery. About all he'd volunteered was that he'd recently been working on a ranch in Arizona.

"So, John," Tyler asked while they waited for Ewell Endicott to bid, "you planning on staying around Savannah for long?"

John thought about the question for a minute, then shrugged. "Depends. I'd like to stay a week or so, but I'd have to find work. I was hoping there'd be a job available."

"My company doesn't need a man right now," Ewell put in quickly.

John nodded, and Ewell went back to studying his hand. Despite his frown, he finally raised the bet.

On the far side of the table, Louis, the elderly house servant or slave or whatever he was, arrived with yet another drink for Clayton.

Tyler unsuccessfully tried to catch Clayton's eye. The fresh air, on their drive here, had gone a long way toward sobering Clayton up. But now, with Louis serving the bourbon fast and furiously, it was a wonder Clayton was still conscious. And the last thing in the world Tyler wanted was to find himself driving that horse and buggy back to the other house in the middle of the night.

Clayton took a long sip of the bourbon, set the glass down beside his stack of money, then sat gazing bleary-eyed at his cards.

"See your raise, Ewell, and up you another ten," Beauregard said, throwing more bills into the pot.

The others glanced expectantly at Clayton.

"Clayton?" Beauregard said at last.

Clayton's response was to slowly slide down his chair and crumple into a heap beneath the table.

Tyler groaned silently. It looked as if he'd be driving that damn contraption, after all.

Beauregard nonchalantly bent down and retrieved Clayton's cards. "Straight flush, king high," he announced. "Clayton would have bet on that for sure. Anyone got it beat?"

John shook his head, and Ewell muttered something about lucky drunks.

Beauregard told Louis to pick Mr. Willis up off the floor, then cheerfully collected Clayton's winnings and handed them to Tyler. "Give him this tomorrow," he said. Then glancing around the table, he added, "Well, I guess it's time to call it a night, gentlemen."

"You mind if Ella-Jane and I stay over?" Ewell asked. "You know how I hate driving back to Savannah this late."

"'Course not, 'course not," Beau said. "I like it when all of my girls are around the breakfast table again. And *you* won't be wanting to go till morning," he added, turning to Tyler. "You won't want to be driving a strange road in the dark."

"Ah..." He tried to decide which idea he liked least. Trying that drive back to the root cellar or having to stay in 1850 until morning. He didn't like the thought of either, but there didn't seem to be a third alternative.

Before he'd decided which was the lesser of the two evils, Beauregard said to Louis, "You tend to Mr. Willis for us. Then show Mr. Adams to a guest room.

"'Fraid the place only has six bedrooms, son," Beau went on, turning to John McCully. "But you're welcome to bunk out in the stable with your horse."

"Thanks," John said. "It won't be the first time."

"Good, then we're organized."

Tyler stood rubbing his jaw as the group dispersed. Visiting 1850 had been the experience of a lifetime, but there was something about staying overnight that made him damned uneasy.

He watched John head out to the stable while Ewell collected Ella-Jane from the veranda.

Vallen came in with them, and they all murmured good-nights, then disappeared upstairs.

Tyler waited uncertainly in the foyer. He should probably hang in down here to say good-night to Beauregard, but he wasn't sure where his host had gone. Or maybe he should be helping Louis with the unconscious Clayton.

"Did you enjoy the poker game?" a woman asked softly, startling him.

It was, he realized, the first time he'd heard Sarah speak. She'd merely nodded when they'd been introduced. But he knew that velvet voice was hers. He glanced toward the front door.

She was a tiny little thing, he thought. She couldn't be much more than five feet tall. Tiny but perfect.

Framed in the doorway, wearing her high-necked, long-sleeved white dress, she was a portrait of beauty.

"The game," he repeated. "Ah . . . yes, I did enjoy the game. But I guess Clayton enjoyed it a little too much."

"Louis will take good care of him," she said, glancing across the foyer.

Tyler's glance followed hers. Louis's *good care* involved dragging Clayton unceremoniously to the stairs.

"Can I give you a hand?" Tyler asked Louis.

"No, sir. You wait right there. I'll be back down in a minute. Show you to your room then."

"It's all right, Louis," Sarah told him. "You just attend to Mr. Willis. Put him in the yellow guest room. I'll show Mr. Adams to the blue room. And, Louis, how has Millie been feeling tonight?"

"About the same, Miss Sarah."

Sarah smiled at the old man. "Well, you tell her I'll read to her for a while tomorrow if she'd like."

Tyler stood gazing at Sarah as she spoke, reminding himself that none of this evening was real—including her. But real or not, it was absolutely fascinating—especially her.

"Would you like a little fresh air before you retire?" she said.

"A little fresh air . . . yes. Yes, that would be nice."

She turned and stepped back outside. Tyler followed her out into the night.

"Shall we walk?" she said, taking a lacy shawl from the back of a chair and starting off across the lawn.

It wasn't long past the full moon, and the night was bathed in silver. A cooling breeze had come up, and Tyler doubted either that lacy shawl or the cotton dress Sarah was wearing were keeping her warm.

Back in New York, he'd have offered her his jacket. But here, the men seemed to stay overdressed all the time—even at the poker table. Maybe taking off his suit coat would be considered inappropriate in 1850 Georgia.

Sarah smiled at him—a smile that almost stopped his breathing. He hadn't imagined it earlier. She definitely *did* have the most luscious lips he'd ever seen.

"This is one of my favorite spots," she said, pausing under a huge tree. "Do you have magnolia trees in New York?"

"Not many. We don't have many trees at all, outside of the parks. You've never been to New York, then?"

"No, I've never been farther north than Atlanta. It must be interesting to travel a lot. I envy Clayton—he's almost never home. But how long will you be staying with him?"

"Not long at all. I have to be back to work on Monday."

For a moment, there was a question in Sarah's eyes, and then she gave a delightful little laugh. "And how will you ever get back to New York by Monday? Fly?"

"Of course."

The words weren't fully out before he realized his mistake, but she merely laughed again, then said, "Do all Yankees have such a droll sense of humor?"

He managed a smile of his own and told himself to be more careful. He'd gotten through the entire poker game without slipping up, but he was suddenly finding it hard to think straight.

"And what do you do up in New York, Mister Adams?"

"Tyler...please."

"Tyler," she repeated softly. "And what do you do, Tyler?"

"Commodities. I..." He hesitated. He could hardly say he was a futures trader when there'd been no commodity futures markets in 1850.

"I buy and sell commodities," he tried. "You know, things like coffee, sugar, pork bellies."

"You're a broker," Sarah said.

He nodded. That was close enough.

"And cotton?" she said. "Surely you deal in cotton as well. Why, the port of Savannah alone ships hundreds of thousands of bales north every year."

"Of course," he agreed quickly, although cotton wasn't nearly as important in 1993 as it had been in 1850.

He stood gazing at her, not knowing where to take the conversation from here. Back home, he'd ask her what *she* did. But, living in 1850, he didn't imagine she *did* anything—aside from probably making every man she met wonder what kissing her would be like. That was sure what she had *him* wondering.

She shivered, and he decided to take a chance. "You're cold," he said. "Would you like my jacket?"

"Why, thank you...Tyler. That's most kind of you."

Slipping his suit coat off and moving nearer to drape it over her shoulders, he was enveloped by the smell of her perfume. It made him think about spring in the country. He had the strongest urge to kiss her. But that, he was *certain,* would be considered inappropriate in 1850 Georgia.

"It's too bad you won't be here long," she said. "There's a lot to see in Savannah, and I could have shown you the city."

For one crazy moment, he wondered if maybe he *could* stay a day or two longer. After all, he'd probably never get another chance to travel through time. But he doubted Clayton would go for the idea. Especially not when he had that poker party to host tomorrow night. In 1993.

"I know Savannah quite well," Sarah added. "I go in to help out at the Georgia Historical Society once or twice a week."

Tyler smiled down at her. He wouldn't have thought there'd have *been* much Georgian history before 1850.

She shyly lowered her gaze from his, saying, "I guess we'd best get back to the house. It's almost midnight."

He didn't move for a second, just watched her start off. She was so small that his old-fashioned suit coat drowned her. He'd thought it was long on him but, on her, it almost reached to her ankles.

Not that he could see them, hidden under her long dress. But he'd bet her ankles were as terrific-looking as everything else about her.

"Coming?" she asked, glancing back.

He nodded and started forward. That damned party of Clayton's wasn't until tomorrow *night.* Maybe he could stay a little longer. "Sarah?" he said.

"Yes, Tyler?"

"I was just wondering if you were free tomorrow. During the day, I mean. I *would* like to see something of Savannah before I have to leave . . . that is if Clayton doesn't object.''

Sarah gave him another of her devastating smiles. He decided that if Clayton *did* object, Clayton was going to have a hell of fight on his hands.

SOMEONE SHOOK Sarah awake. She resisted, trying to cling to the dream she'd been having about that gorgeous Yankee who'd appeared out of nowhere last night.

She could picture him perfectly, standing there looking at her with his beautiful slate-blue eyes. She'd always thought of slate as being cold, but his look had been so warm it had practically melted her insides.

Someone shook her again.

She grudgingly opened her eyes and said, ''Vallen, what are you doing?''

''I need your help,'' Vallen whispered.

Sarah pushed her hair away from her face and tried to focus more clearly.

The light streaming through her bedroom window was still pale. She doubted the rooster was even up yet. And Vallen liked to lie in until the rest of them had breakfast half eaten. So what was she doing here, still in her nightdress, with a pleading expression on her face?

''You need my help with what?''

''It's about those noises that were coming from my room in the middle of the night.''

''What noises?''

''Oh, Sarah, don't josh. This isn't at all funny. It's awful. Just awful. I've been terribly upset for hours.''

Sarah peered closely at Vallen. She didn't look at all upset.

"Sarah, you *must* have heard noises coming from my room."

Funny. She didn't recall hearing a thing, but it wasn't prudent to disagree with Vallen unless there was no alternative.

"You *must* have heard them, Sarah. How could you not have when your room is right across the hall from mine?"

"Well . . ."

"Oh, I *knew* you had." Vallen threw her arms around Sarah and hugged her. "And now you have to help me. Come on." The hug turned into a tug.

Sarah resisted. "Come on, where?"

"Come and talk to Papa with me. And tell him you heard the noises."

"Vallen, I don't think—"

"It's *important*, Sarah! Oh, you can be so mean-spirited. You *have* to come with me."

Which would be worse? Helping Vallen wake their father raised the possibility of getting yelled at. But refusing carried the certainty of incurring Vallen's wrath.

Besides, Vallen was Papa's favorite. She could never do any wrong in his eyes. So, as long as Vallen did the waking . . .

Deciding, Sarah pushed back the sheet and swung her legs over the side of the bed. "Just let me get my robe and—"

"There's no time," Vallen said. She grabbed Sarah by the arm and practically dragged her out of the room and along the hall to their father's door.

Quietly, she opened it, then shoved Sarah inside.

"Don't push!" Sarah whispered, but Vallen had already run past her and was standing beside the bed. Fearlessly, she started to poke at her father.

He snorted in his sleep.

Sarah took a backward step toward the door.

Vallen saw the motion and froze her sister with a glare. Then, turning again toward her father, she whispered "Papa" into his ear.

When that didn't work, she poked and hissed at the same time.

Papa was suddenly awake, flailing his arms as if he were being attacked.

"Oh, Papa," Vallen wailed, throwing herself into his arms and sobbing against his chest.

He looked at Sarah.

She shrugged, and considered taking another shot at escaping. But since Papa didn't seem about to yell, she might as well find out what Vallen was up to.

"There, there," Papa was saying, patting Vallen's back. "What's the matter, darling?"

"Oh, it's dreadful," Vallen cried. "So dreadful I can't tell you."

Sarah rolled her eyes, hoping they weren't in for a lengthy theatrical performance. Her bare feet were more than a mite cold. And she didn't like being out of her room, wearing only a nightdress, when there were strange men staying in the house.

"Tell him about the noises, Sarah," Vallen ordered.

Papa looked over expectantly.

"Well . . ." Sarah said.

"She heard noises coming from my room in the night," Vallen elaborated. "And they were because...because...oh, it was that Yankee friend of Clayton's, Papa. And it was so dreadful! Oh, my, I think I need smelling salts, just remembering."

Vallen's words had Sarah really confused. *That Yankee friend of Clayton's?* What about him? Whatever was Vallen talking about?

"What?" Papa said, his voice suddenly loud. "Are you saying that Yankee trifled with you?"

"Oh, Papa, worse than that. He...he forced himself on me."

"What?" Papa shouted.

Sarah simply stood staring at the two of them, not able to believe what she'd heard. Tyler Adams wasn't that sort at all. When she'd been alone with him, he'd been a perfect gentleman. But surely even Vallen wouldn't concoct a story of this magnitude.

Papa bolted out of bed, his face purple with anger. He grabbed his shotgun from the wardrobe and headed into the hall, bellowing, "Ewell! Get out here! We've got a family matter to deal with!"

Sarah ran into the hall after her father, her head spinning. Nightshirt flapping around his ankles, he marched along toward Ella-Jane's old room.

Then Ella-Jane's door opened and gangly Ewell rushed into the hall.

The nightshirt Papa had lent him was one that had shrunk considerably in length, and Ewell's bare legs were sticking out beneath the garment like a pair of white croquet mallets.

Sarah could feel herself blushing, but she wasn't about to go to her room and miss all the action.

She glanced back, looking for Vallen. She was clinging to the doorway of Papa's room, her expression terribly distraught.

"Oh, Vallen," Sarah murmured. She hurried back to her sister and put her arms around her, assuring her that everything would be all right.

Vallen sniffed loudly.

Along the hall, Papa was telling Ewell what had happened. "Only two things we can do, Ewell," he concluded. "Think I should shoot the varmint straight away?"

Ewell glanced at Vallen.

She sniffed even more loudly.

Ewell said, "Calm down before you go straight to shooting him, Beau. And let's consider this for a minute. That Yankee isn't married. He mentioned that last night. And he had a pile of money at the poker table. And being a friend of Clayton's, he's probably got a lot more where that came from. I'll bet he's got more money than Fitzhugh Farnsworth will ever see. 'Course, he *is* a Northerner. Don't know as how we'd want one of *them* in the family."

"Papa?" Vallen said, wiping her eyes. "Papa, how can I ever show my face after what that Tyler Adams did to me? You know how gossipy Savannah is. I'll be shunned by proper society. And you can't expect Fitzhugh to marry me now that...now that..." Vallen burst into tears.

Sarah hugged her sister tightly, feeling terrible. How could she have thought, even for a minute, that Vallen might have fabricated her story? And how could she have been so mistaken about the Yankee? That horrid Tyler Adams was no gentleman.

Papa cocked his shotgun.

Sarah's heart leapt to her throat.

"I think you're right, Beau," Ewell muttered. "Shooting the varmint straightaway is the thing to do. The more I consider it, the less I think I want to be related to a Northerner. Even if it *is* only by marriage."

Then Ella-Jane poked her head out into the hall. "Papa? Papa, what's happening?"

"What's happening," he said, brandishing the gun, "is that Vallen won't be marrying Fitzhugh Farnsworth, after all. Sorry, Ewell, but you'll have to make the best of it. I'm going to have me a rich Yankee for a son-in-law."

TYLER GROGGILY CLOSED his eyes again. A commotion in the hall had roused him, but the noise had abruptly stopped.

He was just rolling over when his door was thrown open. Tyler looked up in fright.

There was a cast of thousands pushing into the bedroom, led by Beauregard Booker in a nightshirt. And Beau was waving a shotgun. It didn't take a rocket scientist to realize this wasn't a display of Southern hospitality.

"Sir?" he managed, struggling into a sitting position and eyeing that gun anxiously.

"You Yankee cad!" Beauregard roared. "How dare you besmirch Southern womanhood with your Northern indecency? How dare you sully my daughter?"

Do *what* to his daughter? Tyler looked at Sarah.

She looked away.

"Sir?" he tried again.

"Do you have *anything* to say for yourself, you Yankee swine?" Beau snarled.

"Yes, sir! I only took off my suit coat and lent it to Sarah last night because she was cold. I didn't mean a thing by it, sir."

"What?" Beauregard yelled. "What's he talking about?" he demanded, glancing at Sarah.

"That was earlier," she said.

"I don't care about earlier," Beau hollered, turning back toward the bed. "I care about later. I care about what you did to Vallen."

Tyler looked at Vallen in utter confusion.

She said, "Oh, how *could* you have, when I begged you not to touch me?" Then she hugged her father's arm, looking up at him with a helpless expression. "Oh, Papa, I don't know if I can *face* marrying him."

"What?" Tyler yelped, full-blown panic replacing his fear of the shotgun.

"'Course you'll marry him," Beauregard snapped at Vallen. Then he turned again to the bed.

"Get dressed, Mr. Adams," he told Tyler. "I'll expect you downstairs in fifteen minutes. We'll discuss the wedding then."

Beauregard turned and trooped back out of the room, followed by the cast of thousands. The last one out slammed the door.

Tyler sat on the bed, his mind reeling. He told himself to calm down, to get the facts straight. All right. Exactly what *were* the facts?

Well, for starters, he belonged in 1993 but he was in 1850. And that Vallen woman had obviously claimed he'd...but why in hell would she have done that? And now they expected him to marry her?

He had to get out of here. Just as fast as his legs could carry him. He had to get back to that damned root cellar and back to 1993. But he'd only been to the cellar once. In the dark. How was he going to find it again?

Clayton! Of course, Clayton could get him out of this mess. Clayton could explain to Beauregard that . . . that what? That his daughter, Vallen, was a lunatic? That she'd made up her story?

Well, Clayton would damned well have to think of something to make Beauregard see reason. If Clayton hadn't had one too many, and made them stay in 1850 overnight, none of this would have happened.

Tyler scrambled out of bed and into his clothes. Last night, Sarah had told Louis to take Clayton to the yellow guest room. And he was undoubtedly still sleeping off the effects of all the alcohol he'd drunk. But which bedroom was the yellow one?

Quietly, Tyler opened his door. There was nobody in sight. Unfortunately, all the doors in the hallway were closed, and he didn't have the slightest idea which room was which.

He eased his way along, trying to figure out if he should knock or just peek into the rooms.

Peek, he decided. If he knocked, someone was bound to hustle him downstairs for his meeting with Beauregard. Oh, God, he had to find Clayton.

Barely breathing, he stopped at the first door, slowly turned the handle, and cracked the door open half an inch. The bit of wall he could see inside was green. He silently pushed the door shut again, then edged along to the next one.

The second room was wallpapered in pink.

His heart pounding, he crossed the hall to the row of rooms that overlooked the front lawn. The more rooms he eliminated, the better his odds. He opened the door a fraction and almost sagged with relief when he saw the yellow paint.

Quickly, he pushed the door fully open, stepped inside, and was greeted by a sharp intake of breath.

"My God," he whispered.

On the far side of the four-poster bed stood Sarah—wide-eyed and wearing nothing but some kind of corset thing that left little to the imagination. And she looked like she was about to scream.

CHAPTER THREE

SARAH GRABBED the dress that was lying on the bed and held it up in front of her. She looked terrified.

"Please don't scream," Tyler whispered desperately, shoving the door closed. "I'm sorry. I didn't mean to burst in on you. But your room's yellow."

"Get out!" she whispered. "I should yell for Papa this second."

"Oh, God, don't. If he thinks I was trying something again, he'll use that damned gun on me for sure."

"He should!"

"No! Listen, I didn't do it. I didn't even touch Vallen. I didn't—"

"You just said you did."

"What?"

"How could you?"

"I didn't!"

"You just said—if Papa thought you were trying something *again.*"

"No, I didn't mean I'd been trying *anything.* I meant he *thought* I was."

"Get out!"

"Oh, God, Sarah, just tell me which room Clayton is in. Please. I've got to talk to him. I didn't lay a finger on Vallen, and I only came barging in here because I thought this was the yellow *guest* bedroom."

She glanced at the yellow-painted wall, and a flicker of uncertainty appeared in her eyes.

"Honest," he insisted. "You've got to believe me." He didn't remember ever begging anyone for anything before, but all he could think about was an enraged Beauregard holding that shotgun.

Sarah gazed at him for another minute, then slowly said, "Either you are lying about this or Vallen is."

"It isn't me."

"You expect me to believe a stranger...a *Yankee*...over my own sister?"

Oh, God. That *was* expecting a lot. "Sarah, I don't know what's going on here. I went to bed last night and fell fast asleep. The next thing I knew, people were piling into my room with murder in their eyes."

Sarah assessed him for what seemed to be an eternity. "Clayton," she said finally, "is in the last room on this side of the hall...that way."

When she pointed the direction, the corner of the dress she was holding slipped from her hand, revealing bare skin again.

She grabbed it back, blushing furiously.

Clayton swallowed hard. He was no longer thinking of Beauregard holding his gun. "Thank you," he murmured. "Thank you, Sarah. I swear, I really *am* telling the truth."

He opened the door an inch, peered out into the still-empty hall, then raced from Sarah's room and along to the last door at the end.

When he threw it open, Clayton was half lying, half sitting on the bed—as if he'd been trying to get up but hadn't quite been able to manage it.

He watched, with bloodshot eyes, as Tyler hurried into the room and closed the door. Then he put his head in his hands and groaned.

Tyler leaned against the door, breathing hard. He'd never been in such a damned fix in his life, and the only guy who could get him out of it obviously had the mother of all hangovers.

"My head," Clayton moaned. "Pills . . . jacket pocket."

Tyler dug through the pile of clothes on the floor, found the bottle of pills, then poured a glass of water from the pitcher beside the bed.

His hands unsteady, Clayton took the glass and downed some of the pills. "They'll start working in a sec," he whispered. "God, my head hurts."

"Clayton, listen to me. I'm sorry, but I don't have time to hear about your headache. My life is on the line."

Clayton squinted at him, not looking nearly interested enough to suit Tyler.

"Beauregard thinks I raped Vallen."

"Did you?"

"Of course not!"

"For God's sake, don't yell," Clayton said, clutching his head again. After a minute he asked, "So, if you didn't do it, why does Beau think you did?"

"Because she said I did. But I didn't."

Clayton started to shake his head, then groaned and began massaging his temples. "Tyler . . . are we talking one of those date-rape things here? Where she said no and you didn't think she meant it and now she says she did?"

"Dammit, Clayton! What we're talking here is a Southern belle with a perverse imagination. I wasn't anywhere near Vallen Booker. I've never touched her. I've barely even looked at her."

"Then why did she say you raped her?"

"How the hell should I know? All I know is that her father stormed into my room with a damned shotgun in his hand and told me that I was going to marry her."

"Oh."

"Oh? Is that all you can say?"

"Well . . . see, that's how this sort of thing was handled in the Old South. You couldn't go around defiling women from good families without having to do the honorable thing."

"Clayton! I didn't *defile* her. And I don't need a lecture on Old Southern values. What I do need is to get back to that damned root cellar."

"Tyler, relax, okay?"

"Relax? Beauregard is waiting downstairs to discuss the wedding plans."

"Fine. You go talk to him." Clayton sat up straight and looked at Tyler. "Thank God, the pills are finally starting to work. I'll be mobile soon. In the meantime, just agree to marry Vallen. Whatever Beau suggests, go along with it. Then you and I will head off to my place and hit the root cellar. I'll make a quick trip back here tomorrow and explain that you disappeared. Ran off in the middle of the night."

Tyler rubbed his jaw thoughtfully. Clayton's plan was perfectly reasonable. There was actually no problem at all. Why hadn't he realized that?

Probably because being eyeball to eyeball with an irate father brandishing a shotgun tended to push other things from your mind.

"Okay?" Clayton said.

"I guess. But do you have to tell them I slithered off into the night like some snake in the grass? I'd hate to sound like a jerk. Maybe you could tell them I had a heart attack and died or something."

"Tyler...just go pacify Beau so we can get out of here, okay? This is Saturday. I've got a poker party to host tonight."

SARAH HOVERED NEAR the closed study door with Vallen, Ella-Jane and Ewell, wishing she could hear the conversation inside.

Papa and Tyler Adams had been in there long enough to discuss a dozen weddings. And the longer they took, the more Sarah kept thinking about how sincere the Yankee had sounded earlier.

Of course, she'd hardly been in any condition to judge his sincerity. Not when he'd caught her in that mortifying state of undress. And she scarcely knew him. On the other hand, she *did* know her sister.

"You don't imagine Papa will change his mind, do you?" Vallen asked Ella-Jane.

"I certainly hope he does," Ewell snapped. "I don't want a damned Yankee in the family."

"You know Papa never changes his mind once he's decided on something," Ella-Jane said quietly. She sat down in one of the wing chairs that flanked the fireplace, and Vallen gave her a conspiratorial smile.

Sarah couldn't help feeling unsettled. She knew she was being disloyal to her sister, but she couldn't help wondering if it was possible that Vallen had made up the whole terrible story.

She couldn't forget about those scraps of conversation she'd overheard last night and they were adding to her anxiety.

Was it possible Vallen had wanted to make Clayton pass out? So that he and Tyler would have to stay the night? So that Vallen could claim . . . after all, she *really* hadn't wanted to marry Fitzhugh Farnsworth. Now she wouldn't have to.

But surely Ella-Jane wouldn't have been party to such a plan.

Although, what had she said, exactly? That she sympathized with Vallen. And that she wouldn't want to marry Fitzhugh, either.

Someone knocked on the front door and Louis hurried across the foyer to answer it. John McCully was standing outside, looking a little uncertain.

Behind him, Sarah could see his horse hitched to one of the posts beyond the veranda.

"Oh," Vallen murmured, "how could Papa possibly have invited that man to stay the night? Even in the stable. He's so positively uncivilized."

Sarah gazed at John McCully, trying to decide if uncivilized was the word she'd use. She didn't think so. He was just a cowboy—from his hat and his denim shirt and trousers, right down to his boots.

He *was* wearing a Colt .45 hand gun, but most people out West probably did. And surely they weren't *all* uncivilized.

Actually, she felt he looked quite attractive. He was tall, with dark good looks she'd call rugged, rather than uncivilized. Of course, he was nowhere near as fine a looking man as Tyler Adams.

Sarah blushed at that thought. How could it possibly have popped into her head?

Tyler Adams might be a fine-looking man, but he was an unprincipled bounder. And he was also betrothed to her sister. Which meant no other woman should think about him at all. Particularly not Sarah.

Ella-Jane rose from her chair and started across the foyer. "Please come in, John," she said with a warm smile. "Breakfast will be served soon. Will you join us?"

"Why... thank you, ma'am," John said, removing his hat and stepping inside.

Just as he did, Clayton Willis wandered downstairs, looking decidedly pale. He glanced toward the study, saying, "Beauregard still talking to Tyler?"

The words were barely out before the study door opened. Sarah watched Tyler Adams follow her father into the foyer.

"All settled, Vallen," Papa announced. "The wedding will be in two weeks, as planned. We've just got us a different bridegroom."

Sarah wasn't surprised to see that Tyler looked as pale as Clayton.

"Well," Clayton said, "glad you've worked everything out, Beauregard. Ah... does this mean I won't be losing my lease on the house, after all? I mean, since Tyler and Vallen will probably be living up North, they won't need—"

"No," Beauregard interrupted. "Sorry, Clayton, but you'll still have to find a new place to live by the wedding day. I'll be giving that house to Vallen and Tyler as their wedding gift, just as I intended to give it to Vallen and Fitzhugh. Tyler has agreed to come live down South.''

"Oh," Clayton said, looking disappointed. "Well, at any rate, I guess Tyler and I will be heading back to my place now.''

"Not so fast," Papa told him. "Tyler isn't going anywhere. He'll stay right here at Booker's Knoll.''

That turned Tyler's face positively white. "Sir?" he said. "We didn't discuss anything about my staying here.''

Ignoring Tyler, Papa continued talking to Clayton. "No offense meant to you, but Tyler's going to stay right here until we've had the nuptials. After all, you *are* always coming and going. And I'd hate my future son-in-law to take it into his head to go someplace *with* you.''

Beau looked around the room and noticed John, his gaze resting for a moment on John's gun. He motioned the cowboy away from the others and into the study.

He didn't close the door—likely, Sarah decided, so he could keep an eye on Tyler. Her father wasn't taking any chances with the reluctant bridegroom.

She eased a little closer to the doorway. Luckily, even when Papa whispered, he had a loud voice.

"You got women kin?" he asked the cowboy quietly.

"A mother," John McCully said. "And three sisters.''

"I see. And what would you do if some varmint had his way with one of your sisters?''

"I'd make him marry her, sir.''

Sarah could see just enough to catch her father's smile.

"And what if the cad took it into his head that he didn't want to marry her?"

"Why, I'd shoot him, sir."

Papa clearly liked John's answers. "You pretty good with that Colt you're wearing, son?"

"Yes, sir."

"Well, then, I've got that job you were asking about last night. Right here at Booker's Knoll. With this wedding coming up, I'll have to spend some time in Savannah. There's all manner of arrangements to take care of. And then we'll be busy meeting guests at the train station and such. So I'm going to need someone to watch my future son-in-law for the next while. We've got to be sure he doesn't stray before we've got him safely hitched."

Sarah glanced at Tyler Adams. He was standing on the other side of the doorway, eavesdropping as intently as she.

She wouldn't have believed his face could have gotten any whiter, but it had.

SUDDENLY ONLY LOUIS and Sarah were left in the foyer. Papa and John McCully were still in the study, and everyone else had dispersed so quickly her head was spinning.

Tyler had dragged Clayton upstairs. Then Ewell had decided that he and Ella-Jane would forgo breakfast so they could start for home immediately.

And while Sarah had been kissing Ella-Jane goodbye, Vallen had run outside so fast she'd forgotten to take a parasol.

Sarah only wished Ewell hadn't hustled Ella-Jane away before she'd had a chance to ask her a few questions. If Tyler Adams was guilty, that was one thing. But if he wasn't...well, she wasn't quite sure where that would leave her. Vallen was her sister. And Sarah loved her, despite her mercurial temperament. But if Tyler Adams hadn't actually done anything, then it just wasn't fair that he should have to marry Vallen and change his entire life.

"Miss Sarah?" Louis said. "Miss Sarah, I told Millie you said you'd read to her later. She'd like that."

"Fine...she's feeling better?"

"A little, Miss Sarah. I was just going to see her now—while Mr. Booker is busy." Louis headed off toward the back of the house, where he and his wife had a room off the kitchen.

Sarah glanced into the study, torn between her worry for Tyler and her concern about Louis's wife, Millie. She'd been ill for over a week.

Sarah wished there was more she could do but she'd already talked Papa into having the doctor fetched, and then insisted the doctor give Millie laudanum for her pain. So, at least Millie was comfortable.

A moment later, Papa and John McCully came out of the study. Papa called for Louis.

"Yes, sir?" he said, hurrying back into the foyer.

"Louis, Mr. McCully here will be staying with us for the next while. I want you to show him to the room Clayton Willis was in last night."

"Yes, sir."

Sarah didn't know what to do. She might not be sure of the truth, but Papa did have a right to know her doubts.

"Papa?" she said when John McCully had started off with Louis. "There's something I have to tell you."

"Yes?"

"Last night...I didn't hear any noises coming from Vallen's room."

He gazed at her blankly.

She took a deep breath, then went on. "And you know how Vallen is, the way she sometimes...well, I just wondered if she might have only been dreaming that Tyler Adams came into her room...or something like that."

"Lord, almighty, why would you wonder that?" Her father gave her an annoyed frown.

"I...well, I only thought...I thought maybe there was a chance he hadn't really done anything because I didn't hear any noise."

"Don't be ridiculous," Papa snapped. "Why, he went right along with the idea of marrying Vallen. Not a word of objection. He'd hardly have done that if he wasn't guilty, would he?"

"No, I guess not," she murmured. *Of course,* he wouldn't have. Why hadn't she thought of that herself?

Tyler Adams's protestations of innocence couldn't have been sincere, after all. Which made her a fool. A fool to think he might have been telling the truth, and a fool for *wanting* to believe he was.

How utterly naive she'd been, letting his good looks and his kindly smile deceive her into thinking him a gentleman.

Vallen and Ella-Jane were right about her, after all. She *didn't* understand everything the way they did.

She wandered toward the kitchen, planning on reading to Millie for a while. Maybe that would make both of them feel better.

Because, at the moment, knowing she'd misjudged Tyler Adams so badly was making her feel strangely hollow inside. And having suspected poor Vallen of fabricating her story, when that brute of a man really *had* forced himself on her, had her convinced she should throw herself on the floor in front of Vallen and beg her forgiveness.

CLAYTON TRIED surreptitiously to check the old pocket watch that hung on a chain from his vest pocket, but Tyler noticed. His frustration level almost shot through the ceiling.

The only thing Clayton was worried about was getting back in time for that damned poker game he was hosting tonight. Tyler, on the other hand, was worried about *never* getting back.

"Have you thought of a plan yet?" he demanded.

"I'm thinking of one," Clayton said for about the tenth time. "Trust me," he added, pacing across Tyler's room.

"Trust you? Hell, I trusted you when you told me to pretend to go along with this wedding. And look where that got me. How could I have been so stupid? By agreeing to Beauregard's plans, I as much as admitted I was guilty."

"That wouldn't have mattered, if only Beau hadn't come up with the idea of keeping you at Booker's Knoll."

"But he *did* come up with it."

"Well, he can't keep an eye on you twenty-four hours a day."

"No? I'll bet, between him and that fastest gun in the West he's hired, they'll give it a hell of a good try."

"Look, Tyler, I can't see any chance of getting you out of here today. So I'll go and come back tomorrow."

"You'll *go?* And leave me here alone?"

"You won't be alone. You'll be with the Bookers."

"Oh, terrific. The Bookers and that hotshot cowboy with his damned six-shooter."

"Look, I know you're upset, but I can't have the guys showing up for the game tonight and not be there. I mean, coming here now and then is fine, but my real life is in 1993."

"What about *my* real life?" Tyler shouted. "Where do you think *it* is? Dammit, you brought me here. That makes you responsible for getting me back. And I want back now."

"Be reasonable, okay? Even if I stayed, can *you* see getting out of here today?"

"No! I can't see getting out of here at all. And that's scaring the hell out of me. Clayton, maybe I should try talking to Vallen. I don't know why she's doing this, but maybe I could reason with her."

"Uh-uh."

"What do you mean, uh-uh?"

"I mean Vallen isn't the reasoning type. In fact, I recall Ella-Jane once calling her a scheming little vixen. And her scheme, this time, is obviously to marry you instead of Fitzhugh Farnsworth. And she's just like her father. Once either of them decides something, there's no undeciding it."

"Well, I'm not marrying her! Hell, Clayton, what would she be in the real world? About two hundred years old? Look, why don't we go downstairs and explain to Beau about the root cellar and—"

"And expect him to believe we're here from the future? Tyler, the Old South wasn't exactly populated with progressive thinkers. And just imagine if someone had told *you* that people could travel through time, before you'd actually known it was possible. Hell, you didn't even believe it after you'd done it. So why would Beau buy the truth?"

Tyler shook his head. "I'm never going to get out of here," he muttered desperately.

"Of course you will. I'll bet we'll even be able to swing it tomorrow."

"And if we can't?"

"Well...then I'll call New York on Monday and talk to your boss. Tell him you were taken ill, and that you have to stay in Savannah until you recover. That'll take care of things for as long as we need."

"Clayton, I don't want to hear the word *long* in that context."

"Okay, look, I think I've got a plan. And it's real simple. You don't even need me to be here. Just stay cool, wait for your chance, then make a break for it."

"Make a break for it? You expect me to go running across the cotton fields all the way to the next plantation house and find a root cellar I've only seen in the dark? And if I did, when do you figure I go? In the dark, and risk getting lost? Or in the daylight, and just hope to hell I don't get shot by Beauregard's hired gun? You call that a plan?"

"Well . . . it's a starting place."

"Oh, great. And what if I *did* get to the cellar? How do I make it work?"

"Well, there's no real trick to that."

"There *has* to be a trick! Otherwise, every time that slave who looks after the place went down to get some vegetables, he'd end up in the future."

"Oh, yeah...I guess that's true. Well, the only thing I do is concentrate on the year 1850 to get here and on the year 1993 to get back."

"So all I have to do," Tyler said, rubbing his jaw uneasily, "is get to the cellar. But what if good old John McCully kills me? More than a hundred years before I'm even born?"

"For God's sake," Clayton snapped, "nobody's going to kill you. And I'm hardly going to leave you stranded here alone. I told you, I'll come back and help you tomorrow."

Tyler glared at Clayton. He wouldn't be so damned cavalier about this if *he* was the one stuck in the past, staring down the barrel of a shotgun.

"And what if helping me tomorrow turns out to be no easier than helping me today? What if two weeks go by, and there's no chance to make a break for it?" Tyler pressed, trying to sound calm. "What the hell do I do then?"

"I guess you marry Vallen."

"What?" he shouted. To hell with sounding calm.

"Either you marry her or Beau will shoot you. In case it hasn't occurred to you," Clayton added with the trace of a grin, "you're involved in a real shotgun wedding."

"Dammit, Clayton, this is *not* funny."

"Well, it's not the worst thing in the world, either."

"No?"

"No. If you *did* end up marrying Vallen, Beau would give you that plantation next door and—"

"Clayton, don't be insane. I don't *want* the plantation. And I *certainly* don't want Vallen. I want my real life back."

"And I'm going to help you get it back, Tyler. Aside from everything else, if Beau gives you and Vallen the house, that would be the end of my 1850 poker games. Vallen would never stand for me showing up in her root cellar whenever I liked. Hell, I've been worrying about that ever since Beau set the date for Vallen and Fitzhugh's wedding. But knowing her, I figured she'd find a way to get out of marrying him."

"And she certainly did, didn't she," Tyler snapped.

"Well...this wasn't exactly what I figured. But look, there really isn't anything I can do to help you today, what with Beau and that cowboy on red alert. So I'll go for the night, huh? I'll come back tomorrow, and we'll figure something out then."

"Yeah," Tyler muttered. Everything would be fine tomorrow. Clayton sounded just like Scarlett O'Hara in *Gone With the Wind.* Only her entire life had been destroyed—Tyler wanted to keep his life just the way it was.

He sank onto the bed as Clayton left, calculating the risks of trying to find that damned root cellar on his own. And if he did find it, where the hell might he end up? In 1993? Or in some other year?

CHAPTER FOUR

MILLIE HAD FALLEN ASLEEP after Sarah had read for only ten minutes, so she slipped quietly out of the room.

The kitchen was empty. Apparently, in all the excitement, nobody had thought to tell Millie's replacement to start breakfast. Sarah headed upstairs, not hungry, anyway.

At the end of the hall, near Tyler Adams's door, stood John McCully. She found having a stranger with a gun, right outside the bedrooms, most unsettling. Tyler Adams, she reflected, closing her door, must find it even more so. Of course, Mr. Adams was only getting the treatment he deserved.

From her window seat, she could see Clayton Willis on his way home and Vallen heading across the lawn to the house. Simply looking at Vallen made Sarah feel guilty again. She just didn't know how she could have suspected her own sister of being *so* scheming.

When she eventually heard Vallen come upstairs, Sarah hurried across the hall to her sister's room and knocked.

"What?" Vallen said, opening the door.

"I just wanted to be sure you're all right."

"Of course I'm all right. Why wouldn't I be?"

"Well...after what happened...I just wanted to be sure."

"I'm fine, Sarah. But I'm much too busy to stand here talking. I was just discussing the wedding with Papa before I came upstairs, and there's still a lot of work to do. Extra work, now that I'm marrying a different man. Oh, my, it's going to be so difficult for Papa to tell Fitzhugh's relatives they're no longer invited."

Sarah nodded, thinking it was going to be even *more* difficult for Papa to tell Fitzhugh that *he* was no longer invited. She suspected Fitzhugh had his heart set on that plantation Papa had promised as a wedding gift.

"Oh, I *do* hope Millie gets better soon," Vallen continued. "On top of everything, Papa expects me to give the new kitchen servant her daily instructions."

"I could do that for you."

"Thank you. That would help. You go straight down and tell her we want dinner early today. And tell her not to *dare* forget about breakfast again.

"And actually," Vallen went on, gesturing Sarah inside and closing the door, "there's something else you can do."

"Anything." The more she did for Vallen, the less guilty she'd feel.

"Papa is worried that Tyler Adams might decide he doesn't want to marry me, after all."

Sarah simply nodded again. But considering the way Tyler Adams had looked earlier, she knew he'd already come to that conclusion.

"Papa says we all have to be nice to Tyler—even though he behaved abominably. Papa says that when Tyler sees what a wonderful family he's marrying into, he'll be less inclined to consider slinking back up North."

"I guess Papa's right," Sarah said slowly. "But I'm going to find it difficult to be nice to a man who...you know."

"Yes, well, here's what I want you to do to help me. I thought you could tell Tyler what a nice person I am. Point out how pretty I am. That kind of thing."

"How clever you are," Sarah suggested.

Vallen cleared her throat, then said, "I think he's already realized I'm clever. But the problem is, I don't believe he's too fond of me."

"Why ever wouldn't he be? He's the one who did the awful thing. Not you."

"Yes, but that's how men are. Regardless of what he did, he might think he shouldn't have to marry me."

"But he should. That's only fair."

"Of course it is. He had his way with me, so he has to marry me. That's the law."

"I don't think it's actually the law, Vallen. It's just what usually happens."

"Oh? Well it certainly should be the law. But it doesn't matter. Papa's decisions are as good as laws. You can never trust a Yankee, though. And if Tyler decided he didn't want to marry me, he might say any old thing to get out of it.

"He might even try to convince you he didn't do anything," Vallen added with a shifty glance. "But I know you wouldn't take any notice if he said that."

Something in Vallen's voice suddenly made Sarah very uneasy. "Why would he try to convince me?" she asked slowly.

"Oh, I don't know. He just might. I warned Papa he might think of doing it, too. But Papa's too smart to be fooled into believing something like that."

Sarah took a deep breath, knowing it was a dreadful thing she was about to ask, but she *had* to ask it. "Vallen, Tyler Adams *did* have his way with you, didn't he? And tell me the truth, because the very next time I see Ella-Jane, I'm going to ask her what you two were plotting last night."

"Oh, fiddle. You really are *such* a child, Sarah. And I really *do* have an awful lot to do. So please leave now."

"No. Not until you answer my question. And don't lie to me, because you know Ella-Jane will tell me everything."

"All right," Vallen snapped, stomping her foot. "I won't have you pestering me about this for the next two weeks, so no, Tyler Adams did *not* have his way with me. But if any of you actually imagined I'd marry Fitzhugh Farnsworth, you were crazy."

Sarah could barely believe her ears. She'd suspected, but she hadn't *really* thought...

"But it isn't fair," she finally said. "It isn't fair to Tyler Adams."

"Fair? Heavens to mercy, Sarah. If I'd been born in October, like you, I'd have killed myself by now. You Libras are the only people on earth who spend half your time worrying about what's fair, when what's fair doesn't matter a whit. The only thing that matters is that I'd rather marry Tyler Adams than Fitzhugh Farnsworth."

"But you don't even know Tyler Adams! You can't possibly love him."

"What does love have to do with marriage? I've decided Tyler is the man I want for a husband. It's as simple as that."

"It isn't simple for him! And it isn't fair. Vallen, you lied outright! I'm going to tell Papa."

"He won't believe you."

"Yes, he will."

"No, he won't, because I—"

"Never mind *because,* Vallen. Just come with me. Right now." Sarah threw open the door, grabbed Vallen by the arm, and pulled her into the hall.

"Let go!" Vallen yelled.

"No! Come and talk to Papa with me."

"Turn me loose, you hateful little wretch," Vallen screamed, landing a hard kick on Sarah's shin.

"Ouch!" she cried.

Vallen broke free, raced back into her room and slammed the door.

Sarah glanced along the hall. John McCully was still standing at the end of it, and Tyler Adams was in his bedroom doorway. Both of them were staring at her.

"You okay?" Tyler asked.

She could feel herself blushing furiously. She wasn't inclined to physical violence the way Vallen was, but these men must think...oh, mercy, they must think her utterly shameless.

And then Papa was thundering up the stairs, shouting, "What's all the ruckus up there?"

Sarah stopped worrying what the others were thinking and began worrying about what she was going to say to her father.

It was practically risking her life to cross Vallen on something important, but this was by far the most outrageous thing Vallen had ever done.

Papa wheeled into the hall, his face red, and immediately focused on Tyler Adams. "Were you trying something else?" he roared.

"It was me, Papa," Sarah said. "Vallen and me."

He pounded on Vallen's door, shouting her name, and she quickly opened it, wearing her best innocent expression.

Papa gestured Sarah into Vallen's room ahead of him, then shut the door, saying, "Well? Why do I have two daughters screaming like banshees?"

"Oh, Papa," Vallen said, "it's exactly what I warned you might happen. Sarah is so upset that it's *me* Tyler Adams is going to marry that she kicked me. She kicked me right on the shin," Vallen added, bending over and gingerly rubbing her leg through her skirt.

"I didn't!" Sarah said. "It was Vallen who—"

"Enough," Papa roared. "I won't have this, Sarah. Vallen told me how much you fancied Tyler Adams. And I'd already started wondering about that last night, when I saw you out walking in the moonlight with him. But it's your sister he ruined and it's your sister he's going to marry. And I don't want to hear another word about it."

"But, Papa, you don't know what Vallen's done."

"Not another word about what *Vallen's* done. Sarah, when she told me she thought you might make up some crazy story, hoping to get that Yankee for yourself, I didn't believe it. But now that you have, I certainly don't intend to listen to it." Papa turned on his heel and marched back out of Vallen's room, shutting the door behind him.

Sarah glared at her sister, so angry she could spit.

Vallen smiled slyly. "Papa is convinced Tyler Adams is guilty, Sarah. And he isn't going to believe anything you say to the contrary. Didn't it occur to you that I'd make sure of that? Really, you never seem to consider just how smart I am."

"I'm going into Savannah," Sarah snapped. "Right this minute. I'm going to fetch Ella-Jane back here and have *her* tell Papa that you plotted this whole thing, that you're tricking Tyler Adams into marrying you."

"Papa wouldn't believe anything Ella-Jane told him any more than he'd believe you," Vallen said, waving her hand airily.

"He would! When we *both* tell him—"

"He wouldn't," Vallen interrupted. "Because, when I was warning him that you might make up a story, I also told him how Ewell was ranting and raving about not liking the idea of having a Yankee in the family. So Papa wouldn't be at all surprised if Ewell ordered Ella-Jane to make up some silly tale. Anything to keep me from marrying a Yankee."

Sarah felt like scratching Vallen's eyes out. Her sister *always* managed to get things her way. Most of the time, it didn't really matter. But this time . . . oh, there had to be some means of making this right.

The problem was, Papa doted on Vallen. He was blind to her faults, and no matter what anyone else said, he probably *wouldn't* believe she was lying. Not after she'd convinced him that *she* was the only one he could trust to tell the truth. But surely even Vallen couldn't go through with something as wrong as this.

"Vallen," she tried at last, "you simply *can't* do this."

"No?" This time Vallen smiled like a cat who'd been given milk straight from the cow. "Just watch me, little sister."

TYLER STOOD STARING OUT his bedroom window, wondering if the old movie trick of knotting sheets together to make an escape rope really worked.

But even if it did, he'd need a lot more than the two sheets that were on his bed. If he tied them to one of the posts, they wouldn't even reach across to the window. And with the high, old-fashioned ceilings at Booker's Knoll, he was at least twenty feet above the ground, with nothing below the window to break a fall.

Maybe, if he'd been a paratrooper, rather than just having done a stint in the army, he'd risk trying to jump. But that mile or so across the cotton fields to Clayton's would be a hell of a long run with a broken leg.

And he couldn't just go strolling out the front door. The last time he'd checked, John McCully had still been standing guard in the hall—with that gun that seemed bigger all the time.

So, unless Lady Luck came calling, he was stuck here until Clayton arrived back tomorrow. He only hoped Clayton didn't get so drunk at that party of his tonight that he forgot about coming back.

A hesitant knock interrupted his worrying. He opened the door, assuming it was the servant wanting to remove the lunch tray he'd brought up earlier. But instead of Louis, Tyler found Sarah standing in the hall.

"May I come in and speak with you for a minute?" she whispered, sounding as nervous as she looked.

Tyler glanced anxiously along the now empty hall. She'd said *come in,* and he had a damned good idea how Beauregard would feel about his daughter being in a man's bedroom.

"Ah . . . I don't think your father—"

"Papa and Vallen are busy in his study, talking about the wedding," she said, slipping past him into the room.

Wedding. Every time he heard that word, the hair on the back of his neck stood on end.

"And John McCully has gone down to sit in the foyer," Sarah went on. "But you'd better close the door, just to be safe."

Hesitantly, he did, not sure it was the safest thing at all. He didn't know what Sarah wanted, but he'd had enough of Southern women to last a millennium.

Sarah walked over to the window, then stood gazing at him with her big brown eyes. "You're an Aries, aren't you, Tyler Adams," she said at last.

He knew he was frowning at her, but he couldn't help himself. Astrology was about the stupidest thing going. He couldn't stand women who asked men their signs. And he certainly hadn't realized they'd been doing it for the past hundred and fifty years or more.

"You *must* be an Aries," Sarah persisted. "I was certain you were last night when we were talking."

"Yes, I am," he admitted, wondering, despite himself, how she'd deduced it.

"Well, I'm sorry I didn't think to consider that this morning . . . when you told me you hadn't touched

Vallen. It's just that under the circumstances . . . your bursting into my room . . .''

He nodded, remembering how sexy she'd looked in that state of undress.

"I'm sorry I wasn't thinking then, because I know Aries men don't lie. Tyler . . . I know the truth. That you didn't . . . didn't do what Vallen claims you did.''

He stood eyeing her uncertainly. She was on to the truth, all right, but if she'd arrived at it through astrological gibberish, he doubted it would hold much weight with her father. "What made you decide to believe me?''

"I didn't believe *you*, although I know now that I should have. Vallen told me she made up her story.''

Vallen was admitting she'd lied! A chorus of hallelujahs erupted inside his head.

"She's still intent on marrying you, though, Tyler. She doesn't like Fitzhugh Farnsworth and doesn't want to marry him. So she has no intention of telling Papa the truth.''

While Sarah was speaking, the hallelujah chorus died mid-note. But if Vallen had admitted lying to Sarah, then surely *she* was planning to tell Beauregard. That would clear up this crazy mess.

"Tyler, I've been sitting in my room for ages, trying to decide what I should do. Part of me says I shouldn't cross my sister and side with a stranger. But another part says I have to do something about this.''

He began praying that second part had a louder voice.

"And I've decided I'm going to help you escape. If you go out the back way, you can head down to the river and follow its bank along to Clayton's. That way, no one should see you.''

"Escape," he said, trying to smile. After all, she was offering her help. But the smile felt forced. He couldn't help thinking about Beauregard with his shotgun and John McCully with that big Colt of his. What if one of them *did* see him?

"And once you get to Clayton's," Sarah continued, "he can help you get away."

"Ah . . . rather than my trying to get away, wouldn't it be better if you just told your father the truth, so he'd *let* me go?"

"No. Papa wouldn't believe me."

"But you said Vallen admitted—"

"To *me*, not to Papa. And I *did* try to tell him the truth, but he wouldn't listen. Tyler, my father believes Vallen, and she'll make sure he continues to. Even if you and I *both* tried talking to Papa, she'd . . . well, we'd both end up sorry and you'd still be a prisoner here. Tyler, Vallen is a Scorpio. You have to tread softly around Scorpios."

"I see," he said. Not that he saw a damned thing. He wouldn't know a Scorpio from an aardvark. But without even coming close to Vallen he'd ended up in big trouble. So he'd better listen carefully to someone who knew her.

"I have a plan," Sarah said.

He nodded encouragement. Already she was giving him more hope than Clayton had. If she had a plan that would let him get to the root cellar, he'd take his chances about where he'd end up.

"I'll get John McCully out of the foyer," Sarah was saying. "Then you can slip downstairs and through the kitchen. You'll be safely at Clayton's before anyone even knows you're gone.''

This time, his smile felt right. Sarah was an absolute angel of mercy. Last night, he'd thought she *looked* like an angel. And now...

Well, maybe she didn't quite look like one today. Artists always painted angels wearing loose, shapeless dresses. And the top of Sarah's dress fit so tightly he was having trouble keeping his eyes off her chest. The blue silk hugged her figure from her neck right down to her waist. Which was, he noted, the tiniest waist he'd ever seen.

''Tyler?''

He forced his gaze back to her face.

''Shall I go and distract John McCully now?''

''Yes. Yes, of course. And thank you, Sarah. I can't thank you enough. Ah...how exactly are you going to distract him?''

She looked at the floor, clasping her hands in a nervous gesture. ''I thought it would be best to get him upstairs.''

''Into the hall again? But that wouldn't help. He'd—''

''Not into the hall,'' Sarah interrupted. ''I thought...the only place where he couldn't possibly see you is...inside my room. I'll tell him I need his help in there with something.''

Tyler rubbed his jaw thoughtfully. Sarah was still looking at the floor. She was also blushing a vivid pink.

As badly as he wanted out of here, he realized what Sarah was risking. If she lured a man into her room and he made a move on her, she wouldn't have a clue how to handle it. So maybe they'd better revise her plan a little.

"Sarah, let's think about this for a minute, huh? We don't know a thing about John McCully, so your bedroom might not be the best place for you to be alone with him. Maybe you could try suggesting he take a walk with you or something."

"I considered that. But if we were outside, he might see you escaping."

"Well . . . that's true but—"

"I think it *has* to be my room, Tyler. My window overlooks the front of the house and you'll be heading out the back."

"I don't know . . ." Damn. He *really* wanted out of here. So why was his conscience going on about not taking advantage of Sarah?

"There won't be a problem," she said firmly. "I'm not a child. And if John McCully isn't a gentleman, all I have to do is scream and Papa will come running with his shotgun."

"You're right about that," Tyler said sarcastically.

"Fine. Then it's settled. We'll leave your door open an inch, and when you hear mine close, you'll know John McCully is out of the way. Just be sure to creep past my room carefully. There's a creaky board in the hall outside it."

"I'll watch out for it. But, Sarah, one more thing before you go. How did you know I was an Aries?"

"The Ram is a fire sign, Tyler. Ruled by Mars. Aries men are intensely masculine and usually take charge of things. I . . . I simply sensed you were intensely masculine," she added, lowering her eyes from his.

Both what she'd said and the shy way she'd said it made him smile. And that masculine bit...hell, that certainly fit. Maybe there was something more to astrology than he'd believed.

She looked up at him again and gave a tiny shrug, saying, "I guess this is goodbye, then. I hope...I hope everything goes well for you, Tyler Adams."

"Sarah?"

She glanced back, her hand on the door.

"Sarah...thank you for doing this. I hope everything goes well for you, too. And I'm really sorry I'll never be able to see you again. I'd have liked to."

That brought a tentative little smile to her lips. It made Tyler want to kiss her goodbye. Instead, he merely smiled back.

Sarah left Tyler's door open a crack and started downstairs, her heart racing so fast it frightened her.

The study door was closed, so Papa and Vallen were still safely out of the way. And there was John McCully, sitting in one of the wing chairs beside the fireplace.

She'd planned what she was going to say, of course. She just wasn't entirely certain her voice would work. "Mr. McCully?" she made herself begin.

"Yes, ma'am?"

"Mr. McCully, I was trying to close the window in my bedroom, but it's become stuck. I'd be much obliged if you'd help me with it."

He nodded, saying, "Certainly, Miss Sarah." He strode across the foyer and started up the staircase, taking the steps so rapidly she almost had to run to keep up.

From this angle, she thought anxiously, gazing up at his back, he was an intimidatingly large man.

"You just wait right here," John McCully said, glancing back at her when they reached the upstairs hallway. "I'll have a look at that window."

"I'll help."

"That's all right, ma'am, I'll manage."

He headed into her room and strode across to the window. Sarah wrung her hands, desperately trying to decide what to do. He wasn't supposed to have told her to wait in the hall. That hadn't been part of her scheme.

She checked Tyler's door and caught a glimpse of him standing behind it. But he wouldn't be able to make it downstairs with her door wide open. And if she shoved it closed, John McCully would be back out in the hall half a second later, to see what she was about.

There was only one thing to do. Screwing up all her courage, she stepped inside the bedroom and closed the door behind her. She knew exactly what John McCully would think of her actions, but she had no choice.

He glanced around at the sound of the door shutting. Then he effortlessly pushed the window closed and started back toward her, a huge grin spreading across his face.

CHAPTER FIVE

HER HEART IN HER THROAT, Sarah pressed her back against the bedroom door.

The leering grin John McCully was wearing had her frightened half to death. It was all she could do not to scream. But she had to give Tyler enough time to get away.

John extended his hand as if to grab her wrist...but he didn't. He simply reached on past her for the door handle, saying, "I wouldn't have thought there was enough breeze coming in that window to slam the door shut, Miss Sarah. We'd better open it up again fast, though, huh? I know your father wouldn't think it seemly, your being alone in your bedroom with a man."

He pulled the door open as easily as if she weren't leaning against it at all, then let out a low whistle.

"Well, what's going on here?" he said quietly.

Sarah turned toward the hall and her spirits plunged. Tyler Adams was standing not two feet past the doorway, looking as guilty as a fox caught in the henhouse.

"You feeling like a walk, Tyler?" John asked, his hand moving to his holster. "That sounds like a right fine idea to me. I could do with some exercise."

Tyler managed not to swear aloud—but just barely. So much for the great escape. He forced a smile, saying, "Be glad of the company. Would you like to join us, Sarah?"

She shook her head, her dark eyes luminous. She looked as if she was about to cry because her plan had failed.

Tyler wished there was something he could say, but he'd better be damned careful in front of his keeper. If he acted resigned to his fate, it was more likely John McCully would relax his guard.

"Well?" John said. "We going?"

Tyler gazed at Sarah for another second, then started off with John, saying, "I just thought I'd like to have a look around. I've never been on a plantation before."

"No? Me, neither. Not something we have out West. But I guess you've got to learn how they operate and all, since you're marrying into the family."

Tyler swallowed uncomfortably. Funny how words like *wedding* and *marry* had begun striking terror in his heart.

He followed John downstairs, wondering if the man was above taking a bribe. It certainly had to be worth sounding him out.

"Beauregard introduced me to the overseer earlier," John offered as they headed outside. "He's a fellow by the name of Halleck. Horace Halleck. He'd probably show us around if we can track him down."

They started off in the direction of the outbuildings—the slave quarters, consisting of a series of one-room shacks, along with the barn and other structures. The first of them lay several hundred yards to the west of the main house. Tyler groaned inwardly as he realized they were going in the opposite direction from Clayton's place.

With every step, he felt as if he were walking further away from his real life. And he was getting more damned anxious by the second.

To hell with acting resigned to his fate. John Mc-Cully seemed like a regular guy, so maybe it made more sense to be straight with him.

"John?" he said. "Can I talk to you about something?"

"Sure."

"This whole wedding thing . . . I know what Beauregard told you, but it isn't true. I didn't touch his daughter."

"No?" John said, glancing over.

"No. I never went anywhere near her. She made up that story because she was engaged to a fellow she didn't like. And she decided that marrying me would solve her problem."

"That so?"

Tyler tried to read John's thoughts, but his expression wasn't giving away a thing. "John, I'm telling you the truth here. Sarah knows I'm innocent, but she can't convince Beauregard. She's tried."

"Yeah, I can see where Beauregard could be a mighty tough man to convince."

"Exactly. So, the thing is . . . look, I've got a life up North that I have to get back to. And if you could just see your way clear to letting me get over to the next plantation, Clayton would take it from there."

John stopped walking and stood eyeing Tyler, clearly not about to hand over any walking papers.

"Look, John, if you don't believe I'm innocent, how about talking to Sarah? She'll back me up."

"Well, it isn't really a matter of believing you or not, Tyler. It's a matter of my word. I've given Beauregard my word that I won't let you stray. And I've never broken my word in all my thirty-four years."

TYLER AND JOHN wandered around for the best part of half an hour without finding Horace Halleck.

In the fields, Beauregard's slaves were busy picking puffballs of cotton from the waist-high bushes. Tyler tried to avoid looking at them, their white shirts stained with sweat from working in the hot sun, their shoulders stooped under the weight of the picking sacks.

They never did find the overseer, so they headed back to the house. Beauregard and Vallen were sitting on the verandah.

"Taking the measure of the place, son?" Beauregard's voice boomed across the lawn.

There was no doubt which one of them Beau was calling son, and it set Tyler's teeth on edge.

Then, to make matters worse, Vallen smiled over at him in a proprietary way and fluttered her fan.

For some unfathomable reason, his first thought was that if Sarah had fluttered a fan like that, he'd have thought it adorable. When Vallen did it, it sent a chill down his spine—despite the one-hundred-plus heat.

"You tried reasoning with Vallen?" John asked quietly.

Tyler glanced at him, not sure whether John was merely humoring him or not.

The way John shrugged said he might actually have believed the truth.

"Both Sarah and Clayton Willis told me there *is* no reasoning with Vallen," Tyler said.

"Couldn't hurt to try."

Tyler considered that as they crossed the last few yards to the veranda. What was there to lose? He smiled at Vallen. It hurt his face.

"We were looking for Horace Halleck," John said. "Thought he'd give us a tour. But he didn't seem to be around."

"I sent him over to the Farnsworth plantation," Beau said. "To deliver the letter I wrote Fitzhugh, explaining why he won't be marrying Vallen. Hope he takes it well, but I'm afraid the Farnsworths invited kin from danged far off to the wedding. Some of them might be on their way to Savannah already."

"What about *your* kin, Tyler?" Vallen said sweetly. "If we sent letters on tomorrow's steamer for New York, some of your family might have time to get here."

"My kin . . . ah, don't worry about inviting them. Most of them don't travel." *At least not from 1993 to 1850, they don't,* he silently added. And, Lord, but he wished he hadn't, either.

"Well, perhaps we can visit New York after the wedding," Vallen said. "I could meet them then."

Tyler cleared his throat. "Vallen, I . . . would you like to take a little walk with me?"

"Why, Tyler, I surely would." She exchanged the fan for a parasol from beside her chair and flashed a Cheshire cat smile at her father, saying, "Doesn't fate work in mysterious ways, Papa? Why, the more I think on it, the more I think I *want* to marry Mr. Adams, despite what he did last night. I do believe he'll make me a better husband than Fitzhugh ever would have."

Her speech sent an even colder chill down Tyler's spine.

Vallen stepped off the veranda and reached to take his arm, but he clenched it to his side. Trying to reason with her was one thing, but he was already playing fly to her spider. Who knew what she'd do if she actually got her hands on him.

He waited until they were well out of earshot of the veranda, then said, "Vallen, I want to make something absolutely clear. I am *not* going to marry you."

"No?" Her smile didn't even flicker. "That isn't what Papa says. And he's the one with the shotgun."

Tyler's jaw clenched so tightly it was hard to go on, but he made himself try again. "Look, Sarah explained to me that you don't like Fitzhugh Farnsworth. But trying to rope me into marrying you is no solution."

"No? Why, Tyler, it seems like a perfect solution to me."

"Dammit, Vallen..." He tried counting to ten, but it didn't help. He could see Sarah and Clayton were right, there was no reasoning with this woman. So, regardless of Sarah's belief that Aries men didn't lie, he was going to have to try lying to convince Vallen she was playing her cards wrong.

Fixing her with a glare, he said, "Vallen, you're making a serious mistake. You might figure Fitzhugh Farnsworth wouldn't make a good husband, but you let me tell you, I'd be worse. You can ask Clayton Willis—he'll tell you. I lie and swear and drink and..."

He paused, then played his trump card. "And I've been in jail. I'm in and out of jail all the time, in fact, because I've got a violent temper. I'd probably beat you and cheat on you...and dammit, most likely head back up North the first chance I got. Then you'd have no husband at all."

"Oh, fiddle," Vallen snapped. "You are the most dreadful liar I've ever listened to. And even if you weren't, I wouldn't worry a whit about your being terrible to *me,* because I can shoot almost as well as Papa. And do you think I'd mind if you ran back up North? Once we're married, you can go to China for all I care."

He stopped walking and stood staring at her uncertainly. "Vallen . . . you want to tell me exactly what's going on in your head? It's the least you owe me after getting me into all this trouble."

She twirled her parasol for a moment, then shrugged. "I don't suppose it would hurt to explain. It will make you stop worrying about never getting back to your precious North. And maybe then I won't have to listen to your protests. But don't you go thinking about repeating what I say to Papa."

"Absolutely not," Tyler said quickly. "It'll be strictly between you and me."

"Yes, well, even if you *did* say anything to him, he'd only think it was a lie you made up to try and get out of the wedding."

Tyler nodded encouragement for her to continue. Maybe, if he knew where she was coming from, he could figure out how to handle this.

"You see, Tyler, Fitzhugh doesn't like me any more than I like him. He didn't pay me a mite of attention until Papa married Ella-Jane off to old Ewell. But then Fitzhugh started coming around like a hound dog scenting possum. And Papa and old Mr. Farnsworth are good friends. And Papa was just itching to get me betrothed to someone.''

Tyler nodded again, hoping this explanation was going to get clearer as Vallen went along.

''It's the plantation,'' she continued. ''The one next to us, that Clayton has been renting. Papa bought it to give Ella-Jane when she married. But Ewell didn't want it because his business is in Savannah. And he already had more money than the South has cotton. So then Papa decided the plantation should go to either Sarah or me, whichever of us married next.''

''I see . . . so Fitzhugh wants the plantation.''

''Of course. Do you have any idea how much a Georgia cotton plantation is worth?''

''I've no idea,'' he said truthfully.

''Well, landholdings are divided into thousand-acre units. And even a plantation of only one unit is worth at least a hundred thousand dollars.''

''A hundred thousand?'' he repeated, trying to calculate how many millions that would be in 1993 dollars. The numbers became too enormous to figure in his head.

Vallen nodded. ''In fact, even the hundred slaves Papa will provide to work it will be worth that much. So, naturally, Fitzhugh wants the plantation. But I want the plantation *without* Fitzhugh.''

''I see,'' Tyler said. And he finally did. He saw that he'd had her figured entirely wrong. She wasn't a lunatic at all. Far from it. She was one very smart operator.

"I have to marry *someone*, though," she continued, "or else Sarah will get the plantation when she marries. I'm certainly not going to see that happen. And by marrying you, I'll get what I want. Papa will give us the deed, and then you'll be free to leave, Tyler Adams. In fact, I'll insist on it. I certainly don't intend to stay married to a Yankee."

"Let me get this straight," he said slowly. "The way you've got things planned, we get married and then we immediately get divorced?"

"Certainly not. Maybe that's how you'd do it in New York, but respectable women do *not* get divorced in Georgia. I'll simply tell people you had to go back up North, for a while, to wrap up your affairs there. Then, after a few weeks, I'll receive a letter informing me of your unfortunate death. I'll be a rich widow. Which will mean that, if I want a husband, I'll be able to marry any man I fancy."

Tyler stood rubbing his jaw thoughtfully. Even knowing exactly what was going on, he was far from thrilled with the situation. He'd still prefer to get out of here as fast as he could.

But at least it wasn't as bad as he'd thought. Vallen's plan to trap him here for two weeks was a whole lot better than a lifetime sentence.

And if he did get forced into going through with the marriage ceremony, it would be meaningless. Just a scheme to get Vallen the plantation. And it wouldn't make him married in the *real* world...would it? No, that couldn't possibly be, because she'd be long dead by 1993.

"You know," Vallen said, "I do believe explaining things was a wise idea. I'd been thinking I'd have to waste time being charming to you, so you wouldn't take it into your head to try running off. But now that you know you'll be free to go back up North after the wedding, my spending time with you won't be necessary, will it?"

"Ah . . . no. Don't feel you have to waste your time with me, Vallen."

"Heaven knows," she said, shaking her head, "I have enough to do, what with all the arrangements. So you just keep yourself busy for the next two weeks, doing whatever it is you Yankees like to do. All right?"

"Sure. That'll be fine."

"You know, I can hardly wait until that plantation is mine," Vallen went on as they headed back to the house. "I have all manner of plans for it. In fact, I believe I'll ask Papa to start work on one of them even before the wedding. That would likely annoy Clayton Willis a mite, but I'm sure Papa wouldn't worry about that.

"Well?" she said sharply after a moment. "Aren't you interested in what I intend to do?"

"Uh . . . sure."

"Well, I've always thought a pond would look perfect behind that house. Coming right up to the back porch. Maybe I'll have ducks and geese in it. Don't you think that will be nice?"

Tyler nodded. From what he'd seen of Vallen, he could imagine her going out and strangling the ducks and geese for dinner. With her bare hands.

"It won't be all that much work. Papa can just have some of the slaves dig a big hollow and fill in that old root cellar out back. I'll have a new one dug around the side of the house and—"

"Fill in the old root cellar?" Tyler repeated, the words coming out in a horrified gasp as they registered in his brain.

"Of course. If they didn't fill it in, the pond water would pour into it and flood the foundations of the house."

TYLER LEFT VALLEN drinking lemonade on the veranda with her father and John McCully and headed upstairs in a daze.

His mind was still reeling from Vallen's news flash about the root cellar. If he didn't get out of 1850 damned fast, he'd *never* get out.

And he didn't even have until the wedding to escape. Not if Beauregard agreed to start working on Vallen's pond right away.

Tyler started down the hall to his room, then paused outside Sarah's door. He desperately needed to talk to someone, and she was an island of sanity in a sea of madness. He tapped quietly on her door.

She opened it, and he stood gazing down at her for a moment, wondering how two sisters could be so different.

"May I come in?" he said at last.

The way she glanced along the hall reminded him that his suggestion was inappropriate in 1850. But, hell, what could Beauregard do? He could hardly force one man to marry *two* of his daughters.

Sarah opened the door more widely, gestured him inside, then closed it again. "I'm sorry, Tyler," she said.

He simply gazed at her, not knowing what she was talking about.

"I'm sorry I couldn't help you escape," she explained.

Escape. Oh, yeah. She'd tried to help him escape. Vallen's little bombshell had driven thoughts of everything else out of his mind. But Sarah had obviously been dwelling on what had happened, feeling badly because she'd failed him.

"Hey, it wasn't your fault," he tried. "John McCully is smarter than we gave him credit for, that's all."

"No, that isn't what it was," she said, looking as if she were near tears. "It was . . . oh, I practically threw myself at that man, but he didn't fancy me, so he didn't want me in the room with him . . . and then . . ." She stopped speaking and shrugged a miserable little shrug.

"Sarah?" Tyler said uneasily. He wasn't exactly sure why she was so upset, and he had no idea what he could say to make her feel better.

"I saw you walking with Vallen . . . from my window."

He glanced at the window, then back at Sarah. "I was trying to reason with her. But you were right. Reasoning with her is impossible."

"Oh. Oh, I thought maybe you were talking with her because you'd decided that marrying her wasn't such a bad idea, after all."

"Sarah, have you taken leave of your senses? I definitely *do not* want to marry your sister."

"But . . . but Vallen is so very pretty . . . isn't she?"

"Sarah . . . what's this about?" He took a tentative step closer to her, wishing to hell they were in 1993. Not that he could always figure women out there, but here he didn't have a clue.

She shook her head, gazing at the floor.

"Sarah?" he tried again, taking her hands lightly in his. For a second, he thought she was going to pull them away, but she didn't. She simply made an unhappy little noise in her throat.

Whatever the problem was, he had a crazy urge to fold her into his arms and hold her until she felt better. But, he suspected, that probably wasn't allowed in her world.

"I wanted to help you," she murmured at last. "I really did. And if I were as pretty as Vallen, I would have been able to. John McCully would have been happy to be alone in a room with me and—"

"Oh, Sarah," he said, tilting her chin up with his fingers. Her eyes were luminous with tears. "Sarah, you don't really think *that* was the problem, do you? That John left you out in the hall because he didn't think you were pretty?"

She nodded.

"No, Sarah, that wasn't it at all. It was just that John realized what we were up to. I'm sure he thinks you're as beautiful as I do."

"You . . . you think I'm beautiful, Tyler?"

"Sarah, I think you're probably the most beautiful woman I've ever seen."

She gave him a tremulous smile that made him forget everything but his undeniable urge to kiss her. Without being consciously aware of what he was doing, he wrapped his arms around her and drew her near.

Her hair smelled like a fresh meadow, and she was so soft and warm against him it started his heart racing. But she was so tiny that the top of her head didn't quite reach his shoulder.

He was trying to decide how a man should kiss such a tiny, little thing, when she gazed up at him, her chin resting against his chest, and it was obvious. He just bent down and brushed his lips against hers.

They were as soft and warm as the rest of her. Sarah tasted sweeter than any woman he'd ever kissed.

Tentatively, he touched his tongue against her lips.

She gave a startled little gasp and drew away.

Oh, Lord, if she'd ever been kissed before at all, she certainly hadn't been kissed properly. So what on earth was he doing, getting aroused by an 1850s virgin?

Just begging for trouble, that's what.

Maybe Beauregard couldn't force a man to marry both of his daughters. But he could sure as hell decide that shooting a damned Yankee would be a better idea than forcing him to marry *either* of them.

"Sarah, I'm sorry," he murmured, awkwardly removing his arms from around her and stepping back.

She smiled nervously up at him. "I just didn't expect . . . I haven't had many beaux . . . not like my sisters. And then I suddenly remembered you're betrothed to Vallen so I have no right to . . ."

"You mean . . . you mean it wasn't that you didn't like it?"

Her face went scarlet, and he got the answer to his question. She was so adorable, he just couldn't resist kissing her again.

CHAPTER SIX

IF IT WEREN'T for Tyler's strong arms holding her, Sarah wouldn't have been able to stay on her feet. He was kissing her like she'd never been kissed before, and the way he kept caressing her lips with his tongue nearly melted away every last bone in her body.

She was growing positively senseless. She'd forced herself to remember that he was a Yankee. And that he was Vallen's fiancé. And that kissing a man she'd only met last night would be scandalous under any circumstances.

But with every passing second, she was thinking less about her behavior and more about Tyler's kisses. She'd never felt so warm and excited before in her entire life.

And then he suddenly stopped kissing her and looked over toward the window, saying, "What's going on outside?"

Because of the heat, she'd opened the window wide again, after she'd asked John McCully to close it. But she was so swept away by Tyler's kisses, it took a second before she realized there was a loud babble of voices drifting in.

Then Tyler was holding her hand and dragging her across the room. Surprisingly, she could still walk. Her bones hadn't entirely melted away.

"Don't get too close to the window," she whispered, hurrying in front of him. "They'll see you're in my bedroom. Oh, dear," she murmured, peering down at the scene below.

She could see Papa and Vallen stepping off the veranda onto the lawn. Two men on horseback had reined in before them.

"What's going on?" Tyler demanded from behind her. "Who are those men?"

"The older one is our overseer, Horace Halleck."

"He looks like a weasel."

"Tyler, get away from the window," she whispered over her shoulder.

"Who's the other one?" he asked.

"Fitzhugh Farnsworth."

"Fitzhugh Farnsworth? You mean Vallen's fiancé?" Tyler added, his voice sounding a tad uneasy.

"Vallen's ex-fiancé," she reminded him. "Papa sent Horace to the Farnsworths' with a letter telling Fitzhugh that Vallen will be marrying you instead of him. And Fitzhugh has obviously ridden back with Horace."

"And who's doing all the shouting?" Tyler demanded. "I can't see from back here."

"Fitzhugh is shouting at Papa and Horace is shouting at Fitzhugh."

"What are they saying?"

Before she could answer, her father's voice reached their ears. "I have decided," he yelled. "And no one is going to change my decision."

"It wasn't your decision to make," Fitzhugh yelled back. "It's up to *me* to decide if I still want to marry

Vallen. And I do. But first I demand satisfaction! I'll kill that damned Yankee who besmirched my fiancé.''

Sarah glanced back at Tyler. His face was as white as it had been this morning. "Is it the custom in New York," she asked, "for men to duel under these circumstances?''

"Duel?" Tyler whispered.

"Oh, dear," Sarah murmured. "Have you never dueled?''

She looked at him with alarm. The way he began vigorously shaking his head made her wish even more that she'd been able to help him escape.

Except that if he'd escaped, he'd never have kissed her. And she wouldn't have wanted to miss that. Of course, he *shouldn't* have kissed her. The only woman he was supposed to kiss was her sister.

So...oh, her thoughts were all mixed up. But one of them was perfectly clear. She didn't want Fitzhugh killing Tyler Adams. She just didn't know what she could possibly do to prevent it, now that he'd been called out.

She rested her hand on her heart, trying to stop it from racing so fast. "You *do* know how to handle a gun, Tyler.''

"Yes. I was in the army, but—''

"Good. Then don't choose swords.''

"Swords?" Tyler repeated, his voice cracking.

"Choose pistols. Fitzhugh is good with a sword, but he isn't much of a shot.''

"Then why the hell is he challenging me to a duel?" Tyler hissed.

"Because he has to. Especially if he still wants to marry Vallen.''

"Sarah, if he still wants to marry her, why doesn't your father just let him?"

"Because Papa has decided he wants you to marry her."

"Dammit, I can't marry her if Fitzhugh kills me."

"Well, there has to be a duel now that Fitzhugh has demanded one. It's a matter of honor. He might have been able to settle for an apology if what you'd done hadn't been so dreadful. But—"

"I didn't do anything! Remember?"

"Yes, of course, but—"

Someone knocked on the door and they both froze.

"Miss Sarah?" John McCully called quietly from the hall. "Tyler isn't in his room. Is he with you?"

Tyler strode across to the door and threw it open.

John gave him a black look, saying, "You shouldn't be in here. You're just lucky Beauregard sent me up to get you, instead of coming himself."

"Lucky?" Tyler snapped. "Fitzhugh's out there waiting to kill me and I'm lucky?"

"Come on," John said. "Let's get this over with."

Sarah hurried down the stairs after them, her heart racing faster than ever.

By the time they reached the front door, Fitzhugh and Horace had dismounted.

"There you are, you Northern blackguard," Fitzhugh shouted when he saw Tyler. "You think you can just come down South and Yankee Doodle another man's fiancé? I demand satisfaction. Swords or pistols?"

Tyler stared at Fitzhugh Farnsworth, not quite able to believe this was happening.

"Your choice, Tyler," John McCully said quietly.

"Pistols," Tyler said, his mouth dry.

"Papa?" Vallen put in. "I don't think you should let—"

"Quiet," Beauregard snapped. "John, you be Tyler's second. And Horace, you'll have to be Fitzhugh's. Sarah, fetch the dueling pistols. Let's go," he added, motioning everyone to move away from the house.

"I don't know a damned thing about duels," Tyler whispered to John as they walked across the lawn. "What the hell does a second do?"

"I hold your jacket for you. But mostly, I try to keep you from bleeding to death if Fitzhugh only wounds you."

"Terrific!"

"Look, just try to shoot him before he can shoot you. But there'll only be one bullet in each gun, so aim carefully. And you'll get to choose the distance—five paces or ten."

"How about a hundred?"

Sarah hurried back out of the house and across the lawn, holding a black leather case.

Black for death, Tyler thought. *His* death, most likely. But how the hell could he die in 1850, a century before he'd even been born?

Beauregard took the case, opened it and held it out to Tyler. Inside lay two of the deadliest looking old pistols he'd ever seen.

"Pick one," John prompted.

Tyler lifted one from the case and examined it. Shiny new, here. But in his world, it would be an antique.

He'd never thought much about dying, and he'd never thought at all about being killed by an antique.

Fitzhugh took off his suit jacket and handed it to Horace Halleck, so Tyler removed his and gave it to John.

"Five paces or ten?" Beauregard asked, glancing at Tyler.

"Ten." The word almost caught in his throat. For some reason, saying it drove home the fact that unless he came out the winner of this archaic exercise he was going to wind up dead.

He glanced at Sarah. Only minutes ago, he'd been upstairs kissing her. How could things have gone from fantastic to horrific in minutes?

She gave him an incredibly anxious little smile, then Beauregard said, "Places, gentlemen."

Fitzhugh stepped up to Tyler and turned his back on him.

Tyler swung around to face the opposite direction.

"When I reach ten," Beauregard said, "turn and prepare to fire. One."

Tyler forced his right leg forward.

"Two."

He glanced at Sarah again. She was gazing at him, her eyes filled with fear for him. He was seized by the sense that if they'd met in a different time and place, something very special would have happened between them.

"Three . . . four . . . five . . ."

Staring straight ahead, Tyler continued to pace forward, no longer thinking about anything except what would happen when Beauregard reached ten.

"Ten," Beauregard said.

Tyler turned back toward Fitzhugh, his heart pounding and John's words ringing in his ears. *Try to shoot him before he can shoot you.*

After both had walked ten paces, Tyler and Fitzhugh had to be about fifty feet apart, but it was the shortest fifty feet Tyler had ever seen.

"Are you ready, gentlemen?" Beauregard said.

Slowly, Fitzhugh raised his pistol, so Tyler did the same, his brain screaming that what they were doing was insane. He didn't want to kill Fitzhugh any more than he wanted to be killed.

Even so, he aimed his gun at the other man's chest and—

And then he heard the blast of a gun and felt a searing pain shoot through his side.

TIME HAD STOPPED. For a long, frozen moment Tyler waited to die. Then, his right arm still extended, his pistol still pointing at Fitzhugh Farnsworth, he glanced down at his side.

It felt like it was on fire, and with good reason. Fitzhugh's bullet had ripped the right side of his shirt open, about halfway between his shoulder and his waist. A bright red stain was slowly spreading across the white cotton.

He looked back at Fitzhugh. The man lowered his gun.

For another long moment, Tyler stared through the late-afternoon sunshine at his opponent. This man he didn't know, with his too-long nose and his thinning hair, had tried to kill him. And now Fitzhugh Farnsworth expected to *be* killed.

That was the custom in the Old South. That was what everyone was waiting for. And a deep-down animal instinct was telling Tyler that the maxim of kill or be killed was what kept men alive. But Fitzhugh had already taken his best shot.

Finally, Tyler dropped his arm and discharged the pistol into the ground.

When he glanced over at Sarah, there were tears on her cheeks, but she was smiling at him. Then Vallen grabbed her by the arm and hustled her toward the house.

He looked at Fitzhugh once more.

Fitzhugh Farnsworth was collecting his suit jacket from Horace Halleck.

Then he handed the overseer the pistol he'd used and, without a word to any of them, mounted his horse and rode off down the drive.

"Just a flesh wound," John said, checking Tyler's side. "The bullet went right on by. But we'd better head into the house and get the bleeding stopped."

Beauregard took Tyler's pistol, saying, "That was more than the man deserved, son. But his father is a friend of mine, so it's just as well. I doubt Fitzhugh will cause you any more trouble before the wedding."

"Ah...sir, about the wedding. Fitzhugh said he still wanted to marry Vallen. So, since that's the case, I thought you might reconsider making me—"

"Too late for that, son. Too late for that. My mind's made up."

"Well, sir, you could change your mind. I—"

"No, no, I never change my mind. Besides, Vallen's decided she *wants* to marry you and she never changes her mind, either. Not a speck of fickle in her. And I fancy the idea of letting Vallen have the husband she wants. Otherwise, she might act ornery for years.''

With that, Beauregard wheeled away and began marching off across the lawn in Horace Halleck's direction.

"Come on," John said, "let's get going before you bleed to death."

"But dammit," Tyler snapped, wincing as he took a step, "if Fitzhugh still wants to marry Vallen, why the hell should I get nailed?"

"Get nailed?"

"Ah . . . Northern expression. I meant, why should I be forced to marry Vallen when Fitzhugh still wants to?"

"I guess it's what Beauregard said. That he fancies the idea of letting Vallen have the husband she wants. But what I'd like to know is why Fitzhugh would still want to marry her after you—"

"Dammit, John, I told you, I didn't touch her. And the reason Fitzhugh still wants to marry her, even if I *had* done what Vallen claims, is that he wants the plantation Beau's giving as a wedding gift. According to Vallen, it's worth a fortune."

John shot Tyler a sidelong glance. "Then you'd better not count on Beauregard's being right about Fitzhugh not causing you any more trouble. Because if he wants that plantation bad enough, he's liable to come up with some other reason to kill you."

Tyler morosely walked to the house with John, trying to ignore the deep, throbbing pain in his side. If he *had* shot Farnsworth, would his life be a little less complicated? Things could hardly get much worse.

About this time yesterday, he'd been heading for La Guardia Airport, looking forward to a weekend in Georgia, and a poker party Saturday night.

Instead, he was going to be spending Saturday night stuck in the wrong century with a bullet wound in his side. Not to mention the prospect of a shotgun marriage to a conniving little witch. A witch who intended to fill in the root cellar that offered his only escape home.

And to top things off, he'd just been handed an added bonus—Fitzhugh Farnsworth probably wasn't done trying to kill him.

"Look, John," he said as they started across the foyer for the kitchen, "I need a gun. In case Fitzhugh *does* come up with another plan."

John shook his head. "Can't see Beau letting you have a gun when you're his prisoner. But I'll be around. I can take care of Fitzhugh if he tries anything." Pausing at the kitchen door, John added, "Why, Miss Sarah, what are you doing here?"

Tyler looked past John at Sarah.

She was standing beside the kitchen table, gazing at him with a concerned expression. She'd put a long apron on over her dress and had rolled up her sleeves. There were bandages and a basin of water sitting on the kitchen table.

"Our house servant, Millie, has been feeling poorly," she said, not taking her eyes off Tyler. "She's abed. And Vallen has gone to her room because she can't stand the sight of blood. So I thought I'd better see to that wound. Hopefully, we won't need to fetch the doctor."

John glanced from Sarah to Tyler, the trace of a grin on his face. "Well, I was going to tend to it, ma'am." he said, looking at Sarah again. "But I reckon a woman's touch would feel better. I'll just go wait outside until you're done."

Sarah gestured Tyler to a chair beside the table. "You were very gallant, Tyler," she murmured as he sat down. "Very gallant, not to kill Fitzhugh."

Gallant. *Very* gallant. Was he imagining it or was his chest actually puffing up with pride?

Imagining, he decided after a second. Real puffing would have made the pain even worse. But he'd never been called gallant before, and, ridiculous as it might be, she'd made him feel ten feet tall.

Sarah gathered her courage, then nervously said, "You'll have to remove your shirt, Tyler."

"Oh, of course."

He stripped it off, grimacing as he eased the blood-soaked cotton away from his wound, but not seeming a whit embarrassed about removing his clothing in front of her.

She tried to focus on where the bullet had grazed his side, but couldn't keep her eyes from drifting over his chest. The only bare male chest she'd ever seen up close before was Papa's. And it didn't have the effect that Tyler's was having on her.

His chest was extremely broad and muscular. And covered with dark, curly hair. She couldn't keep her gaze from following the trail of chest hair down. It tapered into a V, then disappeared beneath the waist of his trousers.

She swallowed hard, feeling herself blushing. Forcing her eyes to the basin of water she'd heated, she said,

"I'm afraid this will hurt some." She squeezed out the wash rag and tentatively dabbed at the blood on his side.

The more blood she cleaned away, the more relieved she felt. "It isn't too deep," she said at last. "I don't think we need to fetch the doctor. Unless having him tend to it would make you feel better."

"No, I feel fine with you tending to it, Sarah. Just fine."

She washed away the remaining blood, then cleaned the wound itself, so he wouldn't develop a fever.

Once she'd done her best, she pressed a thick pad of cotton against the wound to stop the bleeding. It was a good thing she was almost finished because being so close to Tyler did the strangest things to her. It made her heart pound and her breathing difficult. And it made her think about how wonderful she'd felt when he'd kissed her.

He was Vallen's fiancé, she reminded herself firmly, reaching for the roll of bandaging.

"I do believe," she said, weighing her options, "this pad would stay in place best if I wrapped a strip of bandaging right around you a few times."

But that meant, she realized the moment she began wrapping, that she had to get even closer to him. In fact, when she leaned forward to slip the bandaging around his back, her breasts brushed against his naked chest.

She pulled away, mortified. At the same instant, Tyler inhaled sharply and groaned.

"Oh, I'm sorry. I hurt you."

"No, it wasn't you. I shouldn't have breathed so deeply. Go ahead. Finish."

Gingerly, she leaned nearer again, trying to wrap the bandaging around him without pressing against him. It was impossible. Her arms were too short and his chest was too broad.

"Sarah?"

His face was so close to her own that she could feel the warmth of his breath against her cheek. Nervously, she licked her lips.

He groaned again, but she knew she hadn't hurt him *this* time. She hadn't moved.

"I think," he said, his voice sounding a mite ragged, "that the only way you'll to be able to do this is by sitting on my lap."

She looked at his lap uncertainly, well aware that he wouldn't have suggested John McCully sit on it if *he'd* been doing the doctoring. Of course, John McCully had much longer arms than she did. And she really couldn't see that there was any other way for her to manage.

"I won't be too heavy?" she said at last.

"No, you won't be too heavy."

Taking a deep breath, she eased onto his lap. Then, carefully avoiding the wound itself, she stretched her arms around either side of him. In that position, she could reach far enough behind his back to pass the roll of bandaging from her right hand to her left.

"When I'm done," she told him as she worked, "you go upstairs and rest. I'll give you some laudanum to take."

"Laudanum?"

"Yes, don't you use it up North?"

"Ah . . . I never get sick up North . . . or shot."

"Well, it will ease the pain and help you sleep. The doctor gave me some for Millie, but there's more than enough for both of you. And I'll have Louis take up a dinner tray for you. I don't think you should have to face either Papa or Vallen again until tomorrow."

Wrapping the bandage around him a third time, she tied it off and murmured, "All done." Then she started to slide from his lap, but he caught her hand in his.

"Sarah," he said quietly, "thank you. You're the only good thing about being trapped at Booker's Knoll."

She smiled nervously at him, then did the boldest thing she'd ever done in her life. She leaned closer and kissed him. Right on his lips.

The kiss was every bit as wonderful as it had been earlier. And his woodsy male scent enveloped her in a most intoxicating way.

"Sarah," he murmured, ending their kiss far too soon. "Sarah, I wish the circumstances were different...that maybe we could...but we can't. You're downright irresistible, Sarah, but...well, I guess what I'm trying to do is be gallant again. I don't want you to be hurt. And somehow, I have to get out of here. I can't marry Vallen—I have to get home. And I'll never be able to come back."

Her throat was suddenly so tight she couldn't speak, so she simply nodded.

Whatever had she been thinking, behaving in such an unseemly manner? She'd known how desperately Tyler wanted to get away. And she knew that, if he did, she'd never see him again. But, if he didn't, he was going to become her sister's husband.

CHAPTER SEVEN

"TYLER? TYLER, WAKE UP."

Groggily, he opened his eyes and tried to focus on the five men in front of him.

Then his vision began to clear and he realized there was really only one man. Clayton Willis.

It was dusk outside and the bedroom was dim. Tyler's mind was fuzzy, but if it was almost dark, then it must have been hours since Sarah had given him that medicine and packed him off to bed. That stuff sure worked. His side was barely hurting at all.

"Sarah told me what happened," Clayton said. "Can you walk all right? You'll be able to make it out of here with me?"

"Yeah . . . yeah, make it out of here." But what was Clayton doing back already? He'd said he was going to stay in 1993 until tomorrow. He had his poker party to host tonight.

"Your poker game." The words didn't come out sounding quite the way they should have.

"Yeah, the poker game was great. Too bad you had to miss it. And I guess you had a pretty rough time here, with Vallen playing her game."

"Vallen . . ." All the horrible details began drifting back. Vallen was going to have the root cellar filled in and he'd never be able to leave 1850.

But no, Clayton had come to help him get home. And he wouldn't even have to worry about concentrating on getting to 1993 because Clayton would do it.

Which was a good thing, given the way Tyler's head felt. He shook it, trying to clear his mind a little. Instead, the movement made him dizzy. He tried to get Clayton in focus again.

"Clayton. The root cellar. Is it still there?"

"Of course it's still there. How else would I have gotten back?"

"Yes . . . right." So everything was going to be fine.

"Look," Clayton said, "I'm sorry I couldn't get back earlier. But some of the guys decided we should play all night, and by the time I got rid of them . . . well, anyway, I'm here now."

"All night?" Tyler struggled into a sitting position. The inside of his mouth felt like it had grown fur. "Are you saying this isn't Saturday night?"

"This is *Sunday* night," Clayton said, grinning. "Hell, Sarah mentioned she'd given you a few doses of laudanum, but she must have been in here pouring it down your throat every hour."

"Laudanum . . . she told me it was a painkiller."

Clayton's grin was fading fast. "Yeah, it kills pain, all right."

"Sarah," Tyler said, vaguely remembering her sitting beside the bed, "Sarah was here all the time."

"For over twenty-four hours? I doubt it. Tyler, you don't know what laudanum is, do you?"

"Uh-uh."

"Well, it's opium suspended in alcohol. And it can cause hallucinations."

"Ah...it can also cause addiction, can't it?" he asked uneasily. That disturbing thought went a long way toward clearing his head.

"You wouldn't get addicted in just a few days," Clayton said. "But hallucinations can start immediately. So you were probably hallucinating about Sarah being here."

That was possible, Tyler decided. She'd looked too angelic to be real, sitting there beside him. Of course, he'd thought she looked like an angel the first moment he'd seen her.

"Hell, Tyler, this laudanum could be a problem. I've got a plan, but I didn't expect you to be doped up."

"Plan. What plan? What's all that?" he added, noticing there was a heap of clothes on the end of the bed.

"Oh, that was my excuse for coming here tonight. I brought some of the old outfits from my collection. I said they were *your* clothes, and I'd brought them over since you were staying here now. I brought you this, too, just in case things don't go smoothly."

Clayton rummaged through the pile of clothes and produced a gun. An old Colt. It wasn't as large as John McCully's, but seeing it made Tyler feel a whole lot better.

Not that he wanted to end up shooting his way out of 1850, but if he did run into *more* trouble in this damned century, a gun might come in handy.

"Plan," he said again. "What *is* the plan?"

"This." Clayton reached inside his jacket and pulled out a large silver flask.

"It's brandy, laced with enough liquid tranquilizer to stun an elephant. It tastes like cherries, so I'll tell Beauregard I've brought him a special cherry brandy to try. I figured all we'd have to do was make sure Beau and John McCully enjoy it more than we do. With all the laudanum in your system, though, we'd better come up with an excuse for you not to try *any* of it.''

"How about saying I'm allergic to cherries? Do people know about allergies in 1850?"

"I don't think so. But they know about hives—old Ewell gets them sometimes. So just say cherries give you hives."

Tyler nodded. He might not be much of a liar, but surely he could make a little white one sound convincing.

"Okay," Clayton went on, "so now all we have to do is get Beau and John to drink this stuff. Then they'll pass out and you and I will be on our way to the root cellar."

"Sounds good." And it felt good, too. Clayton had just removed a major weight from his shoulders. The best plans were always the simplest, and they didn't come much simpler than this.

"You get cleaned up," Clayton ordered. "Then come downstairs. I'll get Beau and John started on this stuff."

Tyler rubbed his jaw as Clayton headed for the door. Someone had shaved him while he'd been asleep.

He thought hard and recalled the scent of soap... Sarah beside him with a basin of warm water.

Someone had undressed him, too. He couldn't recall who'd done that, but he'd bet it had been Louis. Sarah would have been too shy.

Although, he had to admit, there'd been nothing shy about that last kiss she'd given him in the kitchen.

She'd sure surprised him with that. And if he hadn't felt obliged to be gallant...

He lit the candle on the dresser, then riffled through the pile of clothes Clayton had brought, amazed the activity didn't make his side hurt worse than it did. Maybe, when he got home, he'd begin a movement to bring back the use of opium as a painkiller.

The brown suit he selected made him think about Sarah again. The suit was a dark chocolate brown. Almost the exact color of her eyes.

Once he was dressed, he slid the Colt into the waistband of his pants, against the small of his back, then blew out the candle. As he started down the hall, he glanced at Sarah's door.

He hated like hell leaving without saying goodbye. But telling her wouldn't be a wise idea. Better if no one knew about Clayton's plan until they were safely out of here.

Very, very reluctantly he started past her door.

And then he stepped on the creaky board she'd warned him about.

THE FLOORBOARD was still squeaking as Sarah opened her door and stood in front of Tyler.

She was wearing white again. This time, her white dress had puffed sleeves and tiny buttons down the front. Its long skirt was so full she had to be wearing a dozen crinolines, or petticoats, or whatever they were called.

Her face seemed paler than normal, and there were dark circles around her eyes.

"You look tired," he said quietly.

"I haven't slept. I was afraid to leave you alone until I was certain you'd be fine. If you'd developed a fever, we'd have had to fetch the doctor right away."

So she *had* been sitting with him for twenty-four hours straight. No one in the world had ever been that concerned about him. At least, not since his parents had died.

But Sarah had stayed with him like his own private guardian angel. Except the dress she was wearing tonight made her look more like a bride than an angel.

Suddenly, the craziest thought popped into his mind. If Beauregard wanted him to marry Sarah, rather than Vallen, would he be quite so intent on escaping?

Of course he would, he told himself. He had a life to get back to.

"You're leaving, aren't you?" Sarah murmured.

"Ah...I'm just going downstairs...to have a drink with Clayton and your father."

She shook her head. "Clayton came tonight to help you get away, didn't he?"

"Well...yes. Sarah, I wanted to say goodbye to you. But I thought it would be best if I didn't."

"Tyler, I've been thinking about what would be best, too. Thinking and thinking, weighing what could happen. And I know how much you want to get back up North, but it might be best if you just stayed here."

"And married Vallen?"

"Marrying Vallen would be better than being killed."

"I'm not so sure." He smiled as he said that, but Sarah didn't smile back.

Instead, she frowned, saying, "Don't josh, Tyler. Papa is no fool. He's half expecting you to try to escape. And if you do, he'll stop you. With that wound in your side you won't have a chance.''

''No, it'll be okay. Clayton has a plan. A good plan,'' he added when she looked skeptical.

''All right,'' she said at last. ''If that's your decision, I'll go sit with Vallen in her room and keep her occupied. Because she'd shoot you every bit as fast as Papa would if she thought you were getting away.''

''Sarah . . . I seem to have spent my whole time here thanking you for one thing or another. But thank you again.''

She merely nodded.

It was his cue to go, but he couldn't seem to make his feet move away from her.

''Tyler . . . be careful. I don't want you to die.''

''I know. You'd rather I married your sister.''

He'd been teasing, of course, trying to lighten the mood, but Sarah's eyes filled with tears.

''Oh, Sarah,'' he murmured, stepping toward her. He had no problem at all making his feet move in *that* direction. He wrapped his arms around her and cuddled her against his side—the one without a bullet wound.

''Tyler,'' she whispered, pressing her cheek against him, ''do you remember what you said yesterday? Before we tried to trick John McCully?''

''What did I say?''

''You said you were sorry you'd never be able to see me again. Because you would have liked to.''

''I still would, Sarah. Incredibly much. But it isn't possible.''

"I know. And I don't want you to stay, because you'd have to marry Vallen. But I don't want you to go, because . . . because I'd like to see *you* again, too."

He hugged her tightly to him. She was such a tiny little thing that he was tempted to just pick her up and carry her off with him.

And then the realization hit him like the proverbial ton of bricks. He really wanted to.

For one insane moment, he considered asking her to go with him. Then the moment passed and reason returned. They were from different lifetimes. And what could he say to her? Something like, *Sarah, please come with me to 1993?*

He gazed down at her again, her cheek resting against him, and almost said the words. But he knew in his heart that he couldn't. Hell, if he started in about being from the future, she'd think he was a madman.

She shifted in his arms and looked up at him, her eyes glistening. "This time it's really goodbye, isn't it?" she whispered.

He nodded, then, unable to stop himself, he leaned down and kissed her, certain he'd never feel so sad again as he did when she drew away.

"I'll just go across to Vallen's room now," she murmured. "Do be careful, Tyler Adams."

Without another word, she turned and hurried across the hall to Vallen's door, knocked, then quickly opened it and disappeared inside.

Tyler stood gazing at the closed door, then finally forced himself to start for downstairs.

By the time he reached the bottom of the staircase, he could hear the men in the parlor. He paused to listen.

It sounded as if Clayton's plan was working. Beauregard was asking something, then John replied. Both of them were speaking loudly but slowly, and their words were slurred.

Tyler glanced back up the stairs, hoping for a final glimpse of Sarah. She wasn't there, of course. She was in Vallen's room, doing her part to help him escape— playing her role in this plan that would mean they'd never see each other again.

Damn but he hated it being this way. He'd never before felt an urge to play caveman, to literally sweep a woman off her feet and carry her away with him. So why, when that urge had hit him, did it have to be a woman he couldn't have?

TYLER STOOD in the parlor doorway, surveying the scene before the others realized he'd arrived.

After a minute or so, Clayton glanced across and acknowledged his presence with a surreptitious thumbs-up.

Clayton looked alert—he couldn't have had much of the brandy at all. But the same wasn't true of Beau or John.

Beauregard was slouched in a huge leather chair, his white hair tousled, his bearded chin resting on his chest and his eyes closed. He was obviously feeling the effects of Clayton's tranquilizer.

John McCully wasn't in much better shape. He took a sip of brandy, carefully holding the snifter with both hands, but when he lowered it to the table beside his chair he almost missed the edge.

He stared at the table for a second, as if he suspected it of having moved, then looked up and noticed Tyler. "Hey," he said, waving a shaky greeting.

Beauregard's head jerked up and his eyes opened, but they were mere slits. "Siddown, son," he said. "Havva drink. Clayton's brought me the bess brandy in the world."

"*Cherry* brandy," Clayton said.

"Oh, damn, I can't have any then. I get hives from cherries."

"That means there's more for us," Beauregard muttered, hiccuping. His chin dropped back to his chest and his eyes closed again.

John McCully took another sip of his drink, gazed at the glass for a second, then mumbled something that sounded like "What the hell," and drained the snifter. This time, when he tried to put it down, he *did* miss the table.

The glass shattered on the wooden floor and John sat staring at the shards, a puzzled expression on his face. "So-o-o tired," he said at last, resting his head against the back of the chair. "So-o-o tired."

John's eyes closed and Tyler glanced over at Clayton.

He held up his hand, fingers spread, indicating they'd wait five minutes before making their move.

Tyler spent the whole five minutes thinking about Sarah. Incredible as it seemed, knowing he'd never see her again was making his heart ache worse than his side.

He'd never believed in love at first sight, but that's what had happened to him. Or, at least, it had been darned close to first sight.

And the way Sarah had been acting, he was pretty sure the same thing had happened to her. But this situation was the catch-22 to end all catch-22s.

He certainly didn't want to stay in 1850. And if he had to, he'd be forced to marry Vallen and wouldn't be able to have Sarah, anyway.

And he was sure Sarah would never go home with him. Of course, he hadn't told her where "home" really was. If he had, though, she wouldn't have believed him. At least he didn't think she would.

But what if he *had* told her? And she *had* believed him? He hadn't even given her a chance. But the future was the only place they could possibly be together, so shouldn't he at least go back upstairs and try the truth on her?

Clayton pushed himself out of his chair and started quietly across the room. He gestured Tyler into the foyer, then closed the parlor door, whispering, "You wait here. I'll go find Louis. He'll have someone bring my buggy around."

"Clayton? I have to talk to Sarah before we leave."

"Don't be absurd. We haven't got time to waste. You wait right here. I'll be back in a minute."

Tyler stood gazing at the stairs while Clayton hurried in the direction of Louis's room off the kitchen.

Sarah was just up those stairs. Of course, she was in Vallen's bedroom. And if he went banging on the door, saying he had to talk to Sarah, Vallen would demand to know what the hell was going on.

Before he could figure out how to get around that problem, Clayton reappeared, Louis in tow.

The house servant looked at Tyler uncertainly, and Clayton said, "Don't worry, Louis, Mr. Adams isn't going anywhere. He's just saying good-night to me."

"Is Mr. Booker still in the parlor, sir?" Louis asked.

"Yes. Now be quick about my buggy."

Louis cast an anxious glance at the closed parlor door, then started out into the night.

"It'll just take him a couple of minutes," Clayton said.

"Ah...Clayton, there's something I should tell you."

"What?"

"Well, it's the damnedest thing. Somehow I've fallen in love with Sarah. That's why I have to talk to her. See, I should have told her we're from 1993. I mean, I should have explained everything and asked her to go back with me. I can't leave until I have."

Clayton stared at Tyler as if he'd just escaped from a loony bin. "Tyler, are you nuts?" he said at last. "We've got to get out of here. Pronto."

"Clayton—"

"Dammit, Tyler. When Beauregard comes to, he'll realize the brandy was spiked. And if we're not gone, I'll be out of here on the end of his boot and he'll chain you to a tree until the wedding."

"Look, all I'm going to do is explain to Sarah about time travel and ask her to come with us. It'll take a couple of minutes."

"A couple of minutes? Tyler, it would take a couple of decades. People in 1850 have never even heard of time travel. H. G. Wells isn't even born yet!"

"But—"

"No! I guarantee that you start in with Sarah and she'll only think you're a raving lunatic."

Tyler could feel his jaw clenching. Like it or not, he was almost certain Clayton was right. Hell, he'd realized earlier what Sarah would think. But now that he and Clayton were actually on their way, it seemed imperative that he try *something*.

"Even if you just asked her to run off up North with you," Clayton was muttering, "it would take her forever to decide."

"But you can't be sure what—"

"Yes, I *can* be sure. And what if she *did* say she'd go with you? You'd have to marry her, you know. Women in 1850 didn't just move in with a man. And you can't marry someone you've only known a few days."

"Why not? I'd marry someone I'd only known a few hours if I thought she was the right one. And you know what? I think Sarah's the right one."

"Oh, hell, Tyler, you're being ridiculous. I once gave this a lot of thought, and . . . oh, never mind."

"What?" Tyler eyed Clayton curiously. "What do you mean you once gave it a lot of thought?"

Clayton shrugged. "Well . . . there was once something between Ella-Jane and me. It started not long after I discovered the root cellar. And that's when I thought about . . . oh, Tyler, use your brain. It's an impossible situation."

"Listen, Clayton, maybe you decided not to bother saying anything to Ella-Jane, but I'm not going to leave without at least taking a shot at it. I'm not walking out of here without—"

Louis interrupted, appearing at the open front door. "Your buggy is waiting, Mr. Willis."

"Well?" Clayton said to Tyler.

He glanced at the stairs once more. Just as he did, a loud thud came from the parlor and Louis quickly started across the foyer.

"Tyler!" Clayton hissed. "Either somebody fell out of his chair in there or one of them is coming around already." He grabbed Tyler's arm and pulled him outside, sending so much pain shooting through his side that resisting was impossible.

A groom was holding the bridle of Clayton's bay mare with one hand and the reins in the other. Clayton scrambled up into the driver's side and grabbed the reins, telling Tyler to hurry.

He didn't have a choice. Dammit, he knew he didn't . . . but no! He *did* have a choice. And he wasn't getting into that buggy until he'd talked to Sarah.

"Going somewhere, Mr. Adams?" a voice asked from behind him.

Tyler wheeled around. The sudden movement caused another searing stab of pain.

A man stepped from the darkness of the veranda into the light spilling through the doorway. A man holding a shotgun. It was Beauregard's overseer—that weasely looking Horace Halleck.

"Louis told me you might be looking to go somewhere, Mister Adams," Horace said, grinning. "And I don't think Mr. Booker would take kindly to that. I reckon," he added, gesturing at Clayton with his gun, "that maybe you should stay around for a spell, too, Mr. Willis. I expect Mister Booker will want a few words with you before you go on home."

CHAPTER EIGHT

SARAH GAZED ACROSS the veranda, watching her father's carriage roll down the drive to the main road. With he and Vallen on their way to Savannah to finalize some of the wedding details, it was the ideal time for Tyler to escape.

She glanced over at him, her emotions in turmoil. How could she still be trying to help him get away when the last thing she wanted was to see him leave? Or was seeing him marry Vallen the last thing she wanted?

He caught her gaze and gave her a weary smile. Her heart started beating faster than a hummingbird's wings. She might not know what she wanted *least,* but she knew exactly what she wanted most.

She'd fallen in love with Tyler Adams, and she wanted *him.* But she didn't see how she could ever possibly have him.

She *could* possibly help him, though. In fact, she was the only one left to help.

Clayton Willis would certainly never show his face at Booker's Knoll again. Not after the way Papa had shouted at him, once the effects of that brandy had worn off last night.

"You've got until the wedding to move out of that house of mine!" Papa had yelled. "And don't you dare set foot on *this* plantation again. You do, and I'll shoot you on sight."

Mercy, Papa had been so loud that she and Vallen had been able to make out every word from upstairs.

So she was the only one left to help Tyler. But every time she thought about never seeing him again, a huge lump filled her throat.

Swallowing painfully, she turned her attention to John McCully.

Letting down his guard last night had clearly made him even more determined that Tyler was going to stay right here. She'd tried to reason with John the entire time Vallen and Papa had been getting ready to go into the city. But John was a most unreasonable man.

She took a deep breath, then began again. "You know, John, Clayton Willis was simply trying to right a wrong last night."

"I don't hold with men lying and tricking people," John said, giving Tyler a black look.

"That brandy was Clayton's plan," Sarah pointed out. "Not Tyler's."

"I'm as much to blame as Clayton," Tyler muttered. "He was only trying to help me get out of here."

Sarah decided to try another approach. "John, Tyler has told you he never laid a finger on Vallen and I've told you the same thing. And why would I lie? Why would I take Tyler's side against my own sister?"

That question made John McCully grin.

His grin made Sarah blush. Had she allowed her feelings for Tyler to be so obvious?

"Why would I take *anyone's* side against my own sister?" she pressed on. "Only because what Vallen is doing isn't right. Keeping Tyler here against his will isn't fair when he's done nothing wrong. Can't you see that? Don't you believe we're telling you the truth?''

John leaned back in his chair and tipped his hat up a little with the barrel of his gun. ''I *do* believe you, Miss Sarah,'' he said at last. ''The more I've seen of people around here, the easier it is to believe that Vallen made up her story.''

''Then you'll let Tyler go,'' Sarah cried, half overjoyed that she'd convinced John, half devastated because it meant Tyler really would be leaving her.

''Well, now,'' John said slowly, ''I didn't say I'd let Tyler go. It's like I told him right off. It's a matter of my word. I gave your father my word that I wouldn't let Tyler stray. So I can't.''

''What sign are you?'' Sarah asked, fearful she already knew the answer. ''Your astrological sign,'' she added when John gave her a blank look. ''What date is your birthday?''

''February 12.''

''Oh, dear, I thought as much. He's an Aquarius,'' she explained to Tyler. ''It's the only sign that values honor and honesty more than an Aries.''

''Aquarius?'' John said. ''And that means I'm honest, huh? Well, I don't know about astrology. But back home a lot of folks do call me Honest John.''

Sarah rolled her eyes. Why in mercy couldn't John have been a Leo? Enough flattery and you could persuade a Leo to go along with anything.

''You know, Tyler,'' John said, ''I really *would* like to help you out here. I don't hold with a woman lying and cheating any more than I hold with a man doing it.''

"John, the only way you can help me out is by turning a blind eye. So I can get the hell away."

"Well . . . I just can't see my way clear to doing that. But there might be another way. I've been thinking, what if we were to figure out something you could do to get yourself into Beauregard's good books?"

"That doesn't sound like much of an idea," Tyler muttered, shooting John a dark look.

"No, I mean, *far* into his good books. Then, if you asked him again about not marrying Vallen, maybe he'd feel obliged to change his mind and let Fitzhugh marry her, after all."

"That just might work," Sarah murmured hopefully. "If you did Papa a big favor, he'd feel honor-bound to repay you."

"You're sure?" Tyler asked, looking decidedly more interested in the idea.

"Yes. But the stumbling block," she said, thinking on it, "is that Papa doesn't have any problems that need solving or anything. He's awfully good at sorting problems out for himself. Unless . . ."

"Yes?" Tyler pressed.

"Well, I help Papa with the plantation's records, and the cotton yields at Booker's Knoll have been down for the past couple of years. I know it's been worrying him a mite."

"That doesn't help," John said. "I don't know a thing about growing cotton. And I recall you saying you'd never been on a plantation before, either, Tyler."

"Right, I haven't. But I know a little about the sorts of things that affect cotton yields. I have to, considering I make my living playing the commodities market.''

"*Playing* the commodities market?'' Sarah said, glancing curiously at him. She knew what brokers did. After all, Ewell Endicott was the wealthiest cotton factor in Savannah and she knew *something* about his business. But she'd never even heard the term commodities market. And brokers bought and sold in a most serious manner. It was hardly play.

"Ahh . . . it's a joke,'' Tyler told her, looking unsettled. "Up North, we sometimes refer to working as playing.''

She smiled wanly, reminded that the South was right to be suspicious of Northerners. They had some very strange ways about them.

Silently, Tyler swore at himself. He'd been careless, making the odd slip and using phrases that hadn't been coined until long after 1850. He'd have to be more careful. Mentioning the commodities market had made both Sarah *and* John look at him strangely.

"Maybe I don't know enough about growing cotton to figure out what the problem could be,'' he said at last. "But looking around the place and asking questions has got to be worth a try. You figure Horace Halleck would cooperate with the idea, Sarah? Especially after last night?''

"Let me think,'' she murmured. "He'd certainly do it if Papa were here and ordered him to. But you'd probably want to get started right away, wouldn't you?''

When he nodded, she said, "All right. I believe Horace is doing something in the stable. I'll go with you and talk to him. Tell him you'd like him to show you the gin house. I'll say you've decided you want to learn all about running a plantation, so you'll know what you're doing...when Papa gives you and Vallen your wedding gift."

Sarah's voice trembled a little on her final words, and Tyler had an almost uncontrollable desire to take her into his arms. He didn't want to even think about being part of a wedding unless it was Sarah he was marrying. But he couldn't tell her, right this minute, that somehow he was going to work things out so he could marry *her.*

Because he wasn't sure that he *could* work things out. Even if he got the other problems under control, there was still the not-so-minor detail of having to explain to Sarah their real destination.

And hell, maybe he was getting way ahead of himself. *He'd* marry someone he hadn't known long, if he figured she was the one for him. He always went ahead and jumped in when something felt right.

Sarah, though, seemed inclined to think about things a lot before she made decisions. Besides, for all he knew, she might not feel half as strongly about him as he did about her.

Maybe she wouldn't even consider the idea of going to *1850* New York with him, let alone 1993 New York—assuming, of course, he could convince her he wasn't crazy.

Sarah picked up her parasol and he rose. His side was still sore when he moved, but he could bear it.

They started out toward the stable. It was situated on the opposite side of the house from the slave quarters just in front of the field that ran down along the river.

John McCully followed along, lagging behind enough to be unobtrusive. He'd obviously realized what had happened between Tyler and Sarah, and he was being cool about it.

John was a good guy. The better Tyler got to know him, the more he liked him.

Of course, he'd like him a *whole lot* more if he wasn't so damned concerned about keeping his word to Beauregard. Because if this plan to make it into Beauregard's good books failed, getting out of here would still be a matter of somehow giving John the slip and getting to the root cellar. Before Vallen had the damned thing filled in.

But giving John the slip was going to be tricky.

The gun Clayton had brought last night suddenly seemed to be pressing harder against the small of Tyler's back. He intended to keep it there constantly, safely hidden by his suit jacket. There was no knowing when he might have to use it.

But if his only way of escaping turned out to be using it on John McCully...

He shook his head, doubting that killing John McCully was something he could make himself do.

"What?" Sarah said.

"Huh?"

"You were shaking your head. I just wondered what you were thinking about."

He gazed down at Sarah, remembering how desperate he'd felt last night when he'd almost been forced to leave without her. And then he recalled Clayton saying, "Even if you just asked her to run off up North with you..."

Well, what if he *did* ask her to go with him? He could explain about time travel later. That way, he could kind of ease into the idea of her leaving with him and see how she reacted to it.

Yes, finding out how she felt about leaving with him *at all* had to be the place to start.

He glanced back, checking that John was still out of earshot, then turned to Sarah again, trying to decide exactly how to put this.

WHEN THEY WERE about halfway to the stable, Sarah stole another glance at Tyler.

The last time she'd looked, he'd seemed lost in thought, but now he was gazing at her as if he wanted to say something and couldn't quite find the words.

He gave her a tentative smile that started her heart fluttering.

''Sarah?'' he finally said.

''Yes, Tyler?''

''Sarah, I was thinking about what you said last night…about not wanting me to stay, because I'd have to marry Vallen. But not wanting me to go because…well, Sarah, when you said you'd like to see me again, did you mean it? *Really* mean it?''

Sarah stared at the hem of her skirt as they walked on. She shouldn't have said that last night. With things as they were, she'd had no right. It had been most unseemly and improper. But somehow the words had slipped out.

''Sarah…Sarah, I can't believe this has happened so fast, but I've fallen in love with you.''

That declaration startled her so much she almost tripped. He'd fallen in love with her. Just as she'd fallen in love with him.

Oh, mercy, she hadn't meant to admit that. Not even to herself. But it was true. She'd fallen in love with a Yankee. And, worse yet, she'd betrayed Vallen by doing so.

"Sarah . . . I need to know how you feel about me."

She stopped and looked at him, stunned. This Yankee fiancé of her sister's wanted her to come right out and tell him how she felt about him.

Whatever should she say? If she admitted she loved him, and he ended up married to Vallen, she'd very much regret speaking the truth.

But if she lied...oh, she couldn't lie to him. And she did want to tell him she loved him, too. But it was too much. She couldn't say aloud that she loved her own sister's fiancé.

"See, Sarah, what I've been wondering is if you'd even consider the idea of coming North with me. Assuming I can get away from Booker's Knoll, of course."

"Of going North with you?" she managed to say, her mind in such a tizzy she could barely speak.

"Well . . . we'd never have any chance of a future together here. Not with Vallen and all, but . . ."

He stopped walking and stood gazing evenly down at her. "Sarah, if you came North we could be married. You could live in New York with me."

"New York?" she repeated inanely. Naturally, marrying him would mean living in New York. That was where his work was. And even if Tyler *would* consider staying, he was right about them having no future here.

It wasn't realistic to believe Papa would relent and change his mind. And even if he miraculously consented to Tyler and her marriage, Vallen would be so spiteful she'd likely set fire to their house the first chance she got.

But living in New York... why, it was chock-full of Yankees, with all those strange ways of theirs. And it was so far from Georgia and her family.

"New York," she said again. "Life in New York must be very different from life at Booker's Knoll."

Tyler nodded, looking uneasy. "I can't lie to you, Sarah. The truth is that your life with me in New York would be so different it would make your head spin. But is the idea something you can even entertain? Do you feel strongly enough about me to consider it?"

She gazed up into the warmth of his blue eyes, knowing she'd never feel as strongly about anyone else as she did about him.

But could she really give up everything to be with him? And why were they even talking this way when Tyler was betrothed to her sister?

If she helped him escape, though, she could go with him. And he'd marry her—not Vallen. Oh, this was all very confusing.

"Well, Sarah? Can you even at least think about marrying me?"

She took a deep breath, gave him a nervous smile and said, "Why... I'd be honored to at least consider the idea, Tyler Adams."

He grinned more broadly than she'd have imagined possible, then murmured, "I want to kiss you, Sarah Booker. But I think it had better wait until my guard isn't around."

Sarah glanced back at John McCully. She'd forgotten all about him, but there he was. He'd had the good grace to pause when they did, staying a distance back, but he was still doing his job.

They started off once more, Sarah desperately trying to figure out how she was going to convince Horace Halleck to cooperate. But all she could think about was being Tyler Adams's wife.

Tyler practically floated on air the rest of the way to the stable. At least, until they reached the kennel that was adjacent to it. Then the uproar caused by their arrival brought him down to earth.

There had to be close to twenty dogs in the big pen. And the ones that weren't barking or howling were snarling, snapping and drooling.

He'd always thought of bloodhounds as kind of passive dogs, but he'd apparently thought wrong. Even the most passive-looking of these ones would make a New York junkyard dog look like a sissie.

"They ever get fed?" he asked, eyeing their bony frames.

"Horace likes to keep them on the hungry side," Sarah explained. "He says it makes them better at hunting."

"You dogs shut up!" a man yelled, stepping out from behind the end of the stable.

"There's Horace now," Sarah said.

The man nodded at them. "Miss Sarah," he offered politely.

Tyler noted the din had died down considerably at Horace's shout. He focused on the man. It was the first time he'd gotten a long, close look at Beauregard's overseer.

During the duel on Saturday, when Horace Halleck had acted as Fitzhugh Farnsworth's second, he'd been across the lawn from Tyler. And last night, when Horace had thwarted Clayton's escape plan, it had been dark.

From a distance, Tyler's impression hadn't been good. Horace looked like a weasel. Up close, the resemblance was even more striking. A forty-odd-year-old weasel with rotting green teeth and tobacco stains on his dingy white shirt. The man even smelled like what Tyler imagined a real weasel would.

When Sarah began explaining what they wanted, it became obvious that Halleck's personality was about as charming as his appearance. And he clearly wasn't keen on giving Tyler an overview of the operation at Booker's Knoll. At least, not just on Sarah's say-so.

"Papa," she insisted, eyeing Horace sternly, "wants Mr. Adams to learn as much as he can before he and Vallen take over the other plantation. He'd have given you the instructions himself, but he and Vallen were in a hurry to leave for Savannah."

Casually, John McCully drew his Colt from its holster and tipped the brim of his hat up with the barrel. "Mr. Booker," he said, not putting the gun away again, "mentioned to me what a cooperative man you are, Mr. Halleck."

"Yeah...well, I guess I got a minute to show you 'round," Halleck muttered. "Come on. You're right, Miss Sarah. Most important thing for Mr. Adams to see is the gin house."

They tromped along under the blazing sun again until they reached the gin house. It was a two-story wooden structure, about eighteen feet by thirty-six feet.

Roughly the size, Tyler couldn't help thinking wistfully, of a large, refreshingly cool, inground pool.

The gin house, though, was as hot as every other place on the plantation.

Half of the ground level was taken up by a huge wheel, turned by four mules trudging in endless circles. A slave with a whip ensured they kept trudging.

From the center of the wheel rose a drive shaft that extended through a hole in the ceiling to power the cotton gin on the second floor.

Following Horace Halleck up the outer stairs, Tyler gulped a few deep breaths of fresh air while he had the chance. The gin house smelled of animals, human sweat and an oily substance that must have come from the cotton.

The air on the second floor was as bad as on the first. And, for an added bonus, it hung far more heavily with dust.

Halleck pointed back through the broad doorway, toward the cotton fields. "The wagons bring baskets of cotton from the fields," he said, giving Tyler a shifty-eyed glance. "Then it gets brought up here to the gin."

Tyler nodded, focusing on the cotton gin. It was about half the size of a small car, and one of its main components was a series of circular saws, set half an inch apart.

Steel bars separated them from a large revolving cylinder, but the teeth of the saws projected through the bars, to within about two inches of the cylinder's surface.

"Cotton goes there," Halleck went on, pointing to the cylinder. "The saw teeth catch at it, and the lint gets pulled through but not the seeds. Then them brushes underneath brush the lint off the saws. Then it goes to that press downstairs—gets packed into bales.''

"Which weigh?" Tyler asked.

The overseer shrugged. "Ain't no standard weight. Maybe four hundred pounds. Maybe four-fifty. Depends on the crop."

"Papa says," Sarah put in, watching the overseer closely, "that our crops haven't been as good as usual the last couple of years. Our yield's been down."

Halleck shot her a black glance. He obviously didn't think women should be privy to such information.

"What would cause a lower yield?" Tyler asked. "Variations in temperature? Amount of rainfall? Those sorts of things?"

"Yeah, that's what does it."

Sarah caught Tyler's eye and said, "Cotton grows best when there's a wet, warm spring and a long, hot summer. That's what we've had the past few years."

Her words earned her a longer, even blacker glance from Halleck. He looked as if he could cheerfully throttle her.

Tyler shifted his weight, putting himself between the two of them.

"Soil's getting old, Miss Sarah," Halleck snapped. "Booker's Knoll ain't fresh land no more."

"So what happens once the cotton is baled?" Tyler asked quickly.

"The bales go down to the river and get loaded on a barge. That's how we get 'em to Savannah. Then they get shipped outta the port to wherever they's going."

"And the bales get weighed in Savannah?" Tyler asked. "And you get paid according to the weight?"

"*I* don't get paid," Halleck said. "I don't have nothin' to do with the money. Mr. Booker gets paid. Direct by Mr. Endicott."

"Ewell Endicott?" Tyler asked Sarah.

"Yes. He's the major cotton factor in Savannah."

"So," Tyler said, turning back to Halleck, "what else do I need to know about?"

The overseer took time to spit a juicy brown wad of tobacco onto the floor before he answered.

"Mr. Adams," he said at last, "owning a plantation ain't gonna be hard work for you, even being a Yankee. You got a thousand acres of land and a hundred slaves. You got horses, mules and a gin mill. And you got an overseer to make it all work right. Ain't nothin' more you need to know."

Tyler nodded. Halleck obviously figured he'd done enough to qualify as being cooperative. "Well, thanks, then, Mr. Halleck," he offered. "I'll be sure to tell Beauregard how helpful you were."

ON THE WAY BACK, John McCully didn't lag behind. And as soon as they were several yards away from the gin house John said, "So? You think there could be something amiss, Tyler?"

Tyler glanced a question at Sarah.

She hesitated. She wasn't accustomed to men asking her opinion about anything, but Tyler Adams actually seemed to believe she had a brain.

Of course, she'd read in some of her magazines that Northern men were more liberal in their thinking. Mercy, if she ever went North with Tyler, she was going to find things *so* different.

"What do you think, Sarah?" he asked, when she didn't speak right up.

"Well," she said, twirling her parasol uncertainly, "I hadn't given it much mind until you asked about Papa having problems. But now that I've started thinking on it... I just can't see any logical explanation for our getting lower yields when the weather has been ideal."

Tyler rubbed his jaw as they walked, finally saying, "What about Halleck's theory that the soil is getting old? Does it wash?"

Did the soil wash? She looked at Tyler uncertainly.

"Oh, sorry, another Northern expression," he muttered. "I mean, what Halleck said about old soil explaining a drop in yield. Is it likely?"

She shook her head, trying not to worry that, sometimes, the North and the South didn't even seem to speak the same language. "On some plantations that would be true, but not at Booker's Knoll. Papa uses very progressive methods. He fertilizes with potash, phosphates and sulfuric acid before every spring planting."

"So..." Tyler said, "if someone wanted to skim off the top... I mean, if someone set out to cheat your father, set things up so he didn't get all the money the cotton was actually worth... is there a common way a fellow would try to do that?"

"I don't think so," she said slowly. "Of course, all I know about it is what I've overheard from Papa's conversations with other planters. But everyone knows that some overseers will try to steal, so they watch out for it."

"How?" John asked.

"Well, at Booker's Knoll, we have a weigh scale down at the river. It's where the barge collects the bales. So they're counted and weighed before they leave the plantation."

"And who supervises that?" Tyler asked.

"Papa does."

"And who checks that the records match the ones in Savannah? That the number of bales sent is the number received? That the total weight is the same?"

"Papa does that, too. I mean, he *used* to, back when he dealt with one of the smaller cotton factors. But since Ella-Jane married Ewell, Papa uses his company. So now he has kin right there in Savannah to make sure everything is aboveboard."

"You're saying that your father doesn't check his shipping figures against what's received anymore?"

"Well, he *could* go into Ewell's office and check if he wanted to. But there's no need. Ewell is always waiting on the wharf when Papa's shipments come in."

Tyler glanced over Sarah's head at John, saying, "You thinking what I'm thinking?"

John nodded.

"What?" Sarah said. "Ewell would never cheat *anyone,* let alone Papa."

"Not Ewell," Tyler said. "But Ella-Jane married Ewell a couple of years ago, didn't she?"

"Yes."

"And that's when the yields dropped?"

"Well . . . yes," Sarah said again.

"And Horace Halleck...would he have figured your father wouldn't check the records once his son-in-law was looking after his interests?"

"Well...yes, I imagine he probably would have. I mean, Ewell is family. If Papa were to check his company's records, it would be an insult. It would be questioning Ewell's honesty. And no Southern gentleman would ever do that to his own kin."

"Then I think maybe we're on to something," Tyler said, a broad grin lighting up his face. "What if some of the cotton *went missing* between here and Savannah? If there's nobody checking if what leaves here is exactly what arrives there..."

"No," Sarah said hesitantly.

"No?"

"No, you see, Papa knows almost exactly what the cotton is worth before it leaves Booker's Knoll. The price per pound doesn't fluctuate much in a few days. And Ewell always pays Papa about what he's expecting to get. Sometimes even a little more. So Ewell must be receiving everything we ship."

"Oh," Tyler said, his grin completely gone.

"There's still something amiss," John muttered. "There's still what Sarah said before. About there being no logical explanation for getting lower yields when the weather's been ideal. That means something unusual *must* be going on. Either with the shipments or the records. We just have to figure out what."

"You could be right," Tyler said. "Maybe if we had a look.... Sarah, is there any way we could see your father's books for the last couple of years?"

"Ah..." She hesitated, feeling dreadfully anxious. If Papa ever caught her...

"Sarah?" Tyler said quietly. "If we can solve your father's problem...."

"Papa's records are in his study," she finally said before she could change her mind. "The last few years don't take up many pages. And he'll be so busy with the wedding, he won't be looking at them until after it's over. But Ewell's records are in *his* office, and I can't imagine how we'd get to look at them."

"What about Ella-Jane?" Tyler asked.

"Oh, my," Sarah murmured. "Oh, my, I don't know whether she would help or not. Or even if she *could* help."

"Let's try to come up with a way that she could," Tyler said.

CHAPTER NINE

TYLER HAD BARELY slept all night, and now his stomach muscles were so tight he could scarcely eat breakfast.

Before Beauregard and Vallen had returned from town yesterday, Sarah had taken the records they needed from Beau's study. And they'd come up with a plan for comparing his figures on the cotton shipments to Ewell's. But things had to go their way before their plan could get rolling.

Both Sarah and John were sitting on the far side of the dining room table, avoiding any eye contact with Tyler. He knew, though, that they were anxiously waiting for him to deliver his opening line.

At last, Vallen stopped chattering about when she was being fitted for her wedding dress, and he had his chance.

"Beau?" he said.

Beauregard glanced across the dining room table, coffee cup halfway to his mouth.

"Sir, I've been thinking that I should see some of the area around here. So that when folks talk to me at the wedding they won't think I'm a dolt."

His gaze flickered to John as he said "dolt." That had been John's word, and he smiled slightly.

"I mean," Tyler hurried on, "I should at least see something of Savannah, so I can talk intelligently with the guests."

"Oh, that's a good idea, Papa," Vallen said. "Why, I certainly wouldn't want people to think I'd marry a dolt."

Tyler held his breath. He could use Vallen's help, as unwitting as it might be. But if *she* offered to take him into town, that would sink the plan.

"I wouldn't mind making a trip into Savannah myself," John said. "Haven't had a chance to look around yet."

"Fine," Beauregard said, allowing Tyler to breathe again. "John, you just let Louis know whatever day you want to go and he'll have the buggy brought around."

"Actually," Tyler said, "I was thinking about going today... leaving in about half an hour. That way, I'd be there before lunch time. See, Beau, I'd like to take Ewell out to lunch. Get to know him better, since he's going to be my brother-in-law."

Beau grinned. "Lunch? That's one of them new-fangled Northern words, isn't it."

"Ah..."

"Son, you're going to be living down South so you've got to talk like a Southerner. Down here, dinner is still dinner, and supper is still supper. But taking Ewell out to dinner isn't a bad thought. You want to show him a Northerner can be hospitable, huh? That your idea, son?"

"Exactly," Tyler said, trying not to flinch at the way Beau kept calling him son.

"Well, that's a mighty fine idea. Mighty fine. Ewell is a member of the Savannah Men's Club. You just suggest eating there. Ewell will like that."

Tyler seriously doubted Ewell ever liked anything, let alone being invited to lunch—or dinner, as was apparently the case—by a damned Yankee, but he resisted saying so.

"You wouldn't mind if I rode along, would you, John?" Sarah said. "It's been so long since I've done any work for the historical society that everyone there will be thinking I up and died."

She'd managed to sound so casual Tyler wanted to lean across the table and kiss her. He resisted doing that, as well.

"If Sarah's going with you, John," Beau said, "then take the carriage. I won't be needing it today. Now, Vallen," he went on, "what do we still have to arrange for?"

Vallen immediately began babbling about the refreshments for the wedding.

She seemed to have Beau's undivided attention, so Tyler risked a glance over at Sarah and John. Sarah gave him a tiny smile; John a slight nod.

Barely half an hour later, the three of them were on the dirt road that led to Savannah. Like the three musketeers of Georgia, Tyler thought—John driving, Sarah sitting between them.

The heavy four-wheeled family carriage provided a slower ride than Clayton's two-wheeled buggy had. It wasn't much smoother, though. But Tyler barely felt the bumps and jolts. Phase one had been a success, and what was the odd bump and jolt on the way to phases two and three?

He glanced at Sarah and smiled. Hell, every time he looked at her he smiled. He'd asked her to marry him and she hadn't said no.

Of course, there were still a few minor difficulties to deal with before she actually said yes. But they were working on them, and it felt so damned good just to be with her.

She'd put on a hat for the trip into town...no, a bonnet, she'd called it. It was the same pale blue as her dress and had a wide front brim and a big white bow tied at her throat.

He hadn't yet figured out how she always managed to look so cool when the humidity was as high as the temperature. But right now she looked so beautiful he'd have loved to have captured her forever in a photograph.

He almost told her that, then caught himself. He wasn't sure whether cameras existed yet. Lord, things were going to be so much easier once he'd explained things to her. That is, once she understood about time travel.

That nagging little fear about how she'd react reared its head again. He forced it out of his mind and took her hand.

She blushed, but didn't remove it from his. And if John McCully noticed, he pretended not to.

"Tyler?" she murmured. "What if I can't convince Ella-Jane to help us?"

"You will," he said. And, if she couldn't, they'd think of another way of getting a look at Ewell's records.

Hell, if the numbers didn't match up with Beauregard's, if Horace Halleck *was* playing some kind of fiddle...well, surely finding out about it would put Tyler as far into Beau's good books as it was possible to get.

The trip into Savannah took *about* two hours. When they reached the outskirts of the city, Tyler was amazed. He'd foolishly been thinking in 1990s terms of pavement and skyscrapers. In contrast, Savannah's streets were rutted mud, and the buildings weren't above three stories in height.

"You'll have to give me directions, Miss Sarah," John said.

"Of course. We'll go past Ewell's place of business on the way to the house, so you'll know where it is."

The road they'd been following had paralleled the Savannah River. In town, it became River Street and ran along the top of the riverbank.

There was a sharp drop-off, so the wharf itself wasn't visible from the carriage, but the tops of ships were. There were two steamers, a paddle wheeler and a mixture of barges and smaller boats.

"This is the mercantile section," Sarah said. "The next street over is Bull Street," she went on, pointing to their right. "That big building over there, at the corner of Bull and Bay streets, is the Customs house. And the offices of *The Georgian* newspaper are right there, too. And that's the Exchange clock. It always tells perfect time. Savannah's a bustling city, isn't it?" she added, smiling at Tyler.

He nodded, wondering if there was even a word in her vocabulary that would describe modern-day Manhattan at rush hour.

"There's another street below River," she continued, shifting their attention to the left. "Commerce

Row. You'll be able to see it from Ewell's office. It's right down by the wharf. And that's Ewell's building there.''

Tyler gazed at the relatively impressive warehouse-type building as they passed. It sprawled along a good portion of a downtown block of River, which was undoubtedly prime real estate.

"Turn here," Sarah said. "This is Abercorn Street and it will take us right up to Lafayette Square, where Ella-Jane and Ewell live."

The Endicott home was an elegant three-story brick house with wide marble front steps and stately white pillars. It was set back from the street and boasted a beautiful front garden—as did the other houses on the residential square. The walkway was flagstone, unlike the board sidewalk in the business district.

Ewell's wealth, Tyler decided, had not been exaggerated. He swung out of the carriage and helped Sarah down.

"Good luck," John said, tipping his hat to her.

She nodded, tightly clutching the tapestry bag that contained the pages from Booker's Knoll's shipping records.

"You going to be okay?" Tyler murmured.

"Yes . . . it's just that I've never done anything like this before and I'm . . . I'm a mite anxious."

"You'll do fine, Sarah."

She gave him such a nervous little smile that he simply couldn't resist.

He leaned down and brushed her lips with a kiss. Right in broad daylight in 1850 Savannah. And, Lord, it was the craziest thing, but doing it made him feel positively daring.

SARAH STOOD WATCHING the carriage until it turned off Lafayette Square and headed back in the direction of Savannah's mercantile district.

Tyler's kiss had started her heart racing, and it was still beating in a most irregular manner. But by now, that had as much to do with the task facing her as with his kiss.

She turned toward Ella-Jane's house and gazed at the front door, telling herself not to fret so. Ella-Jane was her sister. And kin did for one another.

Of course, Ewell was Ella-Jane's kin now, too. And what they were asking her to do... well, Ella-Jane would be in a heap of trouble if Ewell ever found out about it.

But these were special circumstances. And Ella-Jane would help. Sarah just knew she would.

She forced one foot in front of the other until she was standing on the top step. Taking a deep breath, she banged the knocker.

Cliffie, the house servant, answered the door and greeted her.

"Is my sister home, Cliffie?"

He hesitated, then said, "Mrs. Endicott is abed, Miss Booker. She be feeling poorly this morning."

Sarah closed her eyes for a moment. Ella-Jane *couldn't* be indisposed. Her help was essential. "It's important that I see her, Cliffie."

The servant moved aside, but looked uneasy about letting Sarah in. "I'll go tell Mrs. Endicott you here, Miss Booker."

"No, no, don't bother announcing me. I'll just go up and see her. It will be quite all right," she assured the servant, noticing his nervous glance at the staircase.

She pushed past Cliffie and hurried up to Ella-Jane's bedroom. The door was closed, so Sarah softly knocked, hoping her sister wastn't too ill.

"Yes?" Ella-Jane called quietly.

She didn't *sound* ill, Sarah noted with relief. "It's me, Sarah," she called back through the door.

"Just a minute," Ella-Jane said quickly. There was a lengthy series of rustling and scuffling noises in the bedroom before Ella-Jane finally opened the door a crack.

"I have to come in and talk to you," Sarah said.

"Sarah, I'm afraid I'm not feeling well."

"It's important, Ella-Jane. *Really* important."

Ella-Jane managed a wan smile and opened the door a little farther.

She was still in her nightdress, with a robe tied loosely over it, and her hair was all tangles, almost covering one side of her face. The drapes were pulled across the windows, so the bedroom was dim.

"What is it, Sarah?"

Sarah stood looking at her sister, feeling incredibly guilty. Ella-Jane really *was* ill. Too ill to get dressed and go out.

"Sarah? You said it was important."

"I . . . it is, but I didn't realize you were this . . ."

"I'll be all right," Ella-Jane murmured, drawing Sarah into the room and shutting the door. "I'm not really sick, only tired. Now, what is it?"

"You're sure you can talk?"

"Yes. I'm fine. I just didn't sleep well last night. Now, what?"

"Ella-Jane, it's about that story Vallen made up about what Tyler Adams did to her. I *know* she made it up. She told me so. And he doesn't want to marry her. And...oh, Ella-Jane, I've fallen in love with him, and I don't want him to marry her, either. It just isn't fair or anything. And he and I have a plan to make Papa change his mind, but we need your help." Sarah stood biting her lip, praying Ella-Jane would say yes.

Instead she shook her head and said, "Mercy, Sarah, I didn't understand a word of that. Now, come and sit on the bed. I want you to start right at the beginning and tell me all about this plan."

Sarah followed her sister and perched on the edge of the bed, trying to collect her thoughts.

"All right, now," Ella-Jane said. "I knew from the beginning that Vallen was lying. I should have tried harder to talk her out of what she intended. And I understand about Tyler Adams not wanting to marry her. Papa and Vallen came by yesterday, when they were in town. They told me all about the duel with Fitzhugh and about Clayton's attempt to help Tyler escape."

Ella-Jane paused.

In the dim light of the bedroom, Sarah thought that a sad look had crept into her sister's eyes. The same sad look she seemed to get whenever she saw or spoke of Clayton Willis.

Of course, it wasn't likely she'd ever be seeing Clayton again. He'd never come back to Booker's Knoll now that Papa had threatened to shoot him if he did.

Fleetingly, Sarah wondered if Papa had told Ella-Jane about that. But before she could mention it, Ella-Jane went on.

"I also understand," she said with a knowing smile, "how you could have fallen in love with a fine looking man like Tyler Adams. But tell me about this plan of yours.''

"It's not just *my* plan," Sarah said slowly, intent on making her explanation plain. "It involves Tyler Adams and John McCully, and you and Ewell, as well."

"Ewell? Oh, Sarah, Ewell would never become involved."

"Well, he won't actually realize he is. You see . . ." Sarah took a deep breath, then dove in and told Ella-Jane all about the plan to get Tyler into Papa's good books. She explained about the poor crop yields at Booker's Knoll and their suspicions that Horace Halleck might somehow be cheating Papa.

By the time she finally got to the part about what she needed Ella-Jane to do, Ella-Jane had begun pacing the room.

Sarah waited until she couldn't stand the silence a second longer. "Well, Ella-Jane? Will you help us?"

Ella-Jane stopped pacing and stood eyeing Sarah for the longest minute. Then she slowly shook her head. "I'm sorry, Sarah. Truly sorry. But I can't. I can't leave the house today."

Sarah's eyes began burning with tears of frustration. She blinked them back, and looked pleadingly at her sister. "But you said you weren't really sick. You said you were only tired. And we can't do this without your help. Ella-Jane, I love Tyler. I want to marry him. I don't want him to be forced to marry Vallen. And, I don't want Papa forcing me to marry someone I don't love, like he did to you. *Please* help me."

Ella-Jane covered her mouth with her fingertips and stood gazing at Sarah. "All right," she finally whispered. "I don't want Papa forcing you into a loveless marriage, either. So I'll help. But it will take me a little while to get ready. I have to hide this somehow.''

She brushed the tangle of hair aside from her face, revealing a huge bruise that ran from her eye down to the bottom of her ear.

"Ella-Jane," Sarah gasped, horror rushing through her. "What happened?"

"Ewell hit me," Ella-Jane said evenly. "Ewell hits me all the time. Now, run downstairs and tell Cliffie to have the carriage readied."

"Ella-Jane, I—"

"Right this minute," Ella-Jane snapped. "Then wait in the parlor for me. I'll be as quick as I can."

Almost ill, Sarah stumbled down the stairs, relayed Ella-Jane's instructions to Cliffie, then went to wait in the parlor.

She hated Ewell Endicott. Hated him with all her heart. And somehow, she was going to help her sister. She stood gazing out onto Lafayette Square, using the passing minutes to regather her composure.

Through the window, she watched one of Ella-Jane's wealthy neighbors stroll past the Endicott residence toward her own elegant house. This square was the most prestigious place to live in all of Savannah, but Sarah was certain Ella-Jane would easily give everything up to be with a man she loved.

"The carriage will be ready in a minute, Miss Booker," Cliffie announced from the parlor doorway.

"Thank you, Cliffie," she murmured, glancing away from the window. "I'm sure my sister will be down shortly."

She continued to stand, gazing outside. There had to be a way of helping Ella-Jane. If only she hadn't married old Ewell. If only Papa hadn't finally lost his temper that day....

The recollection came floating back so clearly it might have happened yesterday, rather than two years ago. Sarah closed her eyes, reliving the scene.

"You three girls are far too particular," Papa had raged. "I've been turning suitors away for almost ten years now, and I'm sick to death of it. I'm the only man in Georgia who has three unmarried daughters in their twenties. And you, Ella-Jane, are twenty-five years old. Why, you're virtually a spinster. And Ewell Endicott is a wealthy man needing a wife."

"But, Papa—"

"No! I know what you're going to say. I've seen you mooning around Clayton Willis whenever he's here. But I haven't heard him asking me for your hand. And even if he did, I wouldn't have a traveling man for a son-in-law. No, Ella-Jane, you are going to marry Ewell Endicott, you hear?"

Sarah opened her eyes again, wishing that Ella-Jane had never given in. But Papa wouldn't have it any other way, and Papa's will was far stronger than Ella-Jane's.

"I'm ready," Ella-Jane said from the doorway. She was wearing a hat with a huge brim, tied down on both sides. It hid all but the center of her face.

"Do I look good enough," Ella-Jane asked, her voice bitter, "to pay a visit to the office of my husband? Savannah's leading business man?"

"WAIT HERE FOR US, Jackson," Ella-Jane told her driver after he'd helped her and Sarah out of the carriage.

"Yes 'um," Jackson said.

Ella-Jane gathered up her skirts and swept regally across the wooden walk to the front door of Ewell's building.

It was all Sarah could do to make herself follow Ella-Jane inside—she was shaking like a leaf. How could her sister possibly appear so calm and composed?

They walked across the main floor of the building, past a number of clerks working at their desks. Every single one surreptitiously glanced up as Mr. Endicott's wife passed by.

Ella-Jane stopped in front of the clerk who guarded the door to Ewell's office and imperiously said, "Good day, William. I've come to see my husband. Please announce me."

"Mrs. Endicott," William greeted her, almost falling over himself trying to get up from behind his desk. "How nice to see you. But I'm afraid Mr. Endicott has gone out for dinner."

Looking back at Sarah, Ella-Jane gave an exaggerated sigh. "Oh, my, Sarah, it's just as I feared. We've arrived too late to join them. Well, William," she added, turning to the clerk again, "my sister and I shall just have to wait in Mr. Endicott's office for him, then."

"Ahh . . . Mr. Endicott doesn't like *anyone* in his office when he isn't there, ma'am. I could have someone fetch some chairs for you out here and—"

"Nonsense," Ella-Jane snapped. "There are chairs in my *husband's* office. Come, Sarah." Without another word, Ella-Jane marched past William and opened Ewell's office door.

"Come, Sarah," she repeated firmly, noticing her sister's hesitation.

Not even glancing at William, Sarah dashed by his desk and scurried into Ewell's office.

Ella-Jane closed the door, then leaned against it, rapidly patting her throat with her hand. "Oh, my," she murmured. "Oh, my, I'm not very good at that sort of thing."

"You were wonderful," Sarah whispered. "Positively wonderful."

With a tiny smile, Ella-Jane pointed toward a long wooden cabinet behind Ewell's desk. The upper section was a series of glass-and-wood doors, behind which sat shelves of ledgers.

"I think all of the records are in there," she said quietly. "You look for what you need. I'll guard the door."

As quickly as she could, Sarah ran her eyes along the volumes until she located one labeled Booker's Knoll. She opened the glass door, cringing when the hinges creaked, and pulled the ledger down.

Hands shaking, she removed the pages of her father's records from her tapestry bag and began comparing the figures.

"Well?" Ella-Jane whispered after a minute.

"I'm still checking," Sarah murmured, her spirits sinking lower with every set of numbers she compared. They matched. As much as she didn't want them to, they *all* matched.

The number of bales and the total weight recorded as leaving Booker's Knoll were the same as the number and weight received at Ewell's wharf. For every single shipment her father had made since he began dealing with Ewell.

She and Tyler and John had been wrong. And their wonderful plan had gotten them nowhere at all. Horace Halleck hadn't been cheating Papa.

Her throat so tight it was aching, she closed Ewell's ledger and shoved it back into its place on the shelf. Then she shut the creaking glass door and turned.

She simply shook her head at Ella-Jane, doubting she could speak without tears of disappointment spilling over.

"Oh, my," Ella-Jane said. "Oh, my. You just sit down, then, Sarah. I'll have William run across the street and fetch us some nice cold lemonade from the Savannah Hotel."

Blindly, Sarah made her way to a chair.

While Ella-Jane opened the door and spoke to William, Sarah sat gazing out the window, blinking away her tears.

The wharf was full of bustling activity. People were loading stacks of barrels and cotton bales onto the docks, and several schooners were moving in or out of their slips. However, all Sarah could think about was that they'd been wrong about Horace Halleck. And now Tyler would still have to marry Vallen.

"Sarah?" Ella-Jane said softly, sitting down beside her and taking her hand. "Sarah, maybe there's some other way."

"I don't think so," she murmured. "We were so sure we'd find out that less cotton had arrived in Savannah than had left the plantation. And we don't have another plan. But, oh, Ella-Jane, enough about my problems. What's Ewell going to say when he gets back? If he's angry we came into his office, he won't...will he?"

"I'll be all right, Sarah. There's usually only trouble when he's had too much to drink. Bourbon does something dreadful to his temper."

Sarah squeezed her sister's hand. "I'm so sorry, Ella-Jane. I didn't know. But there must be something you can do...*we* can do. If only..." She hesitated, not certain whether she should go on.

"If only what?" Ella-Jane said.

"I...I don't know. It's just that I always expected Clayton Willis would..."

"I always expected he would, too," Ella-Jane murmured.

They were interrupted by a knock on the door, and William bustled in with their lemonade.

Ella-Jane thanked him politely, then waited until he'd closed the door again before turning back to Sarah. "You know, I never did understand why Clayton Willis didn't declare himself. I was so sure he loved me. I thought I'd had enough beaux that I could tell. There were several times when he seemed on the verge of asking me something important, but he never did.

"It wouldn't have mattered, anyway," she added with a sad little shrug. "Papa would never have let me marry Clayton Willis. He said so, remember?"

"Yes, I remember. But you know he sometimes says things he doesn't mean. And if Clayton *had* spoken to Papa...what would you have done, Ella-Jane?"

Ella-Jane gazed at the floor for the longest time. When she looked up, her eyes were moist. "I would have married him, Sarah. Even if I'd had to fight Papa over it. I loved Clayton Willis."

Sarah's heart ached for her sister. Imagine loving one man and being forced to marry another. "I think he loved you, too," she finally offered, hoping it would make Ella-Jane feel better.

She was wise enough, though, not to add that she thought Clayton was *still* in love with Ella-Jane. Judging by the way he looked at her every time he came to the plantation.... But he'd never be coming again, so there was no point in mentioning her suspicions.

"Well," Ella-Jane said, wiping her eyes, "it's far too late to be wondering whether Clayton Willis loved me or not, isn't it."

A moment later, the door burst open and Ewell stormed in, glowering at them.

"Oh, Ewell," Ella-Jane said, smiling up at him. "When Sarah told me you were dining with Tyler Adams and John McCully, I thought it might be fun to join you. But we were too late. And we've had to sit in your stuffy old office prattling on for goodness knows how long. Why, if it weren't for that nice William of yours fetching us cold lemonade, we'd have just fainted right away."

Tyler and John were standing behind Ewell in the doorway. Tyler was trying to catch Sarah's eye.

She couldn't meet his gaze. Telling him their plan had failed would wait until they got away from Ewell's office.

Instead of looking at Tyler, she focused on Ewell. Thankfully, he didn't look suspicious. His glower on finding them there had changed to an expression that, for him, was almost pleasant.

"Well, my dear," he was saying to Ella-Jane, "I'm sorry you've had such a tedious time. Had I known you were coming, we would have waited, of course."

"Of course," Ella-Jane murmured, rising from her chair and nodding to Tyler and John. "So nice to see you again, Mr. Adams. Mr. McCully."

She gave Sarah a tight hug, whispered "Good luck" into her ear, then said her goodbyes and left.

"Would you like a tour of the warehouse?" Ewell asked Tyler. "I'm hoping you intend to use my services once you're running your own plantation."

"Of course I will," Tyler said. "But we'd better save the tour for another time. I told Beauregard I wanted to see the city, and so far all I've seen is the inside of the Savannah Men's Club."

TYLER FELT EVERY BIT as discouraged on the ride back to Booker's Knoll as he'd felt hopeful on the way to Savannah.

Maybe if any of them had been able to come up with another plan, he wouldn't feel quite so defeated. But there wasn't even a glimmer of an idea between them.

So somehow he was going to have to make a break for it.

He glanced at John McCully, wondering what his odds were of getting away. And then his gaze drifted to Sarah.

What on earth was he going to do about her? Was there any chance she'd go with him? And even if she would, could he risk trying to take her? What if she got hurt?

But there he was, miles ahead of himself again. Sarah hadn't agreed to go up North with him even if Beauregard *let* him leave. She'd only agreed to think about it.

And he couldn't take her with him without telling her the truth first. He just couldn't deceive her about something so important.

He shook his head, not wanting to think what her reaction would probably be to the thought of traveling 143 years into the future. But maybe, if he delayed telling her as long as possible...

It was late afternoon by the time they got back to Booker's Knoll. When John reined the horses to a stop in front of the house, Beauregard and Vallen were sitting on the veranda, drinking lemonade.

"Oh, do join us," Vallen called sweetly while they were climbing down from the carriage. "You must all be dry as a zephyr."

"A zephyr?" Tyler murmured to Sarah.

"A west wind. There's an awful lot you Yankees don't know, isn't there?" she teased.

"You all must be hot as hellfire," Beauregard boomed. "Come and set here in the shade for a spell. Louis?" he hollered toward the open front door. "Louis, more lemonade!"

Tyler eased himself into one of the wicker chairs, glad to be sitting on something that wasn't moving.

"Well, son," Beauregard said, "Vallen and I were just talking about fixing up your plantation some before the wedding."

Tyler's entire body went on alert. If *fixing up* had anything to do with that stupid pond she'd talked about...

"Vallen's got a right good idea, Tyler. She wants a pond behind the house. She tell you about that?"

He nodded, trying to look calm, but Beau's words had turned the trickle of perspiration running down his back into a torrent. Vallen had told him about it, all right. He remembered every word she'd said, with horrific clarity.

Papa can just have some of the slaves dig a big hollow. And fill in that old root cellar out back, of course.

"So, how does the idea strike you, son?"

"Ah...well, it's certainly something to think about, sir. I guess it's something I might want to do in the near future."

"Why, shoot, son, there's nothing to think about. We just dig you a new root cellar alongside the house and put the pond out back. There'll be a break in the picking in a few days so I'll be able to send some slaves over then. They'll have everything done before the wedding."

The torrent of perspiration running down Tyler's back turned icy cold. There'd be a break in the picking in a few days. How the hell long was a few days? Five? Four? Three?

What if those slaves of Beauregard's picked faster than he expected? What if that root cellar got filled in within the next day or two?

"Oh, Papa," Vallen said, "do we have to wait for a break in the picking? Couldn't you send a few slaves over there in the morning? I'd so like to see that pond started."

"Well, we'll see, darling, we'll see," Beau said, smiling indulgently. "We can probably arrange something."

Tyler sank back into his chair, a sharp dig against the small of his back reminding him of the gun tucked securely there. This little turn of events meant that now, he had to get out of here before morning. But how the hell was he going to ditch John McCully?

CHAPTER TEN

SMELLS OF MELTED WAX and smoke drifted lazily into the parlor. They made Tyler think of a dinner party, but they weren't coming from dining room candles.

In the foyer, Louis was snuffing the candles in the chandelier with a long, polelike extinguisher—bringing the little metal funnel at the end down over each of the flames.

As the foyer grew dimmer, the parlor seemed bright by comparison, even though it was only illuminated by two oil lamps.

Louis left three candles lit. They were no match for the surrounding darkness, though, providing barely enough light for those still up to make their way to bed.

Tyler had no intention of going to bed. That talk about beginning work on Vallen's pond had scared the hell out of him.

He kept trying to convince himself the root cellar *couldn't* get filled in. It still existed in 1993. But if he could take Sarah home with him he'd be changing history. So maybe it could be changed in other ways, as well. Maybe the damned cellar *would* be filled in, and he'd be trapped here.

He couldn't chance that. As soon as it seemed safe to make a break for it, he'd have to head across the cotton fields to Clayton's.

He glanced out into the foyer again, this time at John McCully. John was leaning against the far wall, by the staircase, and he didn't look as if he had any more thoughts about going to bed than Tyler, himself.

Honest John was on the job. And if he didn't take a hike sooner or later... well, Tyler still hadn't figured out what he was going to do.

He turned his gaze to Sarah, sitting quietly in the chair beside his. He didn't know what he was going to do about her, either.

Well, actually, he knew what he had to do. Tell her the truth. The whole truth. And then she'd have to make her own decision. He just hadn't figured out what words to use to explain.

If he didn't find the *right* ones, he hadn't a hope in hell that Sarah would go with him. But he was so afraid the right words simply didn't exist.

Finally, he took a deep breath and murmured, "Sarah?"

"Yes?" she said quietly, smiling at him.

He loved her smile, just as he loved *everything* about her. In fact, he seemed to love her more each passing minute. He just *had* to find the right words. "Sarah," he began once more, taking her hand this time.

It was so tiny and soft. Holding it in his, he couldn't help but recall how wonderful it had felt to have her touching him the other day. Even though he'd been in pain from Fitzhugh's bullet.

But with Sarah sitting in his lap, wrapping that damned silly bandaging around him, he'd barely been aware of the pain. He'd only been aware of her. The soft curves of her body, her meadow-fresh scent, her gentle touch.

He wanted to be close to Sarah for the rest of his life. Wanted to feel her touch, see the warmth of her smile.

"Yes, Tyler?" she said again.

"Sarah . . . with our plan failing today . . ."

"We'll think of another one, Tyler. We still have time."

"No," he said, shaking his head. "No, Sarah, we don't. See, there's something you don't understand. Something I haven't told you."

She gazed at him with her big brown eyes, waiting.

He looked out at John again, making certain he was still out of hearing range. John hadn't moved a muscle.

"Sarah . . . what I have to tell you is very difficult to understand. And just as difficult to believe. But it's the truth."

"Of course," Sarah said, giving him a teasing little smile. "You're an Aries. You wouldn't lie to me."

"Yeah . . . well, keep that in mind, huh?"

Sarah smiled again. She could sense that Tyler wanted to talk to her about the future. About *their* future. Because, somehow, they *had* to have a future together. She just couldn't bear ever to be as unhappy as Ella-Jane.

As soon as they got everything straightened out with Papa regarding the upcoming nuptials, Sarah intended to put her mind to what she could do to help Ella-Jane.

"You see," Tyler went on, "what I have to tell you concerns what I'm doing here."

"You came to visit Clayton Willis," she said, giving him her full attention once more.

"Ah...right. But, Sarah, Clayton doesn't really live here. Not *really.*"

"I know. Why, with all his traveling, he's almost never home."

"No, Sarah, you don't understand what I'm trying to say."

She looked at him curiously. So far, she'd understood every word he'd said perfectly.

"You see, there's something you've never heard of. It's called time travel."

"Time travel," she repeated. She wasn't familiar with the phrase. But then, there seemed to be a lot of Northern phrases she wasn't familiar with.

"Yes," Tyler said. "And what it refers to...well, there are ways that people can travel through time."

"Well, of course, Tyler. Everyone knows that."

"They do?" he said, staring at her with the most incredulous expression.

"Of course. You did it coming to visit Clayton. You must have."

"Sarah...Sarah, I...I..."

"Tyler, why are you stammering? I mean, you must have gotten on a train or boat in New York, then traveled through time until you finally reached Georgia. Why, mercy, you would have traveled through entire days to come all that way. But *everyone* knows it takes time to travel from one place to another."

Tyler released her hand and began rubbing his jaw. She'd noticed he always did that when he was trying to puzzle something out. But she couldn't see anything puzzling in what they were talking about.

"Sarah, I can't figure out exactly how to put this."

"Put it plainly, Tyler. That's always the best way."

"All right." He leaned forward, and gazed at her intently.

"Sarah, Clayton and I actually live in the year 1993. That's where Clayton is when he's supposedly off *traveling*. He's back where he really belongs. And that's where I belong, too. In 1993 New York. But I came to Georgia—1993 Georgia, that is—to visit Clayton. And he brought me to 1850 to play a game of poker and ... well, you know the rest."

"Oh, Tyler," Sarah said, laughing quietly. "You really *do* have the most droll sense of humor. You had me completely fooled. I truly did believe you wanted to talk to me about something serious."

"Sarah, I've never been more serious in my life! I'm not trying to be funny. Look, I'll prove it to you."

He began digging frantically through his pockets, then muttered, "Damn. I left my wallet back at Clayton's, in my own clothes."

"*These* aren't your own clothes?"

"No, these are Clayton's."

Now, Sarah was really puzzled. She knew perfectly well those were his clothes. When Clayton had arrived with them the other night, he'd told her so.

"I brought Tyler's clothes over," he'd said.

So those were definitely his own clothes Tyler was wearing. Why would he say they weren't? And why he was saying *so many* silly things? There was something about the Northern sense of humor that she didn't find amusing.

Perhaps, though, if she tried playing along, she could get into the spirit of his joshing.

"Look," he said, sticking one of his feet up into the air and waving it around in a most foolish manner. "Look at these shoes. They're mine."

"Really? Why, Tyler, I simply assumed those shoes were Clayton's. And what about the socks? Are they Clayton's?"

"No, they're mine. And look at them," he added, pulling his trouser leg up a few inches. "See how smooth they are. A modern machine made these socks, Sarah. A 1993 machine."

She smiled tolerantly, even though the light was far too faint for her to see whether the socks were smooth or not.

"And look at these shoes," he said again. "They don't look much like your father's shoes, do they?"

"Well . . . no, I guess they look more like Northern shoes."

"No, Sarah, they look like 1993 shoes! Because that's what they are."

Oh, dear, this wasn't working at all. "Tyler . . . I'm sorry. I tried for a bit, but I just don't appreciate this type of funning. I'm sure that after I understand Northern humor better, I will. But right now—"

"Dammit, Sarah, I am *not* trying to be humorous!"

"There's no need to use profanity, Tyler Adams."

His lips grew tight, as if he were trying to keep words in. At last he said, "Believe me, there's nothing the least bit funny about this. I'm simply trying to tell you that I have to get back to Clayton's root cellar before Vallen has the damned thing filled in to make her pond."

"Clayton's *root cellar?*"

"Yes. That's how he gets back and forth between centuries. Somehow, you can travel through time in that root cellar. But once it's filled in, I'll never get home. So, I'm trying to tell you that if you want to marry me, you'll have to come with me now. Tonight. But, if you do, you'll end up in 1993, not 1850."

Sarah gazed at Tyler, feeling a mite annoyed. Maybe, if she wasn't so tired, she'd be entertained by this nonsense. But she *was* tired. And she didn't find it entertaining. And since she'd told him she wasn't enjoying it, he should have stopped.

Managing a smile, she rose, saying, "It's so long past my bedtime I can scarcely keep my eyes open. Tomorrow we'll come up with another plan to get you into Papa's good books. I'm sure we will. But before I can think on it, I need some sleep. So... good night, Tyler."

She hesitated, then boldly leaned down and gave him a quick kiss on the cheek. It made her blush, but she was glad she'd done it. She wouldn't want to leave him believing she was *overly* annoyed.

"Sarah?" he said as she started for the door.

She turned back and looked at him, thinking how much she loved him, despite his silliness.

"I... good night, Sarah Booker. I love you. I'll always love you."

She smiled. Then, with his words to dream on, she hurried upstairs.

FOR A TIME after Sarah went up to bed, Tyler simply sat in the parlor, his heart aching. He should have known she wouldn't believe him.

Actually, he *had* known. He'd simply refused to accept it. Clayton had been right. It would take two decades to explain time travel to her. And he didn't have two decades. He had no time at all.

He had no choice, either. He had to leave tonight, even though that meant leaving without Sarah. If he didn't go, he'd be stuck in 1850 forever. Married to Vallen.

He didn't know which of those two experiences would be worse, but the combination would be unbearable.

If only...but there was no point in thinking about what might have been. He'd tried to make Sarah believe him, and he'd failed.

He gazed out of the room at John McCully. He was more slumped than leaning against the wall now, and his eyes were closed. It was impossible to tell whether he was awake or asleep. But he hadn't stirred when Sarah had passed him, so maybe...

As quietly as possible, Tyler started out of the parlor and across the foyer. One step toward the front door...then another...

And then the click of a gun being cocked broke the silence.

Tyler froze.

"Time to turn in?" John said.

Tyler glanced over and smiled. It wasn't easy to smile at a man leveling a six-shooter at him, but he did his best. "Yeah, time to turn in," he said. "How about getting a little fresh air first, though."

When they reached the front door, John opened it and stepped out onto the veranda.

"Just give me one second," Tyler said. "I want to grab a drink from the kitchen pump."

John nodded, turning his attention to the stars above. Tyler started for the kitchen.

He kept his stride easy until he made it through the doorway, then he tore at top speed over to the kitchen door and out into the moonlit night.

Leaping off the back porch, he hit the ground running. He'd head for the river, and follow the bank along to Clayton's, as Sarah had suggested days ago. With the cover of night and a head start on John, he had a good chance of making it.

He was racing along, the dark shadows of the stable twenty feet or so off to his right, when someone started shouting. "Who's there? Who's running there? Stop!"

Instantly, the kennel came alive with frantic barking.

The voice, Tyler realized, belonged to Horace Halleck. What the hell was Beau's overseer doing out in the middle of the night?

And those dogs! It sounded as if there were a hundred of them, not just the twenty or so he'd seen earlier.

Tyler tried to move faster yet but he was already running at top speed.

"Stop or I'll shoot!" Horace yelled.

Seconds later, a gun blasted.

Its roar was terrifying; Tyler discovered he hadn't been running at top speed, after all.

"What's going on?" John McCully shouted from the distance, his voice barely audible above the barking.

"Slave's trying to escape," Horace hollered. "You go after him. I'll free the dogs."

Free the dogs? Horace was going to let loose those huge snarling bloodhounds that looked as if they hadn't had a decent meal in weeks? Hell, when Sarah had said they were kept hungry because it made them better at hunting, he'd thought she'd meant for rabbits.

Tyler reached the field that stretched to the river and started along between two rows of cotton bushes, ducking low as he ran. The damned plants were only about waist-high, and the damned moon seemed to be getting brighter by the minute.

And then he heard a chorus of excited barking and howling, and Tyler knew that Horace had set the dogs on him.

Oh, Lord, maybe being stuck in 1850, married to Vallen, wouldn't be so bad, after all.

Tyler ran down the field, the bushes catching at his suit as he passed. He was getting desperate. There wasn't a tree in sight to climb. Only the stupid little cotton bushes.

Maybe there were trees on the riverbank. Or maybe he could swim across the river and worry about getting back to Clayton's place later.

Dogs could swim, too, though. And if they caught up with him in the water, they'd probably eat him and drown him at the same time.

He ran on, his breath growing ragged, constant pain stabbing at him—partly because of that bullet wound Fitzhugh Farnsworth had given him, partly from the exertion.

Over the hammering of his heart and the noise of his breathing, he could hear the dogs closing in on him. If he'd had any choice of ways to die, being torn apart by a pack of hounds sure wouldn't have been one of them.

There was the Colt, of course. Still safely tucked in his waistband. He could stand and fight. But with twenty dogs and six bullets, there wouldn't be much doubt about the outcome.

A deep gasp of air sent a new searing pain through his side, but, thank God, he could smell the river. Almost there. What should he do if he actually reached it?

Quickly, he scanned the darkness ahead as he ran. Still no trees, but his eyes picked out a tall, shadowy structure in the moonlight.

A scaffold, his panicking mind said. A scaffold to hang runaways that the dogs didn't finish off.

Then he remembered Sarah saying there was a scale at the river, to weigh the cotton before it was put on barges.

That's what the shape was. A large balance-beam scale, its center pole maybe seven feet high.

He headed straight for it, crashing through the cotton bushes that stood in his path. That scale was the only thing that offered refuge from the dogs.

Above, the balance beam stretched across parallel to the ground. The two weighing platforms, suspended from either end, rested in balance, about three feet above ground level.

For a crazy instant, Tyler wondered if three feet would be enough to keep the dogs from reaching him. Then his brain began working again. If he jumped on either of those platforms, it would come crashing down to the earth, just like the end of a teeter-totter.

The only thing to do was get himself right up on the beam itself.

The dogs were so close their baying was ringing in his ears and he could practically feel their hot breath on his heels.

He gathered what little remained of his strength and made a flying leap at the balance beam, grabbing it on either side of the center pole.

It teetered frantically back and forth.

He almost lost his grip but managed to hold on. Then, bracing his feet against the pole, he shimmied up and straddled the beam.

It wasn't thirty seconds before the dogs burst through the bushes and began leaping at him. The entire pack surrounded the weigh scale, a frenzy of noise and motion. Their teeth glinted in the moonlight, ready to tear him apart if he fell.

He closed his eyes and hung on for dear life.

Then he heard Horace Halleck yelling at the dogs to shut up.

Tyler opened his eyes again. He'd never have believed he'd be glad to see that weasely overseer, but he wasn't simply glad—he was euphoric.

His euphoria lasted for about one and a half seconds. That was as long as it took him to realize Horace Halleck was pointing a shotgun at him.

"You one dead boy," Horace shouted as the dogs quieted down. "I don't let no slaves escape. I just gotta decide if I wanna shoot you or let the dogs git you."

"Wait!" Tyler yelled. "Don't shoot. It's me, Tyler Adams."

From beyond the dog pack, Horace peered up through the darkness at Tyler. "You son of a bitch," he finally muttered. "How many times you think Mr. Booker gonna let you off? I say this be the *last.*"

Horace punctuated his words by clicking back the hammer on his shotgun.

The subsequent blast was deafening.

Tyler clung to the balance beam, waiting for pain to seize him.

It didn't.

He looked down again.

John McCully was standing next to Horace in the moonlight, his Colt in his right hand, his left hand holding the barrel of Horace's shotgun straight up.

"Who the hell you think you are?" Horace was yelling into John's face.

"I think I'm the fellow Mr. Booker hired to keep an eye on his future son-in-law. And I don't reckon either Mr. Booker or Miss Vallen would take kindly to your killing him. Now call off your damned dogs, so Mister Adams can climb down from that thing."

TYLER WOKE WITH A START. The first pale fingers of dawn were creeping into his bedroom now, but he'd been drifting in and out of sleep all night, plagued by nightmares.

In some of them, he'd been on the verge of being torn limb from limb by that pack of bloodhounds. Others were replays of what had happened when he and John had arrived back at the house.

Those nightmares featured Beauregard, waving his shotgun around and swearing. In the background, Vallen had been glaring at him, and Sarah . . . oh, the look on Sarah's face had made him feel about two inches tall.

She'd thought he'd actually *wanted* to run off and leave her behind.

He had to explain to Sarah . . . but he'd *tried* to explain about the root cellar and she'd thought he was joking. He forced his thoughts back to the nightmares. There'd been something important in them.

When he woke up, something had been nagging away at his subconscious, but try as he might, he couldn't make it surface.

Once more, he began picturing what had happened last night. He'd been running through the darkness, the dogs in hot pursuit, knowing he'd never get away from them alive. Then he'd spotted the weigh scale and realized he had a chance.

"Oh, my God," he whispered, sitting upright in the bed. It was the scale. It wasn't the shipping records, at all, it was the damned weigh scale. That's how Horace Halleck was cheating Beauregard.

Tyler leapt out of bed and grabbed his clothes from the floor. He'd practically torn his suit to shreds, running through the cotton bushes, but he didn't have time to worry about finding something else to wear. He had to get back to that scale and make sure he was right.

Quietly, he opened his bedroom door.

"Morning," John McCully said. "Up kind of early for breakfast, aren't you?"

John was sitting in a chair not three feet from Tyler's door. "You know," he went on, "I'm a right patient man, Tyler. But, like I told you last night, I'm getting damned tired of your trying to run off. I was hired to do a job, and you sure aren't making it easy."

"The scale," Tyler whispered. "That's how Horace is doing it."

A tiny creaking noise along the hall drew Tyler's attention. It was Sarah. She'd opened her bedroom door a crack and was peeking out at them.

"Get dressed," Tyler whispered to her. "Fast. We have to go outside."

She hesitated a split second, then closed her door again.

Tyler glanced back at John. John looked decidedly skeptical.

"We can't talk here," Tyler said. "Someone will wake up. But once we're outside..."

John shook his head wearily, but shoved himself out of his chair.

A few moments later Sarah reappeared, still buttoning the top buttons on her dress. She pointed in warning at the creaky board outside her room, then they started single file for the stairs.

CHAPTER ELEVEN

THE SUN WAS ON the horizon, and the dew still lay heavily on the ground. And on the cotton bushes, Tyler noted.

"So?" John McCully demanded, breaking the silence as they started down between two of the rows. "What are we doing out here? Besides getting our feet wet?"

"We're going to have a look at the weigh scale," Tyler told him. "I think there's something wrong with it," he added, glancing back and trying to catch Sarah's eye.

She wasn't having any of that. He was surprised she'd even come along, because she didn't look any happier than she had last night—when she'd clearly decided he'd wanted to run off without her.

He *had* to make her believe that's not what he wanted at all. As soon as he got a chance to talk to her without John breathing down his neck he'd try again.

"What do you mean, something wrong with it?" John asked.

Tyler glanced back again. "There was a wooden box or something sitting on one of the weighing platforms last night. But the scale was in balance."

"Yeah?" John said, his tone interested.

"Yeah. It was the last thing I was thinking about then, but this morning I realized the platform it was on should have been resting lower than the other one."

That made Sarah look at him.

"You mean," she said slowly, "you think the scale might be weighing light?"

"Well, something sure doesn't add up. Not unless that box weighed almost nothing."

"Let's get going and have a look, then," John muttered.

Tyler breathed a sigh of relief when they came in sight of the weigh scale. The box hadn't vanished overnight. There it sat, a small wooden chest on the weighing platform closer to the river.

"Well I'll be," John said.

"It's the tool chest they use," Sarah offered. "To adjust the scale."

"Adjust, huh?" Tyler said, lifting the chest with both hands.

The weighing platform it had been sitting on immediately rose a few inches, wavered a little, then settled a couple of inches higher than its counterpart.

"I'd say thirty or forty pounds," Tyler guessed, hoisting the chest up and down to gauge its weight.

He put it back and the two platforms began moving again, finally coming to rest in balance.

"I think you're onto something," John said. "Which side do they put the weights on?" he asked, turning to Sarah.

She pointed to the right-hand platform, the one with nothing on it. "The cotton bales go on the river side, closest to the barge."

Tyler could feel his excitement mounting. "But without the chest sitting there, the first thirty or forty pounds of cotton would only bring the platforms level. Sarah, you said your father supervises the weighing, but when does he arrive? Before they start? Or once they're ready to go? Exactly when?"

"Well, let me think. The bales are all brought here from the gin house. And they just wait on those skids over there until a barge arrives. So that's the time Papa comes down. Once the barge is here and they're about to begin the weighing."

"And I'll just bet," Tyler said, glancing at John, "that the first bale is already waiting on the scale when Beauregard gets here."

John nodded, opening the toolbox and rummaging around inside. He produced a screwdriver and hammer, then dropped onto his haunches beside the right-hand platform. It was maybe four inches in depth—comprised of inch-thick boards nailed together and attached to a metal base.

Using the screwdriver, John pried his way along the side of the base. Then, bending it back a little, he peered beneath the boards.

"Well, well," he said, "you're never going to guess what someone's put in here."

"Thirty or forty pounds of weights?" Tyler said.

With a wry grin, John began hammering the metal side strip back into place.

"Thirty or forty pounds a bale that Beauregard doesn't record," Tyler said. "That must add up to a lot of cotton over a season. So I guess we should go talk to Horace Halleck. And maybe I'll take this tool chest along, just to get the conversation started on the right track.''

Sarah watched him lean over and pick up the chest once more, her mind in a tizzy. They'd done what they'd set out to do, after all. And now Papa wouldn't force Tyler to marry Vallen—she hoped.

But what would Tyler do then? Last night, he'd left her behind when he'd tried to escape. For all his talk about loving her and wanting her to go North and marry him, he'd run away on her. Was that love?

Like it or not, she knew the answer to her question. Tyler Adams didn't really love her at all. That was what it came down to. And when Papa told him he was free to go, that's exactly what he'd do. He'd go back to New York without another thought about taking her with him.

Swallowing hard, she wondered what demon had possessed her to come with them this morning.

"Sarah?" Tyler said. He quickly strode over, put the tool chest down on the ground and took her hands in his.

She knew she should pull them away but couldn't. She simply gazed up into the warmth of his blue eyes, loving him yet almost wishing she could hate him. If she hated him, he wouldn't be able to hurt her. But he *could* hurt her. He'd walked into her life, stolen her heart, and now he was going to walk away again.

She didn't know how she'd bear that. And by telling him about those stupid cotton yields, she'd even been the one to give him his means of escape.

"Sarah?" he said quietly while John finished his hammering. ''This isn't the time or place to talk about what happened last night. We need hours to talk. But, just for the moment, don't forget that I love you, huh?''

Gazing at him uncertainly, she tried to decide if he really meant that. He looked so sincere, that maybe... "You really do?" she finally whispered. "I thought...I thought you'd changed your mind."

"Oh, Sarah," he murmured, shaking his head, "I'd never change my mind. Not in a million years. I love you and I want to marry you. And just as soon as we're finished with Halleck and your father, we'll talk, okay?"

She nodded, trying to contain her excitement. Tyler loved her, after all. He still loved her and still wanted to marry her. And once they'd finished with Horace Halleck and Papa, there'd be nothing left to stand in their way.

THE OVERSEER'S HOUSE sat about twenty yards from the other outbuildings on its own fenced plot of land.

Horace's horse was grazing out back on a grassy patch, which meant he'd been too lazy to stable it last night. A couple of chickens were scratching in the yard, but, at this hour in the morning, those were the only signs of life.

Sarah walked right up to the door with Tyler, while John McCully casually leaned against one of the poles that supported the porch roof.

"I think I'm going to enjoy this," Tyler said. "Especially after last night."

He glanced down at Sarah, giving her a smile that made her feel warm all over. Then he knocked on the door.

Horace snarled something from inside and, a minute later, opened the door far enough to poke his head out.

"I ain't dressed," he snapped when he spotted Sarah.

"I don't want to miss anything," she whispered to Tyler.

"Miss Sarah has seen men in their nightshirts before," he said. "So why don't you just step out onto the porch and tell us about this," he added, shifting the tool chest into Horace's line of vision.

Horace Halleck's grimy face paled considerably, and he yanked the door fully open.

Sarah *had* seen men in their nightshirts before, of course, but she'd never seen a tobacco-stained nightshirt that was so dirty it looked gray. She inched a little behind Tyler. There might be weevils living in that filthy garment.

"Them's our tools," Horace said. "For the scale."

"Uh-huh" was all Tyler said.

"Shudda left 'em there," Horace said.

"Maybe I should have. Moving them kind of left the scale off balance."

"Yeah?"

"Yeah. I thought maybe you'd like to tell me about that."

"I don't have to tell you nothin', *Mister* Adams."

Tyler shrugged. "Well, then why don't we just wander over to the main house, where we can both talk to Beauregard about it."

Horace wiped his mouth with the back of his hand, then said, "Well... maybe you and I can talk about it... just the two of us, huh? Maybe we be better not to bother Mr. Booker about it. You just come on in and—"

"I don't think so," Tyler said. "I figure Beauregard will be more interested than bothered."

Horace gave Tyler a black look. "You just wait here till I'm dressed," he snapped, then slammed the door in Tyler's face.

"Be mighty interesting to hear his story," John said, grinning.

"Yes," Sarah murmured. "I can't imagine how they'd go about taking thirty or forty pounds from each bale before the barge reaches Savannah."

"Oh, I don't think they'd do anything that complicated," Tyler said. "I think Horace must have an ally in Ewell Endicott's firm, so that the weight recorded there is the same as here. That explains why Ewell's records and your father's match. But there's actually always more cotton than either your father or Ewell know about. And somewhere along the line, Horace and his partner cash in."

"No," Sarah said, slowly shaking her head. "I know for certain that when Papa's cotton arrives in Savannah, Ewell always supervises the weighing himself. He says his father-in-law deserves special treatment. So those thirty or forty pounds must disappear between here and Savannah."

"Unless Ewell's scale is set wrong, too," John put in.

Sarah shook her head again. "It couldn't be. If it were, none of the other planters' records would match up. But it would be so difficult to untie those pressed bales, take some of the cotton, and tie them up to look fine again. I just don't know how they'd manage it."

"Well, we're going to find out," Tyler said. "Once Horace starts talking to your father and—"

His words were cut off by the sudden sound of hoofbeats. A second later, Horace Halleck's horse raced around the side of the house, with Horace riding bareback.

Before Sarah could even blink, John McCully had drawn his Colt and shot.

Horace's hat hit the dirt, but he didn't stop.

The Colt erupted again.

This time Horace yelled in pain and the horse reared, dumping him to the ground.

"Nice shooting," Tyler said.

"WAIT OUTSIDE," Beauregard snapped, glaring at Sarah from behind his desk. "This is men's business."

"Ah...sir?" Tyler said, leaning forward in his chair. "We wouldn't have known there was any problem if it hadn't been for Sarah. It's really her you have to thank. And I'm sure she'd like to hear for herself what Mr. Halleck has to say."

Beau didn't look happy, but he didn't tell her to leave again, either.

Sarah risked giving Tyler a sidelong smile of thanks. Northern men really *were* much more progressive.

"You boys damned well better know what you're about," Beauregard muttered, glancing threats at Tyler and John in turn. "If you've shot up my overseer for no good reason, I'll have the two of you horsewhipped."

"That's what they done, Mr. Booker, sir," Horace said. "That's 'zactly what they done. Shot me up for no good reason."

Sarah looked across at the overseer. She'd hardly call that little nick John's bullet had made in Horace's arm shooting him up. Why, the wound Fitzhugh Farnsworth had given Tyler had been far more serious. And Tyler certainly hadn't sniveled and carried on the way Horace was doing.

"Sir," Tyler said, "the facts are exactly as I told you. Your weigh scale has been tampered with. Every bale is under-weighed by some thirty to forty pounds."

"That's four or five dollars a bale!" Beau shouted.

"Yes, sir, I guess it is. And if you'd like to come with us, John and I can show you exactly how it was done."

Beauregard waved off the suggestion and sat eyeing his overseer.

"So?" he finally said. "Don't I treat you right? I trusted you and this is my reward?"

"I didn't want to do it, Mr. Booker, sir. I didn't want to. But he made me. Said he'd get me fired if'n I didn't."

"Who?" Beau demanded, his face scarlet.

"He made me. It weren't my fault. So I can keep my job, can't I, Mr. Booker, sir?"

"Who!" Beau yelled, slamming his fist against his desk.

"Ewell Endicott, sir."

For a moment, Beauregard Booker simply stared at the overseer. Then his face grew even redder, and he said, "Don't you prevaricate to me, Halleck."

Sarah glanced at Horace again, certain he didn't know what the word prevaricate meant.

"You lie, and I'll whip the immortal soul out of you," Beau went on.

"It's the honest to Moses truth!" Horace cried. "Mr. Endicott told me what to do to the scale. That's why he pay your cotton that special 'tention he's always talkin' about. So he can weigh your bales light on his wharf. That way, his records be the same as yours."

"You are telling me that my own son-in-law..." Beau's words trailed off into a snarl, and Horace Halleck's head bobbed up and down like a puppet on a string.

"You!" Beau finally thundered, pointing at John McCully. "You get your horse and take this no-account skunk into town. I want him in the Savannah jail before noon. Now!"

John nodded, grabbed Horace by the shoulder and hustled him out of the study.

Sarah followed them with her eyes. When John opened the door, Vallen almost fell into the room. She'd obviously had her ear to the door.

"And you'll come with me," Beauregard went on, turning his attention to Tyler. "What day is it today?" he demanded of no one in particular.

"Wednesday," Sarah said. Immediately, she wished she hadn't answered so quickly. She didn't want everyone to know she'd been anxiously keeping track of how many days were left until the wedding. Of course, it didn't matter anymore. After all of this, Papa certainly wouldn't force Tyler to marry Vallen.

"Wednesday," Beau repeated. "Ewell doesn't go to his office on Wednesdays. Well that's damned bad timing, but there's nothing for it. Husband or no husband, I won't have Ella-Jane living with that man another day."

"Papa?" Vallen said from the doorway.

Beauregard silenced her with a look, then opened a drawer and produced a pistol. He stuck it into his pocket, saying to Tyler, "You've proved I can trust you, son. So you and I are going to do a little family business. We're going to rescue my daughter from that polecat she's married to."

"Ah...sir?" Tyler said.

Beauregard was already past him, on his way to the study door.

Tyler gave Sarah an uncertain look, then started after Beau.

Sarah gathered her skirt and hurried after both of them.

"Papa?" Vallen was saying as Sarah reached the doorway. "I couldn't help hear, you were shouting so loud. But sending Horace Halleck to jail? Who will be our overseer?"

"Tarnation!" Beau snapped. "We'll make do with the foreman for a few days. Until I have time to get me another overseer. Louis?" he hollered. "Louis, have the carriage readied. Mr. Adams and I are going to town.

"And you," he went on, glancing at the torn clothing Tyler had been wearing during last night's escape attempt. "You go on upstairs and change into a presentable suit before we leave. I can't have my future son-in-law appear in Savannah looking like a vagabond."

"But Papa," Vallen wailed, "what about my pond? Who's going to supervise the slaves if we have no overseer? And you promised they'd start on it this morning."

"Your damnable pond will have to wait," Beauregard shouted. "I have more important things to tend to."

"Oh, fiddle!" Vallen took a moment to stomp her foot, then flounced off toward the kitchen.

Tyler caught Sarah's eye and motioned for her to follow him upstairs. This was working out better than he ever could have hoped.

He'd let Beauregard go into town and take care of collecting Ella-Jane on his own. That way, he'd have hours to sit and talk with Sarah, have the time he needed to properly explain about time travel, to convince her to leave with him. Then they could be safely in 1993 before either John McCully or Beau got back from Savannah.

He waited in the upstairs hall until he saw Sarah appear at the top of the stairs. Quickly, he ushered her into his bedroom.

"Oh, Tyler," she whispered, smiling up at him. "Isn't it wonderful? Everything is going to be fine for everyone. Even for Ella-Jane. Oh, I'm so relieved she won't have to live with awful old Ewell any longer."

Tyler couldn't resist gathering Sarah into his arms and kissing her. Every time he kissed her, he was amazed by the feelings she brought out in him. Tiny as she was, she fit perfectly in his arms. Making love to Sarah Booker was going to be heavenly. And he'd be able to kiss her and hold her and love her for the rest of his life.

Just as she'd said, everything was going to be fine—for Ella-Jane *and* for them. They were actually going to have their chance to get away.

Reluctantly, reminding himself again that they had the rest of their lives, he stopped kissing her. The way her body was molded against his made him hate interrupting the rest of their lives for even a minute. But he had to go back downstairs.

"Sarah?" he murmured. "Sarah, I'm going to go and convince your father to make that trip on his own. I've done my part by blowing the whistle on Ewell."

"Blowing the whistle?"

He waved her question off, saying, "Just an expression. But we need time to talk. And while your father and John are both gone, we'll be able to get away, Sarah. I just have to make you understand about..." He paused, not liking the way she was looking up at him.

"What?" he said.

"You have to go with Papa, Tyler. He'll need your help."

"Against old Ewell? Sarah, I doubt—"

"No, Tyler," she said firmly, drawing back a little. "You saw Papa take that gun. He's expecting trouble, and he'll undoubtedly get it. You don't think Ewell's going to simply stand by while Papa walks out of the house with Ella-Jane, do you?"

"But—"

"No, Tyler Adams. Ella-Jane is my sister. And she's most unhappy with Ewell. I've been worrying myself sick wondering what I could do to help her, and this is my chance. I mean, it wouldn't exactly be *me* helping, but it would be you."

Sarah gave him a devastating smile.

He tried to think. Would Sarah leave with him this afternoon, not knowing whether Beauregard and Ella-Jane were all right? Hardly likely.

And he *had* gotten a reprieve on the root cellar being filled in. As long as the work didn't get started on Vallen's pond, he had until the wedding to get out of here. That was still over a week away.

But there *still* was that damned wedding to worry about.

"Ah . . . Sarah?"

"Yes?"

"About the wedding. You're absolutely sure your father's going to let me out of marrying Vallen, are you?"

"Oh, Tyler, of course he will. My goodness, you could see how grateful he was to you for uncovering Ewell's scheme."

"I don't know, Sarah. He didn't seem all *that* grateful. I mean, he seemed more mad than grateful. And he was still referring to me as his future son-in-law."

"Oh, Tyler," Sarah said again. "After what you've done for him, there's absolutely nothing you could ask that he wouldn't do for you."

Tyler rubbed his jaw. "That's the way things work down South, huh?"

"It's the way things like *that* work down South. Other things work differently," she murmured, drawing his lips back to hers.

He kissed her again, knowing he was done. The rest of their lives was going to have to wait until he'd been to Savannah and back with Beauregard.

CHAPTER TWELVE

TYLER SHIFTED uncomfortably on the carriage's bench seat. The ride into Savannah yesterday with John hadn't exactly been smooth as silk. But with an impatient Beauregard Booker at the reins, it was positively bone-rattling—kind of like being in a helicopter when there was turbulence. And the dust the two horses were raising was an added treat.

By the time they turned up toward Lafayette Square where the Endicott house stood, both Tyler's butt and throat were aching.

"All right," Beau said, stopping the horses in front of the elegant house. "Let's get in there and get my daughter."

He climbed out of the carriage and tied the reins to one of the hitching posts. Then, as Tyler watched uneasily, Beauregard pulled out his pistol.

"Ah...you think that's necessary, Beau?" he tried.

"Don't be fooled by Ewell's appearance," Beau snapped. "Man can shoot faster than a frog can lick flies."

Tyler nodded slowly, glad he still had the Colt concealed against his back. He wasn't thrilled with the idea he might have to use it, though. When he glanced at the house again, it put him in mind of a three-story brick fortress. And it didn't take much effort to imagine rifles trained on them from behind those windows.

"Listen, Beau," he said, "what about reasoning with Ewell rather than just charging in there, spoiling for a fight?"

"Reason with Ewell Endicott?" Beau asked in a tone that made Tyler feel like an idiot.

"Well then, what if we went to the police? I mean, considering the way Ewell's been cheating you..."

"The police? Son, the police are going to blame Horace Halleck entirely. Whether I claim Ewell was involved or not."

"But—"

"Tyler, I'm a respected planter in these parts, but Ewell Endicott is the most important businessman in Savannah. The police wouldn't arrest him if they caught him up to his neck in under-weighed cotton.

"I should have been smarter than to let him cheat me. Since I wasn't, it's best forgotten. But Ella-Jane is a different matter. So let's go in there and get her."

Reluctantly, Tyler swung down onto the street and followed Beauregard up the flagstone walk and past the fluted pillars flanking the wide front steps.

Beau pounded on the door with his fist. Finally, a servant opened it.

The man started to say something, but Beauregard pushed past him and began hollering for Ewell.

Tyler gave the black man an unhappy shrug, then followed Beau into the house.

"Papa?" Ella-Jane called from the second floor.

She appeared at the top of the stairs just as a door opened off the foyer and Ewell stepped out. "What in blazes is going on?" he demanded.

"You get on down here, Ella-Jane," Beau yelled, pointing his pistol at Ewell. "I'm taking you home with me."

"You stay right where you are, Ella-Jane," Ewell snapped.

She froze on the top step, and Ewell wheeled back toward her father. "And you, Beau, what the hell do you think you're doing?"

"I'm taking my daughter away from the rotten scoundrel who's been cheating his own kin."

"Get out of my house," Ewell said.

"Not without my daughter! You're no fit husband for her."

In the blink of an eye, a revolver appeared in Ewell's hand. "I said, get out of my house," he snarled.

"Ewell! Papa!" Ella-Jane cried.

For a fraction of a second they both glanced up the staircase.

Tyler seized the moment, flinging himself at Ewell and knocking him to the floor with a football tackle.

Ewell's gun clattered across the marble floor.

Ella-Jane screamed.

"Hold on to him!" Beauregard yelled, thundering up the stairs.

Ewell struggled, but he was no stronger than he looked. Tyler could easily keep him pinned and still watch the scene unfolding around him.

Beauregard was racing back down the stairs with Ella-Jane. The black manservant was standing in shock at the front door. Two female servants had appeared from somewhere and were staring at Ewell with their hands to their mouths.

Then Ewell yelled "Cliffie!" and the manservant jumped.

"Cliffie, get my gun and kill this skunk holding me," Ewell screamed.

"No, Cliffie!" Ella-Jane shouted. She raced down the last few steps ahead of Beau and dashed across the foyer, scooping the gun up off the floor.

For one horrifying moment, she pointed it at Ewell.

Tyler was certain she was going to shoot. He was just as certain that he was in her line of fire.

Then Beauregard tore the gun from her hand, yelling, "Hellfire, girl, you'll hit Tyler! You get on out to the carriage."

Ella-Jane started for the door like a frightened rabbit.

One gun pointed toward Cliffie, the other aimed in Ewell's direction, Beauregard began backing across the foyer. "Let's go, son," he muttered to Tyler. "I've got both these polecats covered. Get on out and untie the carriage. You can drive."

This was no time, Tyler realized, shoving himself up off Ewell's chest, to make Beauregard aware that he actually *couldn't* drive.

"Fake it," he muttered to himself, running down the walk. "How hard can it be?"

Ella-Jane was already in the carriage, looking pale and frightened.

"It'll be okay," Tyler said, fumbling to get the reins untied.

Once he managed that, he swung up into the driver's side and looked toward the house.

Beauregard was backing quickly down the steps, still brandishing both guns. But what was Ewell doing?

For a split second, Tyler considered his options. He wasn't safely out of 1850 yet, so he still didn't want Beauregard to know about the hidden Colt. But if Ewell was as good a shot as Beau claimed, he undoubtedly had more than one gun in the house. What if he suddenly appeared in the doorway with another?

Deciding, Tyler reached behind his back and pulled out the Colt. He'd barely aimed and cocked it before Ewell stepped into sight, leveling the biggest rifle Tyler had ever seen straight at Beauregard's chest.

"Papa!" Ella-Jane screamed as Tyler pulled the Colt's trigger.

The rifle exploded, but Ewell was already crumpling to the steps.

Tyler watched, feeling sick. He'd never shot at anything except targets before.

Then he realized Ewell was only wounded. And the way he began yelling said the bullet couldn't have done much more than nick him.

"You get back into this house, Ella-Jane," he screamed, struggling to his feet with Cliffie's help.

"She's never going back into that house again," Beauregard roared, still brandishing both guns and hurrying backward down the walk now.

"I'll kill you, Ella-Jane," Ewell shouted. "If you don't come to your senses and get back here, I swear I'll kill you. I'll kill you if I have to wait years for the chance."

"Let's go," Beau snapped, leaping into the carriage.

Tyler cracked the reins, the way Beauregard had done earlier, hoping to hell the horses knew what they were supposed to do.

They took off like a shot, almost pitching their three passengers backward.

"Lord Almighty, son!" Beau said, grabbing the reins. "Don't they teach folks how to drive up North?" he muttered, crawling across Tyler and taking over the driver's seat.

Tyler gladly relinquished the reins, then looked back at Ewell. He was still yelling death threats at Ella-Jane, his face contorted in rage.

"He means what he's saying," Ella-Jane whispered in a terrified voice. "My husband means to kill me, and he won't rest until he has. Not if it takes him forever."

SOMEWHERE ON THE TRIP back to Booker's Knoll, Tyler's heart had stopped racing. But just listening to Ella-Jane tell Sarah and Vallen what had happened had started his adrenaline pumping again.

He glanced at Beauregard, who was being uncharacteristically quiet. Maybe the close call with Ewell had really shaken him up. Lord, people who worried about getting shot in 1993 Manhattan had never visited 1850 Savannah.

"So if it hadn't been for Tyler," Ella-Jane continued, "Papa might be dead and I might be back in that horrid house with Ewell."

"Hell," Beau muttered, "I'd have been dead as a horse thief at a hanging."

"And when we turned onto Abercorn Street and drove out of sight," Ella-Jane went on, "Ewell was still shouting about killing me. I expect he would have come after me right then and there, if he hadn't been wounded. But he always runs to the doctor immediately for any little ailment."

"Oh, Ella-Jane, it's been so awful for you," Sarah murmured, hugging her sister for what Tyler figured to be about the hundredth time.

And each time she'd hugged Ella-Jane, she'd smiled across the parlor at him, so proud of him he could see it in her eyes. It made him feel as if he could have leapt tall buildings in a single bound—that is if there *were* any tall buildings to leap in 1850 Georgia.

"In all the excitement, I didn't think to ask you, son," Beauregard said, "but where did you get that gun?"

Tyler took a deep breath, trying to decide what he'd do if Beau demanded he hand it over. He wasn't giving it up. Yet, if push came to shove, he could hardly shoot Sarah's father in order to keep it.

"I've had it since I arrived," he said at last. "I always carry a gun when I travel."

"Had it all along," Beau said. "Well, I'll be danged. Guess it's safe to let you keep it then, seeing you haven't pulled it on anyone except Ewell."

"I still don't think you should have done what you did, Papa," Vallen said. "After all, Ella-Jane *is* Ewell Endicott's wife."

"I don't want to be," Ella-Jane said quietly. "I never wanted to be, and I'm never going back to that house."

"But, Papa," Vallen went on, "you know Ewell always means what he says. He's going to kill Ella-Jane."

"If he comes here, he'll find himself looking down the barrel of my shotgun," Beau snapped.

"That's right, we'll protect her," Sarah said, smiling at Vallen. She so rarely thought about others that it was nice to see her concerned about Ella-Jane's safety.

"But he *might*," Vallen persisted. "Why, what if he shows up here on my wedding day? He'd disrupt everything."

Sarah refrained from saying anything. Vallen would never change. Instead, Sarah glanced at Tyler, trying to give him a silent message. It would be best to talk to Papa about the wedding while he was still beholden to Tyler for saving his life.

"Sir?" Tyler said. "Could I speak to you in your study for a minute?"

She smiled at him. She'd never before tried giving a man silent messages, but somehow she'd known it would work with Tyler. There was something so wonderful between them that she could scarcely believe it.

"'Course, son," Beau said. "'Course you can speak to me."

"Ah...sir?" Tyler added as Beau started across the parlor. "This discussion involves Sarah. She should join us."

"What?" Vallen snapped, her eyes flashing angrily to Sarah. "Whatever is going on here?"

"Oh, Vallen," Ella-Jane put in, shooting Sarah a conspiratorial smile. "It's a secret. To do with your wedding gift."

"Oh." Vallen smiled. "Something about the plantation. You're going to get started on my pond, after all, Papa?"

Before Beauregard could answer, Ella-Jane took Vallen's hands in hers, saying, "Never mind your silly pond. Even when Papa hires a new overseer, the man will be busy with other things for a bit. But tell me all about the wedding arrangements. Now that I'm back at Booker's Knoll, I can help."

"Well," Vallen was saying as Sarah started after Papa and Tyler, "the out-of-town guests will begin arriving tomorrow. Uncle Emmanuel and Aunt Maria are coming, all the way from Ohio."

"But the wedding's more than a week away," Ella-Jane said.

"Yes, but they're coming early because Uncle Emmanuel has business to conduct in the city. Papa?" Vallen called as he reached the parlor doorway. "You *will* remember to send someone to meet their train?"

Beauregard grunted and Vallen turned back to Ella-Jane. "And they're bringing little Georgie, of course, like they did to your wedding. And everyone who's traveling here will be staying at the Savannah Hotel. We've reserved every single room."

The sound of Vallen's voice trailed off as Sarah followed her father and Tyler along into the study.

She wasn't at all sure Tyler should have suggested she join them. Southern men like Papa simply didn't hold with women being included in things, the way Tyler seemed to.

"So?" Beauregard said, sitting down behind his desk and gesturing Tyler and Sarah to chairs. "What's all this about Vallen's wedding gift?"

Tyler rested his hands flat on his knees and leaned intently forward. "Beauregard, it isn't about Vallen's wedding gift. I have a favor to ask you."

"Anything, son. Anything at all."

Sarah could feel Tyler's relief.

"Well," he continued, "it's about my marrying Vallen."

"Let me say something, son, before you go on. I had my doubts about you, what with being a Yankee and all. But you've proved yourself to me. I'm going to be mighty proud to have you as my son-in-law.''

Sarah glanced uneasily at Tyler, silently telling him that Papa sometimes needed a little convincing.

Tyler cleared his throat. ''Well, sir, that's exactly the point. You see, I don't want to marry Vallen.''

Beauregard's pleasant expression turned sour. ''Little late to be deciding that, isn't it, son?''

''Ah...sir, if you'll think back, I *never* said I wanted to marry her. You just kind of roped me into it. So I thought, well, Fitzhugh Farnsworth said he still *wants* to marry her, remember? And seeing as how I've kind of helped you out here, I thought you might see your way clear to—''

''No,'' Beau shouted, smacking his desk with his fist and sending Sarah's heart sinking all the way to her toes.

''I can't have folks thinking I change my mind back and forth with the wind. Can't go saying Vallen's marrying Fitzhugh, then she's marrying you, then switch back to Fitzhugh again. Can't do that. Just wouldn't look right. No, there's a wedding planned for next Saturday and you're going to be my son-in-law. Best set your mind on that.''

Tyler ran his hand through his hair, then sat rubbing his jaw. ''All right,'' he said at last.

Sarah's eyes flashed to him, but tears formed so quickly he was nothing but a blur.

''All right,'' he said again. ''I'll go through with the wedding. I'll be your son-in-law. But only if it's Sarah I marry.''

''What?'' Beauregard yelled. ''Sarah, what have you done?'' he demanded.

Even with her blurred vision, she could see he was positively glaring at her.

"I told you days ago," he shouted before she could say a word. "I told you not to try getting Tyler Adams for yourself. I told you, it's your sister he's ruined and it's your sister he's going to marry."

"Dammit!" Tyler snapped. "I didn't *ruin* Vallen. Regardless of what she says, I didn't even touch her. And Sarah hasn't done anything. I fell in love with her, without her doing a thing to make me. And I'll marry her. I *want* to marry her. But I'm damned well not marrying Vallen."

Sarah wiped her eyes and held her breath, praying Papa would agree.

Instead, he shook his head, saying, "Letting you marry Sarah would be changing my mind, and I'm not doing it. Besides, Vallen's heart is set on marrying *you*, not Fitzhugh. It's her wedding and you're the groom. And that's how things are going to stay."

"Beauregard, I am *not* marrying Vallen. I don't give a damn what you say."

Beau shook his head. "You know, son, I thought we had this straightened out. In fact, I had half a mind to send John McCully on his way. But if that's how you feel, I guess I'd best be having him stay around and keep an eye on you until after the wedding—just so you won't be getting any ideas."

"But, sir—"

"That's my final word," Beau said, smacking his desk again. "Come next Saturday, you'll marry Vallen. But don't you fret. You'll start to like her in no time at all. Once you get to know her better."

TYLER PACED ACROSS the foyer again, impatiently waiting for Beauregard to let Sarah out of his study. There wasn't any doubt about the lecture she was getting regarding her attempt to steal her sister's fiancé. And the longer Beau took, the angrier Tyler got.

Twice, now, they'd succeeded at what they'd set out to do. But neither success had produced the expected results. Twice he'd gotten himself into Beauregard's good books, only to have him insist that the wedding was still on.

And what on earth was he going to do about Sarah?

He couldn't leave her behind. The way he felt, that wasn't possible. But how could he take her to 1993 when she was convinced he was only joking? Hell, unless she believed him, she'd get the shock of her life. And then what would happen?

But maybe, if she went to the root cellar with him . . . maybe there was something unusual about it. Something that would convince her people really could time-travel through it. After all, it had been pitch black when he and Clayton had been in it, so there could well be *something* about it that would . . . or maybe he was simply grasping at straws.

Taking her there with him, though, was the only thing he could think of doing. And once they were there . . . well, first things first. Even with John McCully off taking Horace Halleck to the jail in Savannah, just getting away from Booker's Knoll was going to be a major feat.

Finally, the study door opened and Sarah came out, looking as depressed as he felt. She closed the door firmly behind her, then crossed the foyer to where he was standing.

Vallen and Ella-Jane had gone upstairs, so he risked taking Sarah's hand in his. "I've got to get out of here," he told her. "I'm going to have to make a run for it. That seems to be the only way left."

"I know," she murmured. "Papa is more determined than ever that you're going to marry Vallen. Oh, I'm so sorry I was wrong about how he'd react."

He wrapped his arms around Sarah and held her close. "There's no point in worrying about that. But look, I want to try and make it to Clayton's. Now, before John gets back from the city. This may be the only time I'll have when he's not around."

"What about Vallen? Where's she?"

Tyler gestured to the second floor, then looked into Sarah's eyes. "Will you . . . will you come with me, Sarah? At least to Clayton's? I know you haven't said for sure that you'd come North with me. And I know you think some of the things I've told you have been crazy. But if we could just talk . . . if I had a chance to explain. . . ."

She took a deep breath, then nodded. "But we can't go through the cotton fields. Papa said he's going to be working in his study for a while, and its windows overlook them. I think the only way. . . Tyler, I'll go and have the buggy hitched up right now. Vallen can't see the front of the house from her bedroom, so we might be able to make it to the road without anyone knowing."

Anxiously, Tyler waited by the front door until Sarah appeared with the buggy. When he hurried out, she slid across the seat so he could drive.

He swung up, wishing she'd kept the reins herself. But this was no time for a discussion about his lack of driving experience, so he clicked the reins and they started off.

He sat rigidly on the bench seat, expecting at any second to hear Beauregard roaring at them to come back. Miraculously, he didn't.

They reached the road, and Sarah shot Tyler a nervous smile. He turned the horse in the direction of Clayton's plantation. With every clip-clop of the horse's hooves, his excitement grew. They were going to make it. He was going home!

Now he had to think of what he should say to Sarah when they got to Clayton's. However, before he could think of anything, he spotted two riders in the distance. They were coming along the edge of the field on the other side of the road from Booker's Knoll. Both men were brandishing rifles.

He shifted a little on the seat. They probably had no interest in Sarah and him, but he liked to feel the reassuring pressure of the Colt against his back.

"Oh, my," Sarah said. She was holding the handle of her parasol so tightly her knuckles were white. "I believe that's Fitzhugh Farnsworth," she murmured. "With one of his brothers."

That news made Tyler look at the two riders far more uneasily. He hadn't forgotten what John McCully had said after the duel. If Fitzhugh wanted the plantation badly enough, he was liable to come up with some other idea for killing Vallen's new fiancé.

Reaching behind his back, Tyler drew out the Colt.

"Tyler?" Sarah said in a frightened voice. "Tyler, rifles have a much longer range than pistols."

She'd barely uttered the words before a shot rang out and a bullet whizzed by the buggy.

Tyler's heart stopped. "Get down!" he yelled at Sarah.

A second shot started his heart again, racing madly now. What the hell was he going to do? Those idiots were as likely to hit Sarah as him. And if he tried to drive on to Clayton's, he'd be driving toward them.

The two men broke into a trot, heading directly at the buggy. Another shot rang out.

Tyler aimed the Colt and fired, but he knew Sarah was right. A pistol was no match for two rifles.

"Dammit to hell!" he swore, pulling the reins sharply to the left.

The horse whinnied and shied. Tyler tried again, this time managing to make the horse turn around.

Yet another bullet whizzed by, so near he could feel the air move beside his ear. He cracked the reins hard.

The horse took off at a gallop, back in the direction of Booker's Knoll.

SARAH HADN'T EATEN a bite of supper. She hadn't been able to swallow. And all evening, every time she'd looked across the parlor at Tyler Adams, it had taken every bit of her resolve to keep from crying.

If it hadn't been for that horrid Fitzhugh Farnsworth, she and Tyler would be on their way north to New York by now. Clayton would have helped them with the arrangements, and they would have been gone before Papa realized it.

Instead, they were back at Booker's Knoll. And Tyler was another step closer to becoming Vallen's husband.

The front door opened, and Sarah peered out into the foyer. John McCully had finally arrived back from Savannah.

"Well," Beauregard boomed as John stepped into the parlor. "Took you so long I thought you'd deserted us."

"Had a mite of trouble," John said. "Ran into a couple of Horace's friends before we reached the jail, and they didn't fancy the idea of my turning him over to the police."

"But you did?" Beau asked.

"Uh-huh. Just had to hole up for a spell. Until they ran out of bullets."

"Good. Good work, then. And now it's time we all went to bed. Things are going to get mighty busy, what with the out-of-town guests beginning to arrive tomorrow. Tyler, our cousins from Ohio will be here first thing. I want you and John to go into Savannah and greet them at the train station. Take them over to the hotel and get them settled in. They'll be anxious to meet Vallen's prospective bridegroom."

Tyler nodded, looking so downhearted Sarah could barely stand it. What if he'd given up? What if he'd decided just to go along with marrying Vallen? If he did that, her heart would break.

But they still had until next Saturday. And he wanted to marry *her*. He'd even told Papa. So surely they could manage to think of something.

"Custer is the cousin's name," Beauregard went on. "Emmanuel Custer. And his wife, Maria. And they'll have their son, Georgie, with them. A big jolly lad. About eleven years old now, I think."

"George Custer?" Tyler said.

"Right," Beauregard said. "Little Georgie. He's full of mischief. Always up to pranks. Why, at Ella-Jane's wedding, Georgie set fire to the minister's buggy. And the lad was only nine then."

"Really," Tyler said. "And what does little Georgie want to be when he grows up?"

Sarah eyed Tyler curiously, wondering why he seemed so interested in an eleven-year-old boy he'd never met.

"He wants to be a soldier," Ella-Jane said. "All he talked about at my wedding was guns and horses and shooting wild Indians. And Uncle Emmanuel said he'll send Georgie to West Point if he's still as interested in soldiering when he's older."

"Well, like I said, it's time for bed," Beauregard muttered. "Louis?" he called. "Louis, come put out the chandelier."

Something told Sarah to hold back a little when everyone started upstairs. Then she realized that Tyler was lagging behind, as well.

"Sarah?" he murmured as they started up after the others. "Sarah, I have to talk to you. We have to decide what to do. I'll come to your room after everyone's in bed."

"Be careful of—"

"Of the creaky board," he whispered. "I'll remember."

She nodded, trying not to think about what would happen if he were discovered in her bedroom in the middle of the night.

Papa would shoot him for sure. And Vallen would probably shoot Sarah herself, just for good measure.

But Tyler was right. They had to decide what to do. So she'd think as hard as she could. And maybe, by the time everyone else was in bed, she'd have an idea.

Once in her room, Sarah quickly put on her night-dress and a robe. Then she waited, thinking, as the house grew quiet.

She and Tyler couldn't stay in Savannah.

Even if, *somehow,* they could convince Papa that *she* should marry Tyler, they couldn't stay here. Vallen would be so vindictive it could never work out. So they had to get away. That was the only solution.

The lone candle on her bureau had burned halfway down before there was a quiet tap on her door. And by then, she'd had time to think of a plan. A good one.

CHAPTER THIRTEEN

As QUIETLY AS A MOUSE, Sarah hurried across her bedroom and opened the door.

Tyler stepped inside, closing the door behind him, and without a single word, wrapped his arms around her and held her so tightly she could barely breathe.

The muscles of his chest strained against the thin cotton of the nightshirt he was wearing, and she loved being aware of his strength and of the security of his arms.

Tyler wasn't the first man who'd ever hugged her, but the others had seemed so awkward and childlike that she'd hated having them touch her.

Tyler Adams, though, was manly and strong. And being in his arms somehow made her feel whole, as if he were a part of her that had been missing from her life until now. She belonged with him.

And if belonging with him meant living in New York, that's what she was going to do. Because she simply couldn't live without him.

She took Tyler's hand, led him over to the bed, and sank onto the shapeless feather mattress, wondering how having him in her room could seem so right. She'd never allow any other man in the world such liberty.

He sat down beside her, gazing at her in the dim glow of the single candle. Then he softly grazed her cheek with his knuckles.

"I love you, Sarah," he murmured, leaning closer and pressing his lips to hers. So lightly at first, then more firmly.

His kiss felt every bit as right as his embrace, so she wrapped her arms around his neck and kissed him back.

When he began teasing her mouth with his tongue, tiny chills of excitement raced through her body.

He smoothed his hands down her back, drawing her nearer as they kissed, and she pressed against him so that her breasts were crushed to his chest. It felt so good to be close to him that she could scarcely believe it.

An aching she'd never felt before began between her legs, making her squirm. But it wasn't an unpleasant ache. Not unpleasant at all. It was a delicious ache that made her want to be even closer to Tyler.

And then he gently brushed his hand along the side of her breast, and the aching between her legs became a sweet, hot throbbing.

"Oh, Lord, Sarah," he murmured, his breath warm against her cheek. "I just *have* to make you understand."

"Mmm," she said, moving her lips to his once more.

He rested his hands on her shoulders and shifted her away a little.

"What?" she whispered.

"Sarah, I can't think when we're kissing, and we've *got* to talk."

"Mmm," she said less happily. She couldn't think when they were kissing, either, but surely they didn't have to think for a few minutes. Or talk right away, either.

Maybe, though, if she told him about her idea, they could go back to kissing. "I have a new idea," she offered. "One that will let us get away."

"Us," he repeated quietly.

"You...you still want me to go with you, don't you?"

He nodded, and the fear that he'd changed his mind vanished as quickly as it had taken hold.

"Then this is what we can do. When you and John McCully go into Savannah in the morning, to meet the train, I'll go with you. You see, Uncle Emmanuel and Aunt Maria won't be coming out to Booker's Knoll for a few days, because Uncle Emmanuel has business in town. So I could say I can't wait to visit with Aunt Maria."

"And then?"

"Well, Savannah is the end of the line. So once the passengers get off, the train starts back north. Tyler, we can be on that train. Tomorrow, we can be heading for New York. All we'd have to do is slip away from John. Or convince him to let us leave."

"Ah...Sarah, it isn't quite that simple."

"But it is," she whispered, taking his hands in hers. "I know John may be difficult, but we'll think of something. If he's helping my uncle with the baggage he won't be paying close attention to us and—"

"No, Sarah...I'm afraid I can't get home on the train."

"But of course you can. Oh, I realize the Central of Georgia won't take us all the way to the state of New York, but it runs almost as far as Macon. And we can—"

"No," Tyler said again, pressing his fingers against her lips this time. "Sarah, listen to me. I'm so damned tempted to just take you with me and not worry about whether you'll like New York until we get there."

"I'm sure I'll like it, Tyler. It will just take a little getting used to."

He rubbed his jaw for a minute, then said, "Well, see, the thing is, it would take you more than a *little* getting used to. And I just can't believe we could build happiness on deceit. I can't risk you hating me for taking you away from your life here."

"Oh, Tyler, I could never hate you. I—"

"Shh... listen to me. I have to make you understand the truth."

"Of course you do," she murmured, smiling at him. "You're an Aries."

"Yes... well... Sarah, last night, I was telling the truth. I'm from the future. Going home, going to *my* home, doesn't mean going to 1850 New York. It means going to *1993* New York. And I can't get there by train or steamer or horse and carriage. The only way I can get there, the only way *we* can get there, is through Clayton's root cellar."

She simply sat looking at him, unable to understand why he was fooling at a time like this. Getting away with him was the most serious matter she'd ever had to deal with.

"Sarah, I've tried and tried to think of how I can prove it to you. If Clayton were here, he could help me explain. But...oh, Lord, he probably wouldn't help at all. He'd just tell me I was crazy even to be thinking about taking you with me.''

"No," she whispered. "No, I *want* to go with you."

"Oh, Sarah, you can't want it any more than I do. I love you so much. But Clayton didn't think that was enough. That's why he never said anything to Ella-Jane.''

"Ella-Jane?" Sarah repeated uncertainly.

Tyler nodded. ''Clayton told me he was once in love with her. Hell, I suspect he still is. But he thought the situation was impossible. And...oh, Sarah, all I can ask is that you trust me. Trust me...and believe me...and love me enough to come to the future with me. But you have to believe that's where you're going.''

Tears of frustration were forming in her eyes, and her throat had grown tight. Why did he keep going on and on about the future? And what did he mean about Clayton? If he'd been in love with Ella-Jane, why hadn't he declared himself?

And Tyler seemed so serious, as if he really wasn't teasing. He seemed truly convinced that he was telling her the truth. Why, being an Aries, he likely *was* convinced of it. But if he *was*...oh, mercy, was it possible the man she'd fallen in love with suffered from a serious disorder of the mind? Or, at the very least, from delusions?

"Tyler, I love you," she murmured, trying to stay calm. "I love you more than I thought it was possible to love someone. And I want to marry you and be with you always. But please stop this silliness about the future. It worries me so."

He looked at her for a long, silent time, then slowly shook his head. "You think what I've told you is crazy, don't you? You think I'm insane."

"I...I don't know...no, not insane, exactly. I mean, I don't think you're insane at all. But I know that people can't travel back and forth between the present and the future, so I don't know why you keep insisting you can."

Tyler ran his fingers through his hair, as if he simply didn't know what to say next any more than she did.

She only wished she knew more about delusions. Maybe she should be offering to go to Clayton's root cellar with Tyler, to prove there was nothing magical about it. But Papa had given John McCully strict orders that Tyler wasn't to go anywhere near Clayton's.

"Tomorrow is Thursday," he said at last.

"Yes," she murmured, relieved to hear him say something rational.

"And the wedding isn't until next Saturday. So I'll figure something out before that. Some way of proving to you that I'm not a madman. I've got to make you understand what you'd be getting into if you came with me."

She blinked hard, but a tear still escaped. For some reason, mad sounded even worse than crazy or insane. And the idea of Tyler Adams being a madman was simply too much to bear.

She'd fallen desperately in love with him. Even though he was her sister's fiancé. And a Yankee. But, mercy, if he was mad as well, how could she possibly run off up North with him? No matter how desperately she loved him?

Gently, he brushed away her tear. Then he kissed her, so tenderly that more tears trickled down her cheeks. How could she possibly *not* run off up North with him?

"Oh, Sarah," he whispered. "Please don't cry. And don't worry. Everything is going to work out. I promise. I love you."

When he gave her a final kiss, then quietly stole out of her room, she buried her face in her pillow and lay sobbing silently into it.

THE SUN HAD BARELY been up an hour before Tyler and John McCully started off in the carriage for Savannah. With the train carrying the relatives from Ohio due in at nine o'clock, Louis had wakened them at the crack of dawn.

Almost the entire trip, through the gathering heat of the morning, Tyler's head was filled with thoughts of Sarah—the same thoughts that had kept him awake most of the night.

What if he never managed to convince her? Could he risk taking her with him, anyway? And just hope she'd handle the shock and adapt?

But, hell, he still hadn't figured out how he was even going to make it to that damned root cellar, let alone take her along.

By the time they were nearing the city, his mind was going around in circles and his frustration level had reached a new lifetime high. To save his sanity, he forced his thoughts from Sarah and began musing about the relatives from Ohio, the Custer family.

The moment he'd heard the boy's name, he'd wondered if this eleven-year-old Georgie was going to grow up to be the General George Custer who got massacred by the Sioux at Little Bighorn.

From what he could recall of history, the boy's age seemed about right. And it sure would be something to meet a historical figure like General George Armstrong Custer. Even as a child.

When the road cut nearer to the Savannah River, Tyler and John could see that the water traffic was already growing busy.

"Must be the steamer for New York," John said, gesturing toward a larger boat that was inching its way through the muddy water.

Tyler nodded. The steamer was about the size of the Staten Island ferry, and its two tall stacks were spewing black smoke that would give a modern-day environmentalist fits.

"That how you came to Georgia?" John asked. "By steamer?"

Tyler shook his head.

"Train, then?"

"Yeah . . . train." Lord, he was sick of lying. But if he said he'd flown, John would think he was as crazy as Sarah did.

"I came most of the way by stagecoach," John said. "From Nevada, I mean. Rented my horse when I got here."

They turned right onto a street with a sign reading West Broad. The red brick Central of Georgia station lay ahead.

Unlike the river, the station was quiet. Even though the Exchange clock said it was after nine, there was no sign of the train they were to meet.

They hitched the horses and went inside.

The long, narrow waiting room seemed cool after their trip under the blazing sun. But by the end of the day, Tyler imagined, the station would be like an oven.

If he ever got back home, he'd never again take air-conditioning for granted. Or comfortable furniture, he silently added, deciding he'd rather stand than sit on one of the hard wooden benches.

He leaned against a pillar and surveyed the scene. There were a couple of dozen people inside. Some, with luggage stacked on the floor beside them, were obviously waiting to board the train for its trip back north. Others were probably just meeting passengers.

Directly ahead of where he was standing sat an old woman, a black cane propped against the bench beside her. She was holding a big white goose on her lap and talking quietly to it. Either she intended to take it on the train with her, or she'd brought it to the station to greet someone.

Before Tyler could decide which possibility was most likely, he heard the faint rhythmic sound of a distant train.

The steam engine's steady chug grew louder. Tyler and John wandered out the rear door of the station, back out into the heat, and stood on the wooden platform, watching the arrival. The engine was belching at least as much black smoke into the air as the steamer had been earlier.

A shrill whistle sounded, and the wheels gradually slowed—with much clanking and screeching. Finally, with a whoosh of steam, the train came to rest.

"Well," John said, "hope there aren't too many folk who look like they could be Uncle Emmanuel and Aunt Maria."

"Can't be too many folk at all," Tyler said. "Not with only three coaches. And there probably won't be many couples with an eleven-year-old boy."

Even before the train had fully stopped, several uniformed porters had swung down from it. They were quickly followed by passengers.

Two well-dressed men emerged from the doorway closest to Tyler, one of whom turned and solicitously helped an elderly man down the steps of the coach.

All of a sudden, a boy leapt from the doorway to the platform, ignoring the coach's metal steps. He landed on his hands and knees, directly beside the elderly man, practically knocking him off his feet.

A kid like that, Tyler thought fleetingly, would be better off in jeans than that short-panted suit he had on.

"Georgie!" a woman called. "George Armstrong Custer, don't you move. You wait right there for me."

George *Armstrong* Custer? Tyler eyed the boy with interest as he picked himself up from the platform. Little Georgie *was* the future general. There couldn't be more than one kid the right age named George Armstrong Custer.

Unless Georgie was deaf, he'd heard the woman call to him. But he paid no attention. The minute he scrambled to his feet he was off and running.

An extremely harried-looking woman was hurrying down the coach's steps.

"Lay you odds that's Aunt Maria," John muttered.

The woman reached the platform and headed off in hot pursuit of the boy. He was already halfway to the station door.

"I'll catch Georgie and Maria," Tyler said. "You figure out which one is Emmanuel and meet us at the carriage."

Tyler started off after the two Custers, keeping his eye on Georgie. The platform was quickly growing crowded, but the way the kid was dodging his way between people, he'd easily make first string with the Knicks. He reached the doorway to the station and darted inside.

Picking up his pace, Tyler ran past Maria. There wasn't much risk of losing her, but Georgie was clearly another story.

Tyler raced through the doorway... then stopped dead. The big white goose that had been sitting on the old lady's lap was on the floor, flapping its wings and honking its heart out. And Georgie was chasing it.

Or else it was chasing Georgie. Which of them was doing the chasing wasn't instantly clear, because they were racing around one of the pillars.

What *was* perfectly clear was the old woman's response to this fiasco. She was tottering toward the boy and goose, waving her cane in the air and yelling, "Young ruffian!"

That meant, Tyler quickly concluded, it was definitely the goose who was being chased. He pushed through the laughing onlookers and grabbed Georgie by the back of his suit jacket.

Georgie wheeled around and landed a solid kick on Tyler's knee.

He sucked in his breath, just managing not to cry out at the pain, and let go of the boy.

Georgie took off like a shot, streaking toward the front door of the station.

"Come back here!" Tyler shouted.

The kid paid as much attention to that as he had to his mother, so Tyler limped rapidly after him, his damned knee almost killing him.

Little Georgie was big for his age. And fast. It was all Tyler could do not to lose ground.

He roared out onto West Broad Street after the boy and caught him while he was looking from left to right, deciding which way to head.

This time, Tyler grabbed Georgie by the back of both shoulders and held him at arm's length, out of kicking range.

"Let go of me!" Georgie yelled.

"Shut up!" Tyler snapped. "Your uncle Beauregard sent me to meet you, not have a damned race with you."

"Who are you?" Georgie demanded, twisting around so he could see Tyler.

The kid had a hawklike nose and the beadiest eyes Tyler had seen in a long time.

"Oh, my," a woman said breathlessly at Tyler's elbow.

He glanced down at a frazzled Maria Custer.

"Thank you," she said. "Georgie gets overly rambunctious when he's forced to sit too long, and we've been sitting all the way from Ohio."

"Think nothing of it," Tyler said, hoping he sounded more civil than he felt. "Is it safe to let go of him now?"

Maria nodded, and Tyler cautiously released Georgie, warily watching out for a second kick attempt.

"You're Mrs. Custer, aren't you?" he said to Maria when Georgie moved away a few steps.

"Why, yes. Yes, I am."

"And who are you?" Georgie demanded again. "Are you the one who's gonna marry cousin Vallen?" he asked, wrinkling up his face.

"Well . . . that's the story."

"Why, then, you'd be Mister Farnsworth," Maria said, smiling. "When cousin Beauregard wrote, he didn't tell us you were such a handsome young man."

Georgie made a rude noise at that, and his mother shot him a quick glare.

"Actually, I'm not Fitzhugh Farnsworth," Tyler muttered. "My name is Tyler Adams."

"Oh?" Maria said.

"It's a long story. Ah . . . is that your husband?" Tyler asked, relieved to see John heading in their direction with another man in tow.

"Yes. Yes, that's Mr. Custer."

"Good. Well, it's only a few blocks to the hotel. And the carriage is right over there."

"Fine," Maria said, fidgeting at the wisps of hair that had escaped her hat. "Then, as soon as we get the baggage, we can go. It shouldn't take long. There are only two trunks and three bags."

THE SAVANNAH HOTEL was a three-story white wooden building with an impressive front entrance, flanked by two large windows. It sat almost directly across River Street from Ewell Endicott's building, which had been worrying Tyler off and on since they'd started for the city.

He could still clearly picture old Ewell standing on the front steps of his house yesterday, aiming that big shotgun at Beauregard. So it wasn't hard to imagine Ewell appearing, with that gun, at the front door of his office building.

But Tyler hadn't had time to think about Ewell during the ride from the train station. The trip took less than ten minutes, but in that time Georgie Custer managed to spook the horses twice and cause a delay by throwing one of his mother's bags down onto the street. Then, for a grand finale, the boy grabbed John's cowboy hat off his head and pitched it directly under the wheel of a passing buggy.

By the time John reined the horses to a halt in front of the hotel, Tyler could have cheerfully throttled young George Armstrong Custer.

John's tight-lipped expression said that if Tyler needed help, John was his man.

"You ever kill anyone with that thing?" Georgie asked, poking at John's big Colt as they swung out of the carriage.

"Not so far," John muttered. "But the idea's been crossing my mind lately." He reached back up to help Maria Custer down.

"Just as soon as we get checked in," Emmanuel said, "I want to buy you a new hat, Mr. McCully."

"Well, what's the use of wearing a gun if you don't shoot it?" Georgie interrupted.

If Tyler hadn't been easing one of the trunks off the back of the carriage, he might have been able to stop the boy. As it was, all he could do was yell, "Don't touch that!" while Georgie whipped the Colt out of its holster.

John swore, grabbing for his gun, but Georgie took off down the street with it, laughing hilariously.

"Son, you get right back here with that!" Emmanuel yelled.

John was already charging after Georgie.

Tyler let the trunk drop the rest of the way to the dirt and started after the two of them.

Georgie ducked behind a carriage and doubled back toward the hotel, leaving John and Tyler in his dust.

"I'm going to kill that boy," John muttered as they wheeled around and started running back in the direction they'd come.

The way Georgie was waving the Colt around, *someone* was likely to get killed. Unfortunately, Tyler thought, forcing his legs to move faster through the merciless heat, it wouldn't be Georgie. He lived on to become a General.

The Colt suddenly roared to life in Georgie's hand.

Simultaneously, the air was filled with earsplitting, shattering sounds—a boom followed by the crackling and tinkling of a rain of glass. Everything from large pieces to tiny shards were hitting the wooden sidewalk.

Georgie had shot out one of the front windows of the Savannah Hotel.

A moment later, his father grabbed him from behind and wrestled the Colt from his hand.

"Hell, what a monster!" John said. "Almost makes you glad to know he gets his comeuppance at Little Bighorn."

"Sure as hell does," Tyler muttered.

For a split second, John's remark didn't really register in Tyler's brain. Then it did and he looked at John.

John was staring at him.

"How the hell do you know about Little Bighorn?" they said at the same time.

CHAPTER FOURTEEN

"WE'LL SEE YOU at Booker's Knoll in a few days, then," Emmanuel Custer was telling Tyler and John. "I'll rent a carriage and we'll come visiting just as soon as my business is taken care of here in Savannah."

Tyler tried to listen politely as Emmanuel droned on, but all he wanted to do was get away and talk to John McCully.

John knew that General George Armstrong Custer got killed by the Sioux at Little Bighorn, even though that wasn't going to happen for another twenty-odd years. So either John was clairvoyant or he was from the future. And not knowing which was driving Tyler crazy.

But they hadn't had even a second to talk privately. First, they'd had to calm down the manager of the Savannah Hotel, assuring him that Beauregard Booker would pay for replacing the broken window.

After that, they'd had to help the Custers check in. And then Emmanuel had insisted on a trip to a haberdashery, to replace the hat Georgie had tossed under the buggy wheel.

The only good news had been that although the noise of Georgie shooting out the window had brought a dozen men running from inside Ewell Endicott's building, Ewell hadn't been among them. He must be taking time off to recuperate from whatever damage he'd suffered yesterday.

Emmanuel finally seemed to be winding down, so Tyler shook his hand in farewell. Then he climbed into the carriage beside John and they made good their escape.

"So?" Tyler demanded as they started off down Bay Street. "What do you know about George Custer and Little Bighorn? And how?"

John fiddled with the brim of his new hat for a minute, then glanced over. "It was 1876. End of June, if I recall right. I was twenty-three years old and everyone was talking about it, even in Nevada. Over two hundred soldiers were killed, and the only Seventh Cavalry survivor was a horse named Comanche."

Tyler couldn't quite believe what he was hearing. If John McCully had been twenty-three years old in 1876, he'd been born in 1853. So John, too, had traveled back in time—to before he was born. Tyler didn't know why he was surprised—after all, he'd done it himself.

"Is that," John said, "pretty much the same as what *you* know about the Custer massacre?"

Tyler shook his head. "That's *more* than I know. I've only read about it in history books. I wasn't born until 1959."

"Until 1959," John repeated. "And what year did you leave when you came to 1850?"

"It was 1993," Tyler said, unable to figure out how John could be taking this so coolly when the idea of John being a fellow time-traveler was absolutely mind-blowing.

"You don't seem awfully surprised by all this," Tyler tried.

"Well, I guess that's because I've known about time travel for a mite longer than you. And someone explained a lot about it to me."

"So you understand how it works?"

"Not entirely. But why don't you tell me how you got here, and I'll see what I can fill in. I *do* pretty much understand how *I* ended up here."

Tyler began with his flight from New York to Savannah last Friday night and told John the entire story.

"So Booker's Knoll still exists in 1993," John said. "And Clayton Willis is the fellow who owns it, then. And he's been time-traveling for years...through a burned-out plantation's root cellar. Well, that's all mighty interesting."

Tyler nodded, wishing John would get on with *his* story. "What about you, John?" he finally urged. "What year do you belong in?"

"1887. I left 1887, heading for the future. But I ran into a mite of trouble and ended up in the past, instead."

"Trouble?" Tyler said uneasily. He already had his concerns about trying to travel back through that root cellar without Clayton.

"Yeah...guess I'd better start at the beginning," John said. "I was working on a ranch in Arizona, but the owners were in the middle of a feud and I just about got killed. So I decided the job wasn't worth my life and lit out for Tombstone to do a little gambling. But instead of ending up in the saloons, playing poker, I ended up in the Tombstone jail, about to be hung as a horse thief."

"You're a horse thief?"

"No, no, it was all a mistake. But that didn't matter much in Tombstone. Fortunately, though, my sister found out what had happened and came after me. She brought an old friend of mine with her—a fellow named Will Lockhart. Will had been living in the future. That's who explained to me about time travel."

Tyler shook his head in amazement. How many people knew about the phenomenon? How many people were out there traveling through the centuries?

"Anyway," John went on, "it's a long story. But basically, Will and my sister, Emma, managed to get me out of jail and we all headed for San Francisco. Then, somewhere along the way, the two of them fell in love."

Tyler couldn't stop shaking his head. Now he was wondering whether men who time-traveled were particularly vulnerable to falling in love with women in the past.

"At any rate," John went on, "Will decided to stay in 1887 and marry Emma. And I decided to go see the future. The main reason I'd left Nevada and gone to Arizona was because I wanted some adventure. But getting killed in a feud, or being strung up by the good folks of Tombstone, weren't the sorts of adventures I'd had in mind. Going to the future seemed like a great idea. At least it did until I ran into the trouble."

"And the trouble was...?"

"Well, from what you've said, it's clear there's more than one way to time travel. Will had done it by going through a tunnel in Nevada's Broken Hill Mine. He told me it was simple. That all I had to do was go down a side tunnel until I saw a shimmering blue light. By following that, I was supposed to end up in the future.''

"But it didn't work . . . You ended up in the past."

"Yeah. See, once I got a ways down the tunnel, I came to a fork. There were three possible ways to go, with shimmering blue lights down all three passages. And I obviously chose the wrong one."

"But can't you get back? You're not stuck in 1850, are you?"

"I don't think so. Not permanently. But in the Broken Hill Mine you can only travel during what Will called blue moons—when there are two full moons in a single month. Luckily, August 1850 is a blue moon month. So I figure I'll be able to get out of here, during the second full moon. In the meantime, I had time to play with, so I came to Georgia."

"Why Georgia?"

John looked uneasy about answering the question. "I'm not sure I should get into that."

Tyler nodded. "I guess we're kind of in the same boat," he offered at last. "Both in 1850 when we want to be somewhere else. 'Course, you know you can get out of here. But when Beauregard gives us that plantation, Vallen intends to fill in the old root cellar and make a pond. I'll be stuck here forever."

"Hmm, First I've heard about her plan," John muttered.

"John?" Tyler said. His heart was hammering, but he had to seize the moment. "John, think about how you'd feel if you were me . . . stuck in the wrong time."

Flicking the reins, John drove on silently for a few minutes while Tyler waited in agony for his response.

"You know," John finally said, "ever since I realized Vallen is such a liar, I haven't felt right. I can't help thinking I was too quick on the trigger—about giving Beauregard my word that I'd keep you from straying. A man shouldn't give his word before he has all the facts. And now that I know there are even more complications . . . Tyler, I think maybe the only right thing to do is let you get away."

Tyler exhaled a long, slow breath. He'd never felt so relieved in his life. "I'd sure appreciate that, John," he said.

They drove along in silence for a while longer, then John looked over. "I've just been thinking. When you asked about why I came to Georgia . . . well, maybe I *should* tell you the reason."

"Yeah?"

"Yeah. See, I'm running kind of short on time here. I've got to make it back to the Broken Hill Mine before the next full moon and it's a long trip. But I *have* to take care of what I came here to do. And you might have some good thoughts on how I ought to be doing it. You're going to find this story mighty tough to believe, though."

"John, at this point, I don't think I'd find *any* story mighty tough to believe."

"Yeah, I guess that's true," John said, grinning. "Well, then, the thing is that my mother grew up in Savannah. She moved to Nevada when she married my father. But, until then, she and Ella-Jane Booker were best friends."

"What?" Tyler said.

He must have looked as confused as he felt because John grinned again. "I don't get born until three years from now, remember?"

Tyler shook his head yet again. This time-traveling made for damned convoluted situations.

"At any rate," John continued, "when I found myself stuck in 1850...well, I realized I had the chance to do some good. You see, I don't remember the exact date my mother told me. She hasn't repeated the story in years now. But I know that sometime this August, Ewell Endicott kills Ella-Jane."

"Good God," Tyler murmured, a chill running down his spine. "He follows through on his threats."

For a moment, Tyler wondered why John's expression was blank. Then he realized John didn't know about yesterday's confrontation with Ewell. John had left to take Horace Halleck into Savannah before Beauregard said anything about getting Ella-Jane out of Ewell's house.

And John had arrived back at the plantation so late that they'd all been heading for bed. So nobody had told him what happened.

"John," he said, "I'd better explain how Ella-Jane came to be at Booker's Knoll last night. And we'd better get back there fast."

"PAPA, LET'S GO," Vallen whined. She inched closer to the edge of the veranda and impatiently twirled her parasol.

Beau leaned back in his chair and shook his head. "Can't go until Tyler and John McCully get back from the city."

"But, Papa, we're already late. And if Mrs. Ramsey doesn't get my dress fitted in time, it won't be ready for the wedding."

"Dammit, Vallen, we can't leave your sister here alone."

"I won't be alone," Ella-Jane said. "Sarah will be right here with me. You just leave your shotgun there by the table. Both of us know how to use it."

Sarah gave Ella-Jane a reassuring smile, but she'd sooner Papa *did* wait. Both of them might know *how* to use a shotgun, but it had been years since she'd actually shot one. Ella-Jane likely hadn't used one for a spell, either. Vallen was the only one of them who liked to shoot.

"Papa," Vallen said, "if we're too late, that overseer fellow Mr. Ramsey is recommending might leave, thinking you don't want to see him."

"Well," Beau muttered, frowning, "I *do* want to talk to him. Sooner I hire a new overseer, the better."

"I'll be perfectly safe, Papa," Ella-Jane said. "Really. I can't have everyone making their lives stand still for fear of what Ewell might do."

"Well . . . I guess those boys *will* be back any minute now."

"Come *on,* Papa," Vallen whined again.

Beau slowly pushed himself out of the chair.

Vallen scurried over to the buggy and up onto the seat.

"You watch for anyone coming down the drive now, you hear?" Beau said.

"We'll watch," Ella-Jane assured him.

"All right. And we'll be back from the Ramseys' plantation before nightfall. 'Less they insist we stay to supper.''

Sarah's gaze followed Papa across to the buggy. When he and Vallen started off, she glanced at Ella-Jane once more.

Her face was pale, and despite her brave words she looked extremely anxious.

"You probably *are* perfectly safe here,'' Sarah tried. "Ewell wouldn't dare come to Booker's Knoll. Vallen was being silly, last night, saying that he might. Ewell knows how good Papa is with a shotgun.''

"But Papa isn't always here. Ewell knows that, too. And mercy, Sarah, I've just realized that he'll even know Papa isn't here right this minute. I've been prattling on about Vallen's wedding plans, and I'm positive I told Ewell that Papa would be taking her to the Ramseys' place today.''

Ella-Jane paused for a sip of lemonade, and Sarah anxiously gazed down the drive after the buggy. She watched it turn onto the main road, wishing Ella-Jane had remembered about her prattling ten minutes ago.

She doubted that either one of them could aim well enough to hit a fat man at ten feet. And Ewell certainly wasn't fat.

"What am I going to do?'' Ella-Jane said, drawing Sarah's attention back to her. "I meant what I said to Papa. I can't expect you all to stop living because of Ewell. And I don't want to live in fear. But he isn't given to idle threats—he *does* mean to kill me. Even if he was to wait years for the chance. So how can I stay at Booker's Knoll?''

"But this is your home. Where else would you go?''

"I don't know," Ella-Jane murmured wearily. "I thought on it all through the night and I just don't know. But I don't want to be always watching down the drive, in case Ewell is coming. And how could I ever go into the city, knowing he might appear around the next corner? Sarah, if I'm living anywhere near Savannah, I'll be like a prisoner."

Ella-Jane picked up her fan, then glanced toward the road. Her face grew even more pale.

Sarah looked down the drive, and tendrils of fear seized her heart. A lone rider was trotting toward the house.

"Is it Ewell?" Ella-Jane whispered.

Blood pounding in her head, Sarah hurried over to where Papa had been sitting and grabbed the shotgun. Then she looked back at the rider.

Relief washed over her. It wasn't Ewell.

"It's Clayton Willis," Ella-Jane said, sounding as if she couldn't believe her eyes.

Sarah scarcely could, either. Not when Papa had threatened to shoot Clayton Willis if he ever again came near Booker's Knoll.

Carefully, she put the shotgun down, then glanced at Ella-Jane once more, trying to remember exactly what Tyler had said about Clayton last night.

She'd been trying to avoid thinking about last night at all. Every time she did, she couldn't help worrying about Tyler's insane talk.

But Tyler had told her something they'd all once suspected. That Clayton had been in love with Ella-Jane. And Tyler thought he still was. And Sarah knew that Ella-Jane had once been in love with Clayton. So what if . . . ?

Clayton reined up in front of the veranda and dismounted.

"Ella-Jane, Miss Sarah," he said, his eyes lingering on Ella-Jane. "I was riding up near the road and spotted your father and Vallen leaving. So I took the opportunity of dropping in. Much as I enjoy your company, I *have* to talk to Tyler Adams."

Sarah's mind was racing. Maybe Clayton had another plan to help Tyler escape. But, in the meantime . . .

"Tyler isn't here right now," she said. "But he'll be back soon. And Papa will be gone for hours, so please wait with us, Clayton. I'll go and make some fresh lemonade, and you just sit down with Ella-Jane. I don't want to leave her alone because she's more than a mite upset. Ella-Jane, while I'm gone, you tell Clayton what happened yesterday."

In her entire life, Sarah had never taken so long to make lemonade. When she finally came back out to the veranda, Ella-Jane was sitting very close to Clayton, her hands in his.

"Ah . . . Sarah," Clayton said, "I'm sorry you went to the bother of lemonade, because I have to leave now. I have something pressing and can't wait any longer for Tyler. But tell him I'll be at the house until the wedding. I won't go off traveling anywhere. And if there's anything I can do for him, anything at all, tell him to get a message to me. Otherwise, just say I hope to see him soon.

"And to see you, Ella-Jane," he added so quietly Sarah scarcely caught the words.

As soon as Clayton mounted his horse and started up the drive, Sarah hurried across the veranda.

"Well?" she demanded, sitting down beside her sister.

"Oh, Sarah," Ella-Jane murmured. "Oh, Sarah, I just don't know what to do."

"What did he say?"

"I . . . well, I told him the whole story. About Ewell cheating Papa and Papa storming the house on Lafayette Square. And about Ewell's threats to kill me."

"And?"

"And . . . Clayton Willis said he loved me, Sarah. He said he always loved me. And that he's been miserable ever since I married Ewell. I've been worried about the way he's been drinking, but he says it was only because he was so very unhappy. And he wants to take me away and marry me himself."

Sarah could feel a smile stealing across her face. Clayton would take Ella-Jane somewhere safe, where she could divorce Ewell and marry Clayton. And she'd be happy.

So why did she look as if she were about to cry?

"Ella-Jane?" Sarah said softly. "Don't you still love Clayton?"

Ella-Jane nodded.

"Then what's wrong?"

A tear trickled down her cheek. "Sarah, Clayton was talking crazy. So crazy I can't even tell you."

"Of course you can tell me. What did he say?"

Instead of replying, Ella-Jane opened her fist. A large silver coin lay in her hand.

"Clayton gave me this," she explained. "He had it in his pocket, and he said . . . well, he seemed to think I should have heard of the woman whose picture is on it. I haven't, but Clayton said she was famous . . . *is* famous. Right now. And he gave me the coin to prove…Sarah, this is the crazy part. He said that if he took me away, he'd be taking me to another time. And there, he owns Booker's Knoll. So I'd be living right here, but in the future. He said that Tyler Adams lives in the future as well, except in New York City. It was positively crazy, Sarah. But this coin…wherever would Clayton get it?''

Sarah took the coin and looked at it. Clayton had told Ella-Jane the same crazy things that Tyler had told her.

Completely unnerved, Sarah forced her attention to the coin. It bore the picture of an an eagle, perched with its wings outstretched. Above the bird was printed United States of America. Beside it, In God We Trust. Beneath it, One Dollar. She turned it over and a tiny shiver seized her. The dollar coin was dated 1980.

Between the date and the word *Liberty* was the profile of a middle-aged woman. She had a sharp nose and wore her hair in a bun. "Ella-Jane, who did Clayton say this woman was?''

Ella-Jane thought for a moment, then said, "Anthony. He said her name was Susan B. Anthony.''

Sarah stared at the image of the woman once more, her heart racing. Ella-Jane might not have heard of Susan B. Anthony, but she certainly had. She always read the magazines Papa got, and Susan B. Anthony was one of the few women writers who'd had her writing published in one of them.

But she wasn't middle-aged. She was young. Only a few years older than Ella-Jane. That's why it was even more astonishing that she was writing the sort of articles about abolishing slavery that made Papa and his friends so dreadfully upset.

Sarah licked her lips uneasily, eyeing the 1980 date again. Susan B. Anthony wasn't middle-aged in 1850. But, after she became a part of history...

"Ella-Jane, when Clayton told you he lived in the future... did he say it was in the year 1993?"

Ella-Jane's eyes grew larger and rounder. She nodded again.

"Oh, my," Sarah whispered. "Oh, my."

"Oh, my, what?"

"Ella-Jane, Tyler's been telling me the same thing. So, either they're *both* crazy, or it's the truth."

"But it can't possibly be the truth!"

"I know," Sarah murmured, unable to stop gazing at the mysterious coin. "But what if it is?"

BY THE TIME they saw Tyler and John McCully turn down the drive, Ella-Jane had repeated every single word Clayton had told her. And Sarah tried to remember everything she'd heard from Tyler.

Neither man had mentioned specific details, but they'd said enough of the same things to convince Sarah that they *must* have concocted the story together. And had that silver coin specially made by a jeweler or silversmith.

Because the only other alternative was that they'd actually traveled through time. And that, Sarah and Ella-Jane agreed, was inconceivable.

But why in mercy's sake would they have fabricated such an incredible tale?

John reined in the horses in front of the veranda, and the two men swung down from the carriage. They both wore the same expression—a peculiar combination of relief and concern.

"Uncle Emmanuel and Aunt Maria arrived safely?" Sarah said. She wanted to broach the subject she was so desperately interested in, but knew she couldn't mention anything in front of John McCully.

Tyler nodded, saying, "Sarah, where's your father?"

"He's taken Vallen to have her wedding dress fitted."

"Good. Because we have to talk. All four of us," he added, glancing at Ella-Jane. "Right away."

"But Tyler," Sarah said, "I have something important to tell you. If we could just walk for a minute, I—"

"No, this can't wait."

"Tyler," she said, dragging out his name, "I have to talk to you... *alone.*" She glanced meaningfully at John McCully.

Tyler waved impatiently and said, "No, no, it's okay. You can talk in front of John. He and I have ... well, we've come to an understanding."

"Clayton Willis was here," she whispered in annoyance, moving closer to Tyler in the hope John wouldn't hear. "And if I tell you what Clayton said, in front of John McCully, he's going to think both of you are mad."

"Clayton has been here," Tyler told John.

"Tyler!" Sarah cried.

"What did he have to say?" Tyler demanded, turning back to her.

She glared daggers at him, then glanced at Ella-Jane, who gave an uncertain little shrug.

Sarah grabbed Tyler's arm and dragged him several steps away from the others. "Clayton said he's still in love with Ella-Jane," she whispered.

"Thank God," Tyler said. "And how does she feel?"

"Why... why, she's in love with him, too."

"Thank God," he repeated. "There's our solution to saving her from Ewell."

"But Tyler, Clayton was talking... I just don't understand, but he was talking about taking her to the future, the same way you've been—"

"He was talking about that because it's where he'd be taking her. Look, I know how hard it is for you to believe, Sarah, but everything I've told you is true.

"Good news," he went on, turning to John. "Clayton wants to take Ella-Jane to 1993."

"Tyler!" Sarah cried again. He was such an infuriating man. She couldn't keep from smacking his arm, but he frustrated her even more by seeming not to notice.

"It really *is* all right to talk in front of me," John said, grinning at her. "You see, I'm from the future, too."

CHAPTER FIFTEEN

SARAH STARED AT JOHN, then to Tyler, then back at John, wondering if the entire male population was going mad or only the men who'd been arriving at Booker's Knoll lately.

First Tyler. Then Clayton. And now John McCully. All claiming to be from the future.

She glanced over at Papa's shotgun. Maybe she should try to casually make her way across to it. Shared delusions, she'd once read, sometimes led to violence.

"Sit here beside Ella-Jane, Sarah," Tyler said, taking her firmly by the shoulders and settling her into a chair. "We're going to get this sorted out once and for all."

He sat down beside her, adding, "I can't seem to find a way to convince you I'm telling the truth. So listen to John's story."

She stole another wistful glance at the shotgun, then turned her attention to John.

"I guess," he began slowly, "I'd better start by explaining how I'm related to Ella-Jane's friend, Abigail."

"You said you were her husband's cousin," Ella-Jane reminded him.

"Well . . . I had to say that. I knew you wouldn't believe the truth. But now that you've heard about time-travel...Ella-Jane, I'm not Bert McCully's cousin. I'm his son. His and Abigail's."

"Abby's son?" Ella-Jane whispered. "But that's not possible. Abby has no son. And if she did, he'd be a little baby."

"Well," John said, "it's like I told you. I'm from the future, the same as Tyler and Clayton. Except it's not exactly the same—I'm from 1887. My mother is going to have me in 1853."

Sarah was still trying to get that straightened out in her head when John pulled a wallet from his pocket.

"Look at these things a friend gave me," he said, producing two small, brightly colored cards. He handed a blue one to Ella-Jane and a gold one to Sarah.

She stared at it, her head positively spinning now, but she forced her eyes to focus on the card. It wasn't made of colored paper, but of a much more solid, shiny material she'd never seen before.

On the back, below lines of printing too tiny to read, someone had written their name. The penmanship was atrocious, though, so she turned the little card over and examined the front.

It had black printing and designs on it. And there were other letters that were gold, like the card, but were embossed.

Tentatively, she tried to bend the card. It gave under the pressure, then straightened out again when she released the edges.

"You won't hurt it," Tyler said, smiling at her. "It's made of something called plastic that gets invented in the nineteen hundreds."

She almost put it down. It felt and looked like something a lot of people would call the devil's work. But it was so fascinating that she couldn't resist letting her gaze drift over the little raised letters. They spelled out a name she didn't know.

"Will Lockhart," she said, tracing the letters with her fingertip.

"Will is the friend who gave them to me," John told her. "He came from the future, and he gave me the cards because I decided to go to *his* time. Since he's staying with my sister in 1887, he won't need them."

"This is all dreadfully confusing," she murmured.

"I know," John said. "But, in Will's world, you use those cards in place of money."

"I have them, too," Tyler said.

"In place of money," Sarah repeated. "But you do *use* money." She was still holding the silver dollar Clayton had left behind. Uncertainly, she extended her hand to Tyler, the coin lying flat on her palm.

Even as she did so, she realized she'd started to believe the dollar wasn't part of a concocted story. That it really had been minted in 1980.

"Right," Tyler said. "We use both money *and* credit cards. But where did you get the Susan B. Anthony?"

"Clayton gave it to me," Ella-Jane murmured.

Sarah glanced at her sister, then handed the coin back to her.

Ella-Jane clutched it tightly, looking as if she didn't know what to believe any more than Sarah did.

The longer this went on, though, the more Sarah was thinking it all just might be possible. But how could anything so inconceivable be possible?

She gazed down at the little card once more, silently repeating the unfamiliar word. *Plastic*.

"In place of money," Ella-Jane was whispering. She seemed to have almost lost her voice entirely.

"Right," Tyler said. "But look, none of these details are important. The important thing," he said, taking Sarah's hands in his and looking deeply into her eyes, "is that you believe me. And John. And Clayton.

"But most of all," he added, for her ears alone, "I need you to believe *me*."

She gazed into the depth of his blue eyes. What he and John were saying was utterly unbelievable. And yet, Tyler was an honest Aries and John an honest Aquarius. And what other explanation could there possibly be that *would* be believable?

"Well?" Tyler said quietly. "Are you convinced?"

Sarah took a deep breath, then whispered, "I think so."

"And . . . Sarah, do you think you can still see your way clear to go with me?"

She took an even deeper breath, one that strained the ties of her corset. She'd fallen so in love with Tyler that she'd go to the ends of the earth with him. But never in her wildest dreams had she imagined the ends of the earth would include the ends of time. If it did, though, so be it.

Slowly, very anxiously, she nodded a yes.

Tyler pulled her into his arms and whispered, "I'm glad, Sarah Booker. More glad than you could ever believe."

He held her for a long moment, then turned to Ella-Jane and said, "What about you? Are you convinced we're really from the future?"

She shot Sarah a frightened little glance, but murmured, "I believe I am."

"Good," Tyler said. "Because something is going to happen in the next few days, Ella-Jane. John's mother told him it would. And we've got to interfere, so that it doesn't."

"*What* will happen... or *did* happen?" Ella-Jane asked, still tightly squeezing the coin Clayton had given her.

"Ella-Jane," Tyler said quietly, "I realize this is going to frighten you, and I'm sorry. But John and I decided we have to tell you. Ewell wasn't bluffing yesterday. If we don't get you away from here, he really *is* going to kill you."

Every speck of color drained from Ella-Jane's face.

Sarah reached over to her sister, certain Ella-Jane was about to faint. She didn't, though.

"Abby told you this?" she said, gazing at John with a dazed expression. "But I don't understand how that could be."

"Ella-Jane," John said, "pretend with me for a minute. Pretend you're looking back from 1887. What you'll see is that, on February 12, 1853, Abby has a son. She names him John."

"You," Ella-Jane whispered.

John nodded. "And years after 1853, Abby tells her son a story about how, in August 1850, her best friend was killed by her husband. Someone wrote to her when it happened, telling her the news."

"She told you? But... ?"

"She told me about it several times while I was growing up," John went on. "You were her best friend, Ella-Jane. Thinking about your death always upset her. That's why I came to Georgia. To prevent it from happening. And, I guess, the way everything seems to be falling into place, the only way to prevent it is by your going to the future with Clayton."

"And with Tyler and me," Sarah said, trying to sound reassuring, even though she felt as confused as Ella-Jane clearly was.

"Oh, Sarah, I wouldn't be brave enough to go without you," Ella-Jane murmured.

"Well, you won't have to go without me. And we'll be just fine." Sarah turned anxiously to Tyler. "Ella-Jane and I will be able to see each other, won't we? Even though you and I will be in New York?"

Tyler shifted his chair even closer to Sarah's and draped his arms over her shoulders. "Sarah, you and Ella-Jane will be able to talk to each other every day if you like. In the future, we have little machines called telephones that let you talk to people anywhere in the world. And there are huge things called planes that carry people through the air. It takes less than two hours to fly from New York to Savannah."

"Oh, my," she said. "Now it takes that long to get from Booker's Knoll to Savannah." She pressed her cheek against the reassuring warmth of Tyler's shoulder, wondering how she was ever going to manage in his world.

"You okay?" he whispered. "Because, if you are, we should get ready to go to Clayton's. Until we're in that root cellar, Ella-Jane isn't safe."

Sarah nodded, trying not to feel so terrified at the thought of leaving her own world behind.

TYLER STOOD IN SARAH'S bedroom doorway, resisting the temptation to tell her that she wouldn't need any of the bonnets she was carefully packing into a hat case. She was so obviously frightened that he didn't want to say anything to add to her fears.

"Sarah," he tried at last, "do you have any mementos you'd like to take? Things that will remind you of your life here? Use whatever room you need to pack them. As soon as we get to 1993, I'll take you shopping and we can buy you an entire new wardrobe."

She gave him a tentative little smile. "An entire new wardrobe? Are you a wealthy man, Tyler Adams? I never even thought to ask."

"Well, I'm not fabulously rich. But I'm a long way from poor. You won't want for anything, Sarah. I have a great condo, right in Manhattan."

At her questioning look, he explained, "I own an apartment in midtown New York. It's almost all windows. And it's on the twentieth floor, so there's not much noise from traffic."

"The twentieth floor," she whispered. "Oh, my, there must be so many stairs to climb."

"No, no, there are elevators. They whisk you up in just a minute or two. And, if you'd like, we could look for a place in the country. Spend our weekends there."

"Weekends?"

He cleared his throat. It seemed as if every second thing he mentioned hadn't been heard of in 1850. "We call Saturday and Sunday the weekend, Sarah. I only work Monday to Friday. Saturday and Sunday I'll be with you all the time. And in the evenings Monday through Friday, of course.''

"Of course," she murmured, packing a long dress Tyler refrained from pointing out she wouldn't need. Then she looked over at him again.

"Tyler, tell me more about the future. Not about things like telephones and planes and weekends, but about people. The way you treat me... well, you treat women differently than the men I'm accustomed to. I thought it was only because you were a Yankee, but now I realize..."

"Well," he said slowly, "I guess if I'm treating you differently it's because women are different in the future."

"Different how?"

"More... more independent. That's probably the best way of putting it. They do pretty much what they like with their lives, just the way men do."

"Really?" she said with such a dubious expression he grinned at her.

"*Really,* Sarah. Women in the future are more or less equal to men."

She looked even more dubious, so he went on. "See, most women have jobs. That means they're not economically dependent the way they are in 1850. And they work in the same occupations as men, and—"

"But what about the children? How could I have a job and care for our children?"

Our children. The words stopped him for a moment. He'd never thought about being a father. Mostly, because the type of women he met in New York had little interest in being a mother.

But Sarah would, of course. He had no doubt that she'd want children. And now that he thought about it, being a father seemed like a great idea. Sarah and him and their children. Just the prospect made him grin.

"Children make out just fine in the future," he said. "And not *all* women have jobs. The point I was trying to make was simply that women have more choice about the way they live. It isn't like here—husbands and fathers don't generally try to run their women's lives."

"But what about husbands like Ewell Endicott? And fathers like Papa?"

"Well, men like your father and Ewell are kind of an endangered species in the future."

"They're a what?"

"Ah...there aren't too many of them around, Sarah. Most women wouldn't stand for being told what to do. They have their own opinions and make their own decisions."

"And men accept that?"

Tyler grinned again. "It's like I said. Men and women are more or less equal. So I guess that's why I've been expecting you to think for yourself. Exactly the way I'd expect John McCully or Clayton Willis to."

"But...but, Tyler, I haven't done an awful lot of thinking for myself. I might disappoint you fearfully. And this idea about having a job. Why, whatever kind of work could I do? Tyler, I just don't know. This is all so frightening to even consider."

Quickly, he crossed the room and folded her into his arms. "Sarah, it's going to be great. You could never disappoint me. Not even a little. And you don't *have* to have a job. But if you want one, we'll figure out what you could do. Sarah, you'll get used to it, in no time. It's just going to be different at first, that's all."

She nodded slowly. "And we can come here some-times."

"Here?" he said uncertainly.

"Clayton told Ella-Jane he owns Booker's Knoll... that she'll be living here."

"Oh, right. Yes, he does. And yes, we can come here."

"Tyler... there's so very much I don't under-stand." She moved away from him and picked up a sheet of paper from the bed, saying, "This note I wrote to leave Papa... I tried to explain, but I couldn't re-ally explain what I don't understand myself. How does Clayton Willis come to own Booker's Knoll? Why doesn't my family still own it?"

"I... well, I'm not sure. Maybe Clayton knows. We can ask him when we get to his place."

"But it's been worrying me, Tyler. Ever since Ella-Jane mentioned it. What if something dreadful hap-pens to Papa and Vallen and I'm not here to help?"

"Ah..." Tyler rubbed his jaw, thinking about the upcoming Civil War, finally saying, "I don't think anything dreadful happens to them, Sarah."

In fact, he'd bet a major poker pot that Vallen came through the war ten times better than even Scarlett O'Hara had.

"But you don't *know* nothing happens," Sarah per-sisted.

"No, but there's the fact that Booker's Knoll is still standing in 1993. And it looks much the same. Whereas the plantation Clayton's been renting was burned to the ground during the war."

"The war?" Sarah repeated.

Her panicked expression made him swear silently at himself. He shouldn't have let that remark slip out. He'd known better than to mention the damned war. If he didn't watch what he was saying, she was going to change her mind about leaving.

"There's a war coming between the North and the South," he reluctantly admitted, trying to make the word *war* sound like a minor altercation.

"When?"

"It begins in 1861."

"And it ends?" she demanded.

"In 1865," he muttered.

"Four years," she whispered, sinking onto the bed. "A four-year-long war? And who wins? The North or the South?"

"Ah...the North."

"Oh, my. Four years of war. Tyler, whatever will happen to Papa and Vallen?"

He sat down beside her, putting his arm around her and drawing her to him once more. "Sarah, I'm sure they'll be all right. Like I said, Booker's Knoll survives in good shape."

"Oh, Tyler, I wish time could stand still forever! I don't want to leave Papa and Vallen. But I know Ella-Jane meant what she said. She really *wouldn't* be brave enough to go without me. And if she doesn't go, Ewell will kill her. But, oh, Tyler, I wish you and I could stay right here, together, and—"

"Sarah?" Ella-Jane said from the doorway. "Sarah, are you ready to leave?"

Sarah squeezed Tyler's hand more tightly than he'd have believed she could. Then she gave Ella-Jane a weak smile and nodded.

WHILE TYLER TOOK the bags outside to load into the carriage, Sarah put the note she'd written to Papa in his study.

She stood gazing at it for a second, sitting there on the middle of his desk. She was tempted not to leave it at all. When he read it, he was going to think she and Ella-Jane were crazy.

But at least he'd know they weren't dead.

She turned and hurried from the study to the kitchen, to say goodbye to Millie and Louis.

She so hated the thought of never seeing the servants again that she gave them both enormous hugs. That made them look even more worried.

"We'll be fine," she told them. "We just have to take Ella-Jane somewhere safe." She gave Millie a final hug, then almost ran to the front door, so neither of them would see her tears.

Outside, Tyler and Ella-Jane were waiting in the front seat of the carriage. John, though, was mounted on his horse.

"You're not coming to Clayton's with us, John?" Sarah said, wiping her eyes and trying to look composed.

"No, I'll ride up the drive with you, but now that I know Ella-Jane is going to be all right, it's time I was heading for Nevada. If I don't get back there by the next full moon, I won't make it to the future."

Sarah glanced at Tyler, wondering what the full moon had to do with anything.

"John's got a different way of time-traveling," Tyler explained. "It's through a mine during special full moons."

He turned to John, adding, "You're sure you don't want to try going through the root cellar with us? Aren't you worried about taking the wrong tunnel again?"

"You took a wrong tunnel?" Sarah said.

"Well . . . yeah, I had a bit of a mishap," John told her. "When I left 1887, I expected to travel to the future, but the tunnel I chose brought me here. 'Course, I'm mighty glad it did, since I was able to help out, but I'm counting on my second try getting me where I meant to go."

Sarah's heart was suddenly skipping erratically. "Tyler?" she said nervously. "Tyler, you didn't tell me there could be mishaps."

"I don't think there can be in the root cellar, Sarah. Clayton's been using it for years."

He didn't *think* there could be? But he didn't sound entirely convinced that there *couldn't* be.

Sarah glanced at Ella-Jane. She looked frightened half to death. But if they didn't leave, she'd be shot *entirely* to death by Ewell.

"I figure," John was saying to Tyler, "I'd feel a lot safer taking my chances with those tunnels again. Even though I got it wrong once, I understand how the mine works."

Tyler swung down from the carriage and helped Sarah up to the front seat.

"Getting the hang of driving yet?" John asked, grinning at the way Tyler fumbled with the reins when he climbed back up.

"You don't drive in 1993?" Sarah said.

"Not a horse and carriage," Tyler told her. "Horses are pretty much obsolete. We drive things called cars. They're machines that...well, you'll see for yourself soon." He clicked the reins and the horses started off.

Sarah's gaze drifted from Papa's matched pair of blacks to John's big brown gelding. How could there possibly be a world without horses?

As Tyler had said, though, she'd soon see for herself. She shifted a little closer to him, and he smiled at her.

His smile made her feel warm inside, the way it always did...and not *quite* so afraid of having to face the strange world he lived in.

When they reached the road, Tyler reined in the blacks and John rode his horse up right beside the carriage. He leaned over in the saddle to shake hands with Tyler, then tipped his hat to Sarah and Ella-Jane.

"Thank you, John McCully," Ella-Jane said quietly. "I still don't understand exactly how you did it, but thank you for helping to save my life."

"My pleasure, ma'am," he told her. "I hope everything goes well for you. For all of you."

"You, too," Sarah murmured past the lump in her throat. She'd grown very fond of John McCully in the days he'd been at Booker's Knoll, and now he was leaving them. Another part of her life that would be gone forever.

He touched the brim of his hat with two fingers in a final farewell, then turned his horse toward Savannah and started off.

Tyler turned the carriage in the opposite direction, and they headed down the road toward Clayton's.

"Do you think John will be all right, Tyler?" Sarah murmured. "You don't suppose he'll have another mishap, do you?"

"I hope not," Tyler said. "But, you know, John's the type of guy who'll make out all right wherever he ends up."

"Look," Ella-Jane said anxiously, pointing ahead down the road.

Sarah stared into the distance. The afternoon sun was so bright it was difficult to make out any details, but there was a tiny cloud of dust moving on the road. It hadn't been there a minute ago, which meant someone was coming *toward* them.

Anxiously, she thought about what had happened yesterday, when Fitzhugh Farnsworth and his brother had appeared.

"You don't think it could be Papa and Vallen, do you?" Ella-Jane asked. "On their way back from the Ramsey plantation already?"

"I don't think so," Sarah told her. "They've barely had time to get there, let alone start back."

"Well, I hope to hell it isn't Fitzhugh again," Tyler said. "Damn, I should have thought to bring a rifle."

Sarah sat gazing ahead at the dust cloud as the carriage rolled on, her heart pounding. It could be anyone approaching, of course. There were several plantations along the road. But, as Tyler had said earlier, until they were in Clayton's root cellar, Ella-Jane wasn't safe.

Tyler pulled out his Colt and drove on with it in his hand.

The cloud of dust gradually grew larger.

Finally, Sarah made out two men on horseback, and her heart began pounding harder yet.

"Do you recognize them?" Tyler said, his voice tense.

She shook her head. "Maybe, when they get a little closer...."

They rode on for a few more yards. Then Ella-Jane gave a frightened squeak.

"What?" Tyler demanded.

"I recognize one of them," she whispered. "The one on the gray horse. His name is Sam Crockett. He works for Ewell, on the wharf."

"Then what the hell is he doing out here, two hours from Savannah?" Tyler said, reining in the horses.

He lowered his gun below the front of the carriage, so the riders wouldn't be able to see it, and they sat waiting as the men drew nearer.

Both men wore revolvers, Sarah noted anxiously, but didn't have them drawn.

They stopped in front of the carriage.

The one Ella-Jane had said was Sam Crockett tipped his hat politely. "Why, Mrs. Endicott," he said. "We were just on our way out to Booker's Knoll. Mr. Endicott sent us along to deliver a note to you."

"But you aren't coming from Savannah," Ella-Jane pointed out, her voice trembling a little. "Is Mr. Endicott not in the city today?"

"No, ma'am," Sam Crockett told her, not quite managing to suppress a grin. "Mr. Endicott had business out near the Ramsey plantation."

Sarah heard Ella-Jane's breath catch almost in unison with her own. Ella-Jane had told Ewell that Papa would be taking Vallen to the Ramsey place today. But surely...

"You said you had a note for Mrs. Endicott," Tyler said tersely.

"Yeah, yeah, I do," Sam said. He dug into his pocket, then handed Ella-Jane an envelope. "Mr. Endicott told us we should wait until you read it."

Her hands shaking, Ella-Jane opened the envelope and unfolded the sheet of paper inside. Her face grew tight as she read.

"Mr. Endicott told me I should get it back after you read it," Sam said.

Wordlessly, Ella-Jane handed him the sheet of paper.

"Thank you, ma'am." Sam dug into his pocket again, this time producing a match. He lit it with his thumbnail and held it to one corner of the note.

His horse shied as the paper burst into flame.

Sam let it drop to the road, and they all watched it burn.

When it was reduced to nothing but a few black scraps, Sam looked at Ella-Jane once more. "Mr. Endicott told me I should tell you to enjoy the rest of your visit at Booker's Knoll, ma'am. And that he'll see you back home tomorrow morning."

Sam flicked his reins, and the gray started off along the road toward Savannah once more. The other man followed, not having spoken a single word.

"What?" Sarah said. "Ella-Jane, what did Ewell's note say?"

"Oh, Sarah," she murmured. "It said that he and his men have seized Papa and Vallen. They're being taken to Lafayette Square for the night. And when I return home in the morning, Ewell will let them go. But if I don't go back, he'll kill them.''

CHAPTER SIXTEEN

"OH, TYLER," SARAH murmured. "Whatever are we going to do?"

Tyler glanced from Sarah to Ella-Jane, both looking at him in wide-eyed horror, and wished John McCully hadn't had to make it back to Nevada in time for his blue moon. Whatever they were going to do, it would have been nice to still have him on their team.

But John was gone. And at the moment, Tyler didn't have a clue about what they were going to do.

In 1993, he'd pick up his car phone and call the police. Tell them that Ewell had kidnapped Beauregard and Vallen and was holding them hostage.

From what Beau had said yesterday, though, Ewell had the police in his vest pocket. So asking for their help would hardly be the way to start, even if he could find a damned car phone in the carriage.

"I'll have to go back to Lafayette Square," Ella-Jane whispered. "Back to Ewell. It's the only solution."

"No," Tyler said, "that's no solution at all. We know that if you went back, Ewell would kill you. So maybe we should do nothing for the moment. He has to be bluffing about your father and Vallen. I mean, he wouldn't really kill *them,* would he?"

"I believe he might," Ella-Jane said. "Tyler, my husband is not given to bluffing. Nor to idle threats."

"But he can't just go around killing people and getting away with it! Not even in 1850. Can he?"

"Ewell would make it look as if he'd had nothing to do with it," Sarah said, her voice trembling almost as badly as Ella-Jane's. "And the police would end up blaming it on vagrants. Whenever they can't, or won't, solve a crime, that's how they explain it."

Tyler exhaled slowly. "All right," he said at last. "What we're going to do is continue on to Clayton's and—"

"We can't leave," Sarah whispered. "Not now, Tyler. Ella-Jane and I can't possibly leave with Papa and Vallen as Ewell's prisoners."

"I know that," he said, squeezing her hand. "I know you can't. But Ewell has given us until the morning. So why don't we continue on to Clayton's and the four of us will figure out what to do."

With a click of the reins, Tyler started off again, hoping to hell they'd be able to come up with a plan. But how many men would Ewell have guarding the house on Lafayette Square? He and Clayton could hardly take it by storm when . . .

An idea began to form in his mind. An utterly crazy idea. Crazy unless they could pull it off, of course.

By the time Sarah reminded him that the turn into Clayton's was just ahead, damned if he hadn't almost convinced himself they *could* pull it off.

Clayton appeared on the veranda, a broad smile on his face. As they drew closer, though, and he saw their expressions, his smile faded.

"What's wrong?" he demanded, helping Ella-Jane down from the carriage and drawing her into his arms.

"You're coming with me, aren't you?" he murmured to her.

"Let's go inside," Tyler suggested. "We've run into a major hitch."

They sat in the parlor, Tyler holding Sarah's hand and Clayton with his arm tightly around Ella-Jane's shoulders, while Tyler filled him in on what had happened.

"I'll have to go back to Ewell," Ella-Jane whispered when Tyler was done.

"No," Clayton said firmly. "You're never going back to him."

"But..."

Ella-Jane paused to wipe away a tear, and Tyler said, "I've got an idea. It's pretty bizarre, but it just might work."

The others focused their attention on him.

"We could use the element of surprise, Clayton," he began. "Ewell told Ella-Jane to come home in the morning. But what if you and I showed up at the house tonight? Made a preemptive strike?"

Clayton shook his head. "Problem is, Ewell's sure to have the house crawling with armed men."

"Yeah, I already figured that. Then I started thinking..." He paused, checking the grandfather clock in the corner. "We've still got most of the afternoon. So what if we made a quick trip to 1993 and picked up a few things?"

He tried to sound nonchalant, as if he actually believed that going from one century to another wasn't much different than making a casual trip to the corner store. In fact, he still didn't like the idea of going through that root cellar even one more time. But

Clayton had said he'd been doing it for years. That there was nothing to it.

"Pick up a few things like what?" Clayton was saying, leaning forward on the settee.

"Oh, for starters, I was thinking body armor and riot helmets."

"Body armor?" Sarah said. "Riot helmets?"

"They're things the police use in the future," Tyler told her. "Protective gear they wear," he elaborated, indicating with his hands how body armor fit. "It covers your body almost entirely and prevents bullets from injuring you. And the helmets have a protective panel that comes down over your face.

"And what about tear gas," he went on, turning back to Clayton. "And stun guns. Stun grenades, even, depending on how cooperative a supplier you can turn up fast."

Clayton grinned, clearly getting into the swing of things. "One of my poker buddies is a detective on the Savannah police force. I think I could turn up a cooperative supplier pretty fast."

Tyler felt a surge of relief at that news. "Hell, if you've got a contact like that, we could have so many elements of surprise on our side that Ewell's men would think we were alien invaders."

"Think you were what?" Sarah asked.

"Creatures from outer space," Tyler explained, grinning at her. "When cops get all decked out in protective gear they look really weird. Hardly human. Especially in the dark of night."

"You know, this isn't bad," Clayton said excitedly. "In fact, it's damned near brilliant. I mean, how many of Ewell's men do you figure would stick around during a space invasion? Even if there were only two invaders?''

"Four," Sarah said.

"Four of them would stick around?" Tyler said, wondering how on earth she'd come up with that number.

"No," she said. "I mean there'd be four invaders. You, Clayton, Ella-Jane and me."

"Don't be crazy," Tyler said, turning back to Clayton.

"I'm not being crazy," Sarah told him firmly, poking him to get his attention again. "I don't know exactly what you're talking about, Tyler Adams, with your body armor and tear gas. But it's my father who Ewell is threatening. And my sister. Even if Ella-Jane and I can do nothing more than distract some of those armed men of Ewell's—"

"No," Clayton snapped, interrupting.

"Yes!" Sarah snapped right back. "Don't you try to tell me what to do, Clayton Willis. I ... I'm doing exactly what Tyler expects a woman to do. I'm thinking for myself. I'm thinking for myself and making my own decisions and not...not letting a man tell me what to do. And I'm thinking that four of whatever these invaders are would scare off more men than two would."

"Good God," Tyler muttered as his own words spilled from Sarah's lips. He'd created a monster. Sarah sounded so damned gutsy he was half proud and half scared to death. What if she was actually going to be stubborn about this?

"And it's my house," Ella-Jane added, not sounding half as brave as Sarah, but clearly trying hard. "I know how to sneak into the back garden. And I know how the house is laid out, of course. Besides, this is my fault."

"It isn't *your* fault," Clayton told her. "It's Ewell's fault. And you certainly can't—"

"Yes, I can," Ella-Jane said. "If Sarah can, I can, too."

"What the hell have you been telling them?" Clayton hissed at Tyler.

He shrugged, feeling every bit as stunned as Clayton looked. He'd created *two* monsters. Sarah had infected Ella-Jane.

"And we know it's perfectly safe for Sarah to help," Ella-Jane went on. "Because, if something did happen, Abigail McCully would have told John about her death as well as about mine. And, I only have to worry about Ewell, not any of those other men. So I just have to stay away from my husband."

"Maybe," Sarah put in, "with your body armor, you won't even have to worry about Ewell."

"Is any of that logic logical?" Clayton asked Tyler, his voice not sounding at all normal.

Tyler simply shrugged once more. Some of what Ella-Jane had just said made sense. Surely if Sarah *had* been killed in 1850, Abigail McCully *would* have told John.

But if it was possible to change history, which was what they were trying to do by attempting to save Ella-Jane, then couldn't other things change, as well?

Maybe Sarah *could* get killed. Maybe someone other than Ewell could kill Ella-Jane. Hell, maybe the four of them could end up dead in Lafayette Square before the night was out.

"I intend to help, Tyler," Sarah said quietly. "I have thought for myself, like an independent woman, and I have made my decision. If you and Clayton go into Savannah, I won't wait quietly at Booker's Knoll while you're off risking your life for my family."

Ella-Jane silently nodded her agreement.

"I just don't know about this," Clayton said, giving Ella-Jane a worried glance. "Let's start by seeing what gear I can manage to get. *Then* we can talk about who's going to do what."

"You'd best be sure you *manage* to get four body armors," Sarah said calmly. "Otherwise, Ella-Jane and I might be killed. Because we're going along regardless."

Clayton glared at her, then took a deep breath, obviously trying to control his temper.

"Look, Tyler," he finally said, "I'd better make the trip back alone. Otherwise, there wouldn't even be a servant here with Ella-Jane and Sarah. Joseph is off taking care of something for me."

"All right. If you think you can manage all the stuff on your own."

"Yeah, there's a van I know I can borrow. Then I'll just toss everything down into the cellar ahead of me and you can help me drag it back up. But, hey, while I'm gone, the three of you had better try to get some sleep. You all look beat, and it could turn out to be a damned long night."

SARAH SHIFTED RESTLESSLY in the bed. She'd pulled the drapes against the afternoon sun, had even unpacked a nightdress and put it on, but she simply couldn't sleep. Her mind was too troubled.

She really did want to go to Lafayette Square with Tyler and Clayton. She had to do whatever she could to help them. Because if anything should happen to Tyler... but maybe she'd been far too bold about insisting on going along.

Maybe she hadn't truly understood what Tyler had meant about thinking for herself and making her own decisions. Maybe he was angry at what she'd done and would decide he didn't love her, after all....

Oh, she simply didn't understand how she should behave to make Tyler happy with her. Mercy, what if he was angry with her right this minute? What if he was lying awake, thinking in his bed, just as she was in hers? What if he was thinking she was a dreadful, headstrong, willful woman?

She threw back the sheet, unable to stand that thought. She *had* to be sure she hadn't made a terrible mistake. If Tyler just held her closely for a minute and assured her that he still loved her, she knew she'd feel so much better.

Quickly, she poked through her valise, searching for her robe. It wasn't there. Either she'd forgotten to pack it or it was in a different bag. She glanced at the chair, where she'd left her dress and underclothing, but she didn't want to take the time to put them on.

She needed to hear Tyler tell her he still loved her right this minute.

Besides, she was going to marry him. So, she decided, heading to the door, the idea of allowing him to see her in her nightdress wasn't *that* shocking.

The hallway was dim and silent. She crept down it, pausing to peek into the room Ella-Jane was using. She was fast asleep, the Susan B. Anthony silver dollar resting on the pillow beside her head.

Sarah quietly closed Ella-Jane's door and continued along to Clayton's bedroom, the room Tyler was using.

She paused outside the door, reconsidering. If he was asleep, she shouldn't waken him. Clayton had been right. They were all tired.

As quietly as she could, she eased open the door and gazed into the room.

Tyler was lying on his side, bathed golden in the sunlight streaming through the window. His face was toward her, the sheet drawn up only to his waist so that his bare chest was exposed.

The gunshot wound had healed quickly, and he was no longer wearing a bandage. But she couldn't help thinking back to that afternoon he'd been shot... thinking about sitting on his lap, wrapping that bandage around him, her body pressed against his naked chest.

And she couldn't help remembering how she'd felt. How she'd wanted him to touch her the way she'd been touching him. How she'd wanted him to kiss her.

Mercy, she was feeling the same way right now, just looking at him lying there. Once they were married, of course, he *would* touch her. He'd... well, she'd asked Ella-Jane all about it, so she knew *exactly* what he'd do.

Ella-Jane said it was odious. But one of Sarah's married friends had confided that it was sometimes quite nice. And there was a big difference between Ewell Endicott and Tyler Adams. Imagining being with Tyler Adams like that...

Sarah could feel herself blushing, but she was very, very curious. Of course, the thoughts she was having were most improper. At least, that was what the instructors at the Chatham Academy had always told their girls.

Although, now that she thought about it, that wasn't what the girls themselves had secretly said. And, given the number of babies born after only a few months of marriage, there were a lot of young women who hadn't paid any heed to what the instructors considered improper.

Sarah could well understand why, if their fiancés had made them feel anything like the way she felt when she was near Tyler.

"Sarah?" he murmured, opening his eyes.

She began blushing even more, worried that he might be able to tell what she'd been thinking.

"Sarah?" Tyler murmured again, not entirely sure she was standing in the doorway. Maybe he was just still dreaming about her. "What's wrong?"

"Nothing," she whispered, giving him a nervous little smile. "I mean...I wanted to talk to you for a minute if you weren't asleep."

"Well, I'm not asleep now, so come in and talk." He started to sit up, then quickly changed his mind and just propped himself up on his side, draping the sheet loosely over his hip. Dreaming about Sarah had left him decidedly aroused.

She closed the door and started hesitantly over to the bed.

When she passed the window he almost groaned. With the sunlight behind her, she might as well be wearing nothing. And for such a tiny woman, she had an incredibly enticing figure. Firm round breasts, an impossibly small waist . . . and, Lord, in that light he could even see the dark shadow between her legs.

As casually as he could, he readjusted the sheet over his hip. He was growing harder still, just looking at her.

She perched herself on the side of the bed and nervously licked her lips.

He almost groaned again, but managed to turn it into "What is it, Sarah?"

"Tyler . . . Tyler, I don't know quite how to put this . . . it's most difficult for me."

"Put it plainly. That's always the best way. I remember someone giving me that advice, only a few days ago."

Sarah smiled, telling him she remembered, as well. "Tyler . . . I've been worrying that I made a mistake. That when I thought for myself and made my decision and . . . well, I've been worrying I didn't understand what you meant and that I did wrong. Did you disapprove of me speaking my mind?"

"Oh, Sarah," he said, taking her hand. "I didn't disapprove at all. I'll admit you surprised me, but it was a nice surprise."

"It was?"

"Yes, it was. I'm not saying I agree with you. I'm not convinced you and Ella-Jane should come with us. That's something we'll have to talk about when Clayton gets back. But I was glad you spoke your mind."

"Really?"

"Uh-huh. I thought it was very brave of you to act like a woman from the future would, when you aren't even there yet. And the fact that you were willing to try...well, it made me very happy. It showed me how much you love me.''

She smiled again, looking relieved. "Oh, I'm so glad, Tyler, because I was so afraid. You see, I'm not sure exactly *how* to act like a woman from your time. I mean, even my coming in here like this...would that be all right? It wouldn't be considered improper?''

"Not at all," Tyler said, wishing to hell they were already married.

"Not *at all?*" Sarah repeated. "Not even a little improper?''

"No. Things are different there, Sarah. If a man and a woman are in love, it's all right for them to..."

"It's all right for them to what?''

"Ah..." He let go of her hand and rubbed his jaw, not comfortable with where this conversation was going. He was fighting now to keep his self-control. And he could never expect a woman from 1850 to—

"Put it plainly, Tyler. It's all right for a man and a woman in love to what?''

"Well...it's all right for them to make love, Sarah. In fact, it's usual.''

"Really?" she said, gazing at him wide-eyed. "It's usual even before they're married?''

He nodded, hoping to hell that was the last he'd have to say on the subject.

"Oh," Sarah said quietly. "And nobody thinks the woman is a soiled dove?''

That wasn't a term he'd heard before, but he had a pretty good idea what it meant, so he shook his head again.

"Oh. Well...I'm glad you explained that, Tyler. I didn't know what was proper. But I thought...well, as

I said, I was worried I'd done the wrong thing. And I thought that if I came in here and you just held me close for a minute, I'd feel better.''

He tried to smile, but it was tough when what she was asking would be utter torture. If he held Sarah close, her wearing that thin nightgown and him wearing nothing, he was going to have one hell of a time keeping in mind that she was an 1850 virgin—who'd undoubtedly been told all her life to save herself until she was married.

"Tyler?" she said uncertainly. "Don't you *want* to hold me for a minute?"

"Of course I do," he murmured, wrapping his arms around her and drawing her near.

The sheet got all scrunched between them, and Sarah reached to move it.

"Sarah," he said, grabbing her hand, "I don't have anything on."

"I won't look. I promise," she whispered, going ahead and moving it so she could slip closely against him, then tucking the sheet over the two of them.

He practically lost it, right then and there.

He'd meant to simply cuddle her beside him. But because of the angle he was at, she ended up as much beneath him as beside him, looking at him with those gorgeous brown eyes of hers. Her merest touch sent a wild jolt of electricity surging through his veins, and it was almost more than he could stand.

He gazed at her, wondering if she felt the same sensations when *he* touched *her*. God, there was so much he wanted to show her once they got out of this century. But, most of all, he wanted to love her.

Silently, he recited the batting average of the Yankee's leadoff hitter, then began working his way through the entire lineup.

It did nothing to take his mind off the fact that Sarah was in his bed and in his arms, or that her breasts were pressing against his chest, setting him on fire. His erection was so hard she had to know what she was doing to him. She couldn't be that naive!

She was all softness, bathed in a fresh-meadow scent, and he wanted to make love to her more than he'd wanted anything else in his life.

Then she nuzzled her cheek against his chest and tangled her fingers in his chest hair.

He stifled yet another groan, but he apparently didn't stifle it completely because she looked up at his face. Her dark eyes told him she loved him, her lips begged to be kissed.

"What's the matter?" she murmured, her breath warm and enticing against his skin

"I . . . I don't know how to put it."

"Put it plainly," she told him with a little smile.

He wasn't sure which of them moved, but suddenly he was kissing her. He tried to keep it gentle, but that was impossible. He had to possess her with his kiss.

And then she was kissing him back, her tongue teasing his and completely driving away his concerns about her being an 1850 virgin. She was a woman. *His* woman. Nothing else mattered.

He smoothed his hand down her body, drawing her even closer to him. As he brushed his palm across her breast, her nipple hardened and she moaned.

When he stroked it with tiny circles, Sarah wriggled against him, driving him crazy.

She felt so soft and luscious he had to kiss her and touch her all over....

Oh, Lord, a tiny voice of sanity was reminding him he'd left almost *everything* behind in the future, including protection.

But maybe he could just try withdrawal and...

No. He began repeating the word to himself, making a damned mantra of it. He wanted her first time to be as perfect as he could make it.

Doing it practically killed him, but he stopped kissing her. "Mmm," Sarah murmured, drawing Tyler's lips back to hers. She'd never in her entire life felt anything so wonderful as the way Tyler was making her feel.

"Sarah," he whispered, his voice sounding strangled, "Sarah, we have to stop."

"What?" she murmured, kissing his neck.

"We have to stop."

She stopped kissing his neck and looked at him. This hardly seemed the time to be joshing. And he wasn't smiling. "But you said it was all right," she tried uncertainly. "You just said that in the future..."

"But we're not in the future."

"I...but I thought..." Her throat grew so tight she doubted she could say more. He didn't want her. And if he didn't want her he couldn't really love her. But he *had* to love her because she'd die if he didn't.

"But you said," she whispered, forcing her voice to work. "You said you thought I was brave to try and act like a woman from your world. And you said it made you happy that I was willing to. You said it showed you how much I loved you. I just wanted to show you that, Tyler."

The last words were barely out before her tears escaped. Tyler didn't love her, and she'd just behaved like the most shameful fool in the world.

She tried to push herself away from him, but he grabbed her wrists and pressed her body to the mattress with his own, kissing her so hard she couldn't breathe.

"Dammit, Sarah," he finally murmured, releasing her. "Don't be an idiot. I love you so much that I think the only reason I came through time must have been to find you.

"I didn't stop kissing you because I wanted to. I stopped because I don't have anything to use. You understand what I mean? I don't have anything to make sure you won't get pregnant."

She swallowed hard. He *did* love her. And he wanted to make love to her. And she wanted him to.

"We're in Clayton's room," she whispered. "Maybe he has something."

Tyler barely dared to hope, but he rolled over to check the little stand beside Clayton's bed, praying.

He opened the drawer... then offered up a second prayer. This one of thanks.

CHAPTER SEVENTEEN

SARAH LAY IN THE WARMTH of Tyler's arms, not wanting to move for the rest of her life.

"Well?" Tyler said at last, gently brushing her lips with his fingers.

She couldn't resist capturing and kissing them.

"You okay?" he said, gazing at her.

"Yes ... yes, it wasn't at all odious."

"What?"

"Oh, Tyler, it wasn't even 'quite nice.' That's just not an apt description."

"Sarah...Sarah, I didn't hurt you, did I? I tried not to."

"Oh, no, Tyler. No, you didn't hurt me at all. In fact..."

She could feel herself blushing, but she wanted to tell him how wonderful it had been for her. "But I thought...you see, I'd been told...it wasn't like that, though. It was wonderful. Positively wonderful. I felt ... I felt as if you were part of me," she murmured, burying her face against his chest.

"I am, Sarah," he said softly. "And you're part of me. For ever and ever."

"And nothing will go wrong," she whispered, hoping that saying it would make it so. "We'll rescue Papa and Vallen. And then we'll go to the future. And then—"

"Shh," Tyler said, tilting her face to his.

"Not so fast with the *we'll* rescue bit," he told her after kissing her into silence. "I know you want to help, but I really think you and Ella-Jane should stay right here where you'll be safe. Clayton and I will take care of things at Lafayette Square."

Sarah propped herself up on her elbows, not even bothering to cover herself, and regarded Tyler seriously.

"I want to be with you," she said.

"No, listen—"

"No, Tyler, it's important to me. The only reason you're going to do this is because of me...because I'm part of you. And I want to be there with you because you're part of me. And there's something else."

"What else?"

"I'm not sure I can explain it, but helping you rescue Papa and Vallen would be like nothing I've ever done before. It would be something I'd never have thought I'd be brave enough to do. I...maybe it's that I have to prove to myself I'm brave enough to go to the future with you. Or maybe it's more that I need to know you honestly believe I *can* become an independent woman who makes her own decisions. But whichever the reason, it's very important to me to go with you."

He rubbed his jaw for a minute. "All right," he said at last. "*If* Clayton gets four sets of gear. But only if he does."

"You promise?"

"Yeah. I don't like it, but I promise."

Sarah released her breath, not realizing until then that she'd been holding it, and then she kissed Tyler—a long, slow kiss to tell him how very much she loved him.

She would have done more than kiss him, but Clayton had just arrived downstairs, calling for Tyler to come and help him in the root cellar.

Tyler scrambled into his clothes, then hurried downstairs. Clayton was already hauling stuff up from the cellar.

"You get everything we'll need?" Tyler asked, grabbing the carton Clayton was climbing out of the cellar with.

"Yeah, only one problem. It was a lot trickier to get than I expected. Turned out the only *supplier* available was the Savannah police force itself. And lending stuff to civilians isn't exactly smiled upon. My detective buddy had to pull serious strings. And even then, I handed out some serious bribes for a few cops to look the other way. But we've got some great stuff. Official police gear. The only drawback is that we have to have it back before midnight. No ifs, ands or buts."

"That shouldn't be a problem, should it? It's pretty well dark by nine, so if we hit Lafayette Square then...two hours to get back here..."

"No," Clayton said. "I mean we have to get it back into the police equipment room in 1993 Savannah. Which means we've got to be back here well before eleven."

Tyler could feel his jaw clenching. If they had to hit Ewell's house before dark, it was bound to be more dangerous. "There's no way around the deadline?"

"Uh-uh. The shifts change at twelve, and my buddy can only cover me until then. The cops are busting a booze can in the middle of the night and they'll be using riot gear. So if everything's not there, my buddy's butt will be in a sling. And mine right along with his."

Clayton headed down into the cellar again, leaving Tyler swearing to himself. He wished to hell he hadn't promised Sarah she could go along. But back there in bed with her, he'd probably have promised her the moon if she'd asked for it. Maybe he'd lucked out, though. He'd agreed that she could go *only* if Clayton got four sets of gear.

"Clayton?" he called down into the cellar. "How many sets of body armor did you get?"

"Four," Clayton called back. Tyler started swearing again.

"But look," Clayton went on, reappearing with another carton, "now that we'll have to do this in daylight, I really don't want Ella-Jane and Sarah along, okay?"

"Ahh . . ." Tyler said uneasily. "There's one other problem I guess I'd better mention."

IT WAS A LITTLE before dusk when they pulled Beauregard's carriage and Clayton's buggy into the small park behind Lafayette Square. They hitched the horses and began unloading everything from the carriage.

There was no one in sight. Sarah hoped that was a good omen, but she was so frightened she was certain the others could hear her heart pounding.

She tried to tell herself everything would be all right. Tyler and Clayton had real guns with them as well as the stun guns.

But Ewell's men would have real guns, too.

"All right, you've both got it straight?" Tyler said quietly as he and Clayton helped Sarah and Ella-Jane put on their body armor over their dresses.

"Clayton and I are in charge of Ewell and whatever guys he has helping him. You two are responsible for your father and Vallen. As soon as they come out of the house, grab them and run like hell. And don't forget to throw all your gear into the buggy as soon as you get back here."

"It's going to be a damned tight fit, getting it all in there," Clayton muttered.

"We'll manage," Tyler said.

Sarah took the helmet Clayton handed her, trying to keep her hands from trembling. She didn't like the idea of being separated from Tyler, the idea of going back to Clayton's in the carriage while Tyler and Clayton went in the buggy. She didn't want to be separated from Tyler for one minute, let alone for several hours.

But he and Clayton had figured out the best plan. They had to get back to the root cellar quickly. Not that she'd exactly understood why it was essential to be back at the 1993 Savannah police station before midnight. They'd completely lost her when they'd tried to explain what "busting booze cans" meant.

The basic point, though, was that Clayton's buggy would be faster than Papa's heavy carriage. Besides, as Clayton had teased Ella-Jane, he wanted his own buggy so that Papa couldn't be in charge and tell him what to do.

But what if something went wrong? What if something happened when Tyler and Clayton went to the future to return these things? What if something happened and Tyler didn't come back for her?

She ordered herself to stop worrying. Of course he'd come back for her. Nothing would stop him. Besides, if she was going to worry, she should worry about what would happen when they reached Ella-Jane's house.

"Okay," Clayton said, "helmets on."

Sarah pulled her helmet down over her head, then gazed at the others. Tyler had been right. Dressed in these things, they didn't look human. They looked like monsters.

She almost smiled, thinking what a fright they'd give Ewell and his men. But there was really nothing to smile about. This was a most serious undertaking.

The padded armor would protect their bodies. Clayton's police friend had said they could only get hurt if someone shot into the armor at point-blank range. But they could still get wounded in an arm or leg.

"Here," Tyler said, flipping up the tinted protective shield on the front of her helmet. "It's easier to see without that down."

He handed her and Ella-Jane each a little black stun gun. Sarah took hers anxiously, careful to keep her fingers away from the button that was the trigger.

It didn't look anything like a real gun, was just a little oblong shaped thing. But Tyler said that if she touched someone with the two metal prongs sticking out of the end, they'd be paralyzed for at least twenty minutes.

The idea of being able to paralyze a grown man made her dreadfully nervous.

The four of them started across the park, heading for the gate in the stone wall at the end of Ella-Jane's garden. The armor was lighter than Sarah had expected and only a tiny bit awkward. But it was so hot that she was almost suffocating.

When they reached the metal gate, Ella-Jane slid her arm between two of the bars and retrieved the key from its hiding place in the wall.

The gate creaked when she pulled it open, making Sarah's pulse race with fear.

And then a man called, "Who's there?" and her heart leapt to her throat.

Tyler waved them against the wall, motioning them to pull down the shields on their helmets.

They crouched there, staring at the open gate and listening to someone moving through the back garden.

The sound of footsteps stopped. The man was so near the wall that Sarah could hear him breathing. She imagined him looking around, trying to see if anyone had come into the yard.

Then she saw his arm reaching for the gate.

All in the same moment, Tyler leapt forward and the man collapsed onto the ground.

Sarah stared at him lying there—then she looked at the stun gun in Tyler's hand. She couldn't believe it— the man had dropped like a stone.

"Come on," Tyler said to Clayton. "We don't want this guy walking around when we're trying to get out of here."

Tyler and Clayton dragged the man over to the nearest tree, wrapped his arms around its trunk and handcuffed his wrists together.

"One down," Tyler muttered, heading back to the gate.

Single file, they slipped through the opening. Then, as they'd agreed, Sarah and Tyler started quietly up one side of the house, Clayton and Ella-Jane up the other.

"That's the kitchen," Sarah whispered as they neared the first window.

Tyler nodded. He peeked through one corner, then murmured, "Nobody in there."

Even so, they ducked down and passed beneath the glass.

"Dining room," she whispered as they neared the next windows.

Again, the room was empty. They had assumed Ewell had Papa and Vallen in the parlor, on the other side of the house. The worrisome question was, how many armed men did he have in there with him?

Tyler reached the front of the house and motioned Sarah to stop. Cautiously, he peered around the corner then drew back, holding up two fingers, indicating there were two men on guard outside. Sarah clutched her stun gun tightly, hoping she wouldn't have to use it.

Tyler leaned down and picked up a stone, then tossed it toward the flagstone walk that ran in front of the house.

There was a small thud when it hit.

"What was that?" a man said.

He was standing, Sarah guessed, either on or near the front steps.

"I'll go check," a different voice muttered.

Sarah stood behind Tyler, barely breathing. She could hear the man coming in their direction. Then, suddenly, just as before, Tyler made his move and the man fell to the ground.

"What's wrong?" the other man called. Tyler ducked back behind the side of the house.

They could hear someone begin to run. Tyler sank to his hands and knees, pulling Sarah down with him. A second later, a man charged around the corner, a pistol extended in front of him.

Tyler lunged forward and the man dropped.

Sarah was shaking, but she managed to smile.

"Not bad, huh?" Tyler said, shoving up his shield and grinning at her.

"Not bad at all," she murmured.

"I guess there's no point in suggesting you stay right where you are, is there?" Tyler said.

She shook her head. Even though staying put sounded like a wonderful idea, she had a job to do.

Gas lamps were lit on either side of the front door. And it was growing dim enough now that, on the far end of the house, they could see light glowing through the parlor window.

Sarah and Tyler had only taken a few steps along the front of the house when Clayton and Ella-Jane appeared at the other side. Clayton gestured to them and they crept quietly forward.

"They're in the parlor like we figured," Clayton whispered. "Ewell, Beauregard, Vallen and three men wearing guns. And there's one more armed guy in the foyer. The parlor door's open, so we could see through to it."

Tyler nodded, then reached beneath his armor. First, he pulled out a single heavy work glove and put it on his left hand. Then he dug out a tear gas canister.

Clayton pulled out one as well. "You take the parlor's side window," he whispered. "It's only about four feet from the front of the house. I'll take the door. Ella-Jane's given me the key, and I know where the guy in the foyer is standing.

"You and Sarah," he told Ella-Jane, "get over there behind that wall. And stay down. There's sure to be shooting."

The word *shooting* sent a chill down Sarah's spine. As she and Ella-Jane hurried over to the low stone wall, she reminded herself the armor would protect them from everything but a point-blank shot.

"At the count of twenty let 'em rip," Tyler quietly told Clayton.

Clayton nodded, then started toward the front door.

Tyler moved along to the corner of the house and disappeared down the side.

Silently, Sarah counted. When she reached five, she was overcome by the most fearful feeling. For a second, she simply stared at the corner of the house. And then she started after Tyler.

When she reached the corner, he was already standing in front of the side window, waiting.

And then, from the shadows behind him stepped a man—aiming a rifle directly at the center of Tyler's back.

The words *point-blank range* flashed into her mind, and she moved faster than she'd ever moved before. Covering the few feet between herself and the man, she put her finger on the button of the stun gun.

Suddenly both the man and Tyler were turning toward her.

She shoved her hand forward, catching the man in the stomach with the gun, and he fell to the ground.

"My God," Tyler whispered.

Then he was turning back to the window, smashing it with his gloved hand, and pitching the tear gas canister into the parlor.

SARAH COULDN'T RECALL making her way back to the wall, but she must have because she was soon waiting with Ella-Jane again, peering around to see what was happening.

Tyler and Clayton were standing on either side of the front door, pretty much hidden by two of the pillars that graced the house. They both had their guns out now and were watching the door.

Clayton, she realized, must have pulled it closed after he'd thrown the tear gas into the foyer.

Inside, people were coughing loudly, but nobody had come out yet.

"What if they stay inside?" Ella-Jane whispered.

"They won't," Sarah said. They just couldn't.

As if her willing it made it happen, the front door burst open and four men spilled out and down the steps, coughing and spluttering, shooting their guns without trying to aim at anything. She doubted they even realized Tyler and Clayton were there.

"But where's Papa?" Ella-Jane murmured.

As she spoke, he appeared. His face was beet-red, and he was making a dreadful hacking noise.

Vallen was clinging to his arm, coughing and crying at the same time.

Behind them came Ewell, coughing as well, but holding a gun unsteadily on Papa.

"Oh, my," Sarah whispered.

The three of them started down the steps.

The moment they got by the pillars, Tyler and Clayton threw themselves at Ewell.

For a second, everything was a blur of motion. Then Ewell lay in a crumpled heap, while Tyler and Clayton were standing by Papa and Vallen, looking like a matched pair of monsters in their gear.

Papa glanced around in confusion, then grabbed Vallen's arm and started backing away from Tyler and Clayton. Vallen had begun screaming.

Ewell's four hired guns realized something was happening and started shooting wildly again.

"Sarah!" Tyler yelled. "Get them out of here!"

"Come on, Ella-Jane," Sarah said, starting for Vallen and Papa.

"Stay away from us!" Beau roared as they neared him. "Devils! Demons! Fiends from hell! Stay away from us!"

Only then did Sarah remember that she and Ella-Jane looked as much like monsters as Tyler and Clayton did.

"Papa, it's me," she called. "It's me and Ella-Jane." She risked lifting the shield on her helmet for a second as they reached him.

He stared at her face in disbelief.

Vallen was screaming so loudly it hurt Sarah's ears.

"Come on!" Ella-Jane said, taking Papa by the arm.

Sarah grabbed Vallen. Vallen kicked at her hysterically.

"You stupid goose!" Sarah yelled. "Come on." She gave Vallen a hard shove to start her off, and the four of them scuttled along through the noise of guns shooting and men shouting.

Sarah wheeled around the side of the house, then paused for a second to check on the others.

Amazingly, nobody seemed harmed. Papa still looked frightened half to death and Vallen was still crying, but they didn't seem hurt.

"We did it!" Ella-Jane whispered. "Sarah, we did it."

"We're not safe yet," she said. "Come on."

They started off again, running along the side of the house and down the garden. Then through the park to where the carriage and buggy were waiting.

Papa stood blustering and flustering, asking questions and demanding answers, while Sarah and Ella-Jane tore off their helmets and armor and threw everything into the buggy.

"Get into the carriage," Sarah ordered, ignoring Papa's questions. "We have to go to Clayton Willis's."

While they were in the midst of piling into the carriage, Tyler and Clayton came charging across the park.

Sarah felt such relief at seeing Tyler safe that she almost began to cry.

He tossed his helmet into the buggy and swept her into his arms, pressing her tightly against the bulk of his armor, murmuring that he loved her.

"That's my fiancé!" Vallen screamed from the carriage. "Sarah! You get your damnable hands off my fiancé!"

"What in tarnation is going on here!" Papa roared. "Tyler Adams, you unhand my daughter! And Clayton Willis, you unhand my other daughter!"

Tyler grinned down at Sarah. "Sorry we have to leave the explaining to you, but we don't have any choice. We'll be back just as soon as we can, love. A little past midnight at the very latest."

He gave her a hard, fast kiss, then leapt up into the buggy.

Clayton clicked the reins and his bay mare started quickly out of the park.

SARAH GLANCED WEARILY at the clock in Clayton's parlor. She hadn't been imagining it. She and Ella-Jane really *had* spent two hours answering Papa's questions.

But Papa and Vallen still didn't believe that it was possible to travel through time. When Papa heard what John McCully had said, about Ewell actually killing Ella-Jane, he'd simply shaken his head and muttered something about men who spent far too much time with their horses.

Of course, neither Papa nor Vallen could explain the helmets and body armor. Or the stun guns. Or the tear gas.

"Tricks," Papa kept saying. "Yankee tricks, that's what they were using."

But neither of them could explain where the men had gone, either, when they found that Clayton's buggy and his bay mare were in the stable.

However, Papa was positive that, wherever Tyler and Clayton had gone, it hadn't been through the root cellar and into the future.

"I'm going to prove this once and for all," he finally said. "Come on."

He marched his three daughters from the parlor, through the kitchen, and out onto the back porch.

"You're trying to tell me this takes people to the future?" he demanded, lifting the door of the root cellar. "You look down there, Sarah, and tell me if you think that's really possible."

She gazed down into the blackness. What little she could see looked like an ordinary root cellar. The cool air drifting up from it carried only an earthy vegetable smell.

"Well?" Papa said.

Sarah said nothing. It *was* difficult to believe anyone could get to the future through a hole in the ground. But just because it *looked* ordinary didn't mean it was.

She glanced off into the surrounding night, remembering what Tyler had told her about Clayton bringing him through the cellar to 1850.

This house was lovely now. But in 1993, Tyler had said, it was only a charred ruin. It had been burned to the ground in that war he'd told her about, and almost all that was left of it, in his world, was the cellar door— lying amid rubble.

"Liars," Papa declared, letting the door slam down. "Clayton Willis and Tyler Adams are nothing but liars. Either that or they're crazy. Maybe both." Looking at Sarah and Ella-Jane, he added, "And you two, why, you've taken leave of your senses if you truly believe anything else."

Papa gestured them all back inside, muttering, "I should never have rented this house to Clayton Willis.

Should never have rented it to a traveling man. Can't trust them. Or those damned Yankees, either. But how could I have known my girls would be so gullible?''

"I wasn't gullible, Papa," Vallen said. "I never liked Clayton Willis. And I never trusted Tyler Adams. I told you he'd try to run off on me, didn't I? And now he has. They've both run off."

"They haven't run off," Sarah said as they reached the parlor and sat down once more. "I've told you a hundred times, they're coming back to take Ella-Jane and me to—"

"They're not taking you anywhere," Papa snapped. "Not unless it's over my dead body. If they *do* come back, I'll have it out with them. But they won't be coming back. They've made fools of you two girls and now they're gone for good. I don't know why we're even still waiting here. We should go home."

"Papa, please," Ella-Jane said. "You told us that Tyler's bullet barely grazed Ewell. If he comes looking for me he'll go to Booker's Knoll. You know we're all safer here."

"Of course we're safe," Papa snapped, picking up the shotgun he'd purloined from Clayton's study. "I can look after you all perfectly well."

"We know you can," Ella-Jane said. "But Clayton and Tyler *are* coming back. So please, let's just wait for them."

"I have been waiting. But, dammit, it's almost two o'clock in the morning. How much longer do you expect me to wait?"

"They *aren't* coming back," Vallen said. "And it's all your fault, Sarah. Tyler Adams made you believe he'd fallen in love with you when all he wanted was to escape. And you were so dumb you helped him. You let my fiancé run off. You're a mean, awful sister and I hate you."

Sarah didn't even glance across the room. She'd seen enough of the malevolent look in Vallen's eyes. She simply sat rubbing her temples with her fingertips, trying to make the terrible throbbing in her head go away.

It was keeping perfect time with the ticking of Clayton's grandfather clock. And with every tick of that clock, she was growing more worried.

Tyler had told her he'd be back a little past midnight. So why wasn't he here? Something awful must have happened to him. Either that or... she closed her eyes, refusing to think that Vallen might be right.

Tyler *did* love her. He hadn't merely wanted her to help him escape. But where was he?

Ella-Jane, she noticed, was staring at the clock, too. Her face was pale, and she looked every bit as worried as Sarah felt.

"I only hope," Papa muttered, "that neither of you two girls allowed those rotten scoundrels any liberties."

Sarah closed her eyes again, thinking back to the afternoon. She hadn't allowed Tyler *liberties*. She'd made love with him. And it had been the most wonderful experience of her life. And if he didn't come back for her, if he never loved her again, she wouldn't want to live.

"Well, I've had enough of waiting," Papa said, picking up Clayton's shotgun. "I'm going upstairs to find a bed to sleep in."

"Me, too," Vallen said, gathering up her skirts and marching out of the parlor after her father.

Sarah and Ella-Jane remained where they were, the silence broken only by the ticking of the clock.

It struck two. Then two-thirty. Then three.

All the doubts she'd had over the past while kept drifting in and out of Sarah's mind. She kept hearing Papa saying Tyler and Clayton were liars and insane. And Vallen insisting Tyler had only wanted help escaping.

Then John McCully's voice was saying, "I had a bit of a mishap... didn't end up where I meant to go."

If there could be mishaps in John's mine tunnel, who was to say there couldn't be a mishap in the root cellar? And if there hadn't been a mishap, then the only other conclusion was that Tyler had deserted her.

Ella-Jane rose, crossed the room and sat down on the settee beside Sarah. "Sarah?" she murmured. "Sarah, I don't think they're coming back for us."

Ella-Jane's eyes were wet with tears, and her bottom lip was trembling.

Sarah put her arms around her sister, thinking of the warning John McCully had brought them. It was still August 1850—Ella-Jane wasn't safe. If they didn't get her away, Ewell was going to kill her. If Tyler and Clayton didn't come back, she was going to die, after all.

Surely they wouldn't simply leave Ella-Jane here, knowing what would happen.

"They're coming back," Sarah whispered, her throat so tight she could barely get the words out. "I know they're coming back."

But she didn't know that at all. And she had a strong suspicion that something had gone dreadfully wrong. The more she thought about never seeing Tyler again, the worse her heart ached.

CHAPTER EIGHTEEN

SOMETIME AFTER 4:00 a.m., Ella-Jane murmured, "Sarah? I'm going upstairs to try to sleep. I'll feel safer if I'm closer to Papa and his shotgun. I...oh, I just know Ewell isn't going to give up. And when he finds we're not at Booker's Knoll, this is the next place he'll come looking."

Sarah hugged her sister, then curled up on the settee and gradually drifted off into a troubled sleep. Why hadn't Tyler come? What had gone wrong?

She tossed and turned, trying not to think about how unhappy and meaningless her life would be if she had to live it without him.

The clock struck six and she opened her eyes. Outside, the sky was just beginning to grow light.

She closed her eyes and drifted off once more. And then she woke with a jolt of fear. The dark shape of a man was looming over her.

For a panicked instant, she thought it was Ewell. Then he whispered her name and she realized it was Tyler.

He swept her up off the settee and into his arms. She clung to him, crying against his chest—tears of relief that he was safe, that he was here, his body so reassuringly strong against hers.

Softly, he stroked her hair. "Everything's going to be all right, Sarah. It's going to be fine."

She wanted her tears to stop but they wouldn't.

"Hey," he said, "what's wrong? Ella-Jane's still all right? She's here?"

"Upstairs...asleep...so are Papa and Vallen."

Tyler brushed his fingers across Sarah's cheeks, trying to dry them, but his gentle touch only made her cry harder. She loved him so much and she'd been so afraid.

"You know," he said, "if you keep on crying like this, I'll think you aren't happy to see me."

"Oh, Tyler," she managed, wiping her eyes, "you can't possibly know how happy I am to see you. I thought...but what happened? What went wrong? And where's Clayton?" she added, all at once realizing he wasn't there.

"He's in jail," Tyler said. "That's what went wrong. When we got to 1993, the van he'd borrowed to tote the gear had a flat."

Sarah shook her head, not understanding what he'd said.

"Doesn't matter," he told her. "But that meant we didn't make it back to the police station on time, and all hell broke loose. They finally let *me* go, because I'd had nothing to do with borrowing the stuff. So I hopped into Clayton's Ferrari and headed back to the root cellar. But he and his detective buddy are still sitting in a cell."

"Oh, mercy. Whatever will happen to them?"

"Nothing serious. Clayton's well connected, and he called the best criminal lawyer in Savannah. The guy said he could straighten everything out in the morning. For both Clayton *and* his buddy. But I knew how worried you'd be, so..."

"So you came back on your own," Sarah murmured, running her fingers along his granite jaw. Every time she was near Tyler, she had an aching need to touch him, and this time it was worse than usual. Somehow, touching him made her more certain he was real.

"Yeah, I came back on my own," he said, grinning down at her. "Even though I was scared spitless that I wouldn't be able to make the cellar work right."

"You were scared spitless, but you came, anyway."

"Yeah. I guess being in love makes idiots of people, huh?"

Sarah gave her idiot a long, loving kiss.

"Oh, Lord," he whispered, his breath enticingly warm against her throat. "Once we get out of here, I'm going to spend the rest of my life kissing you."

"Only kissing me?" she teased softly.

"No, that'll just be for starters. First, I'm going to kiss every inch of you. Then we'll take it from there."

Her face grew hot, just imagining the pleasures.

"Promise me something?" Tyler said, grinning again.

"What?"

"Promise that when we're living in New York, and you're becoming a woman of the nineties, you won't change *too* much. I love it when you blush. In fact, I love everything about you."

She nuzzled his chest, so happy she felt she would float on air if she weren't clinging tightly to him.

"Sarah, I'd be happy to stand here holding you for about a million years," he finally said. "But I don't think we should push our luck too far. If your father wakes up, he's liable to cause trouble. So let's get Ella-Jane and get the hell out of here."

"I'll wake her," Sarah said, "and you can start carrying our luggage down to the root cellar. It shouldn't take us more than two or three trips."

For a second, she thought he was going to say taking the time for those two or three trips would be pushing their luck too far. But he simply nodded and they started for the stairs.

Ella-Jane had changed into a nightdress, but when Sarah woke her she began putting her clothes back on as if there was a prize for speed.

"You're absolutely positive Clayton is all right?" she asked again, buttoning her dress.

"Yes, I told you Tyler said he has the best criminal lawyer in all Savannah. He'll be out of jail in a few hours."

"Criminal . . . jail . . ." Ella-Jane murmured, throwing a final few things into her valise. "Oh, I've caused so much trouble."

"Well, it's almost over," Sarah said.

Ella-Jane nodded. "I'm ready. We'll just wake Papa and Vallen to say goodbye and then—"

"No," Sarah said, picking up the valise. "It's too risky, especially after the way Papa was behaving last night. We're going to have to let that note I left at Booker's Knoll serve as our goodbye."

They'd only taken a step or two toward the door when Papa's voice boomed forth.

"Why, you Yankee swine!" he was bellowing in the hall. "You *have* come back! And just where do you think you're going with that case of my daughter's?"

"Oh, no," Sarah whispered, her hand flying to her throat.

TIME STOOD STILL while Tyler stared down the barrel of Beauregard's shotgun. Beau had stepped out of the last bedroom and was blocking the path to the stairs.

Then Sarah and Ella-Jane came piling into the hallway, behind the men. Tyler risked a glance back. They both looked terrified.

"Papa," Sarah whispered. "Papa, don't shoot him. We explained everything to you last night. We're going to the future with—"

"The hell you are!" Beau roared. "You're going back to Booker's Knoll with me. And Mr. Tyler Adams is going to meet his Maker. With my help."

"Papa?" Vallen said.

For a split second, Tyler thought Vallen's interruption would give him a chance to escape. But Beauregard's gaze didn't even flicker toward Vallen.

"Papa?" she repeated.

Tyler glanced back to see what she was up to.

She was standing at the far end of the hall, gazing out the window that overlooked the front lawn.

"Papa, I think we've got trouble coming," she said. "A carriage has turned onto the drive, and I do believe it's Ewell Endicott's. And there are men riding alongside with rifles."

"Oh, Lord," Tyler said. "Beauregard, you have to let us get out of here right this second."

"I don't have to do any such thing," he snapped. "I'm in charge here. This property belongs to me, and I shall deal with Ewell Endicott."

"Papa, he's going to kill me," Ella-Jane cried. "Please, let us go."

"He is *not* going to kill you, Ella-Jane. I just finished telling you I shall deal with him. Wasn't it me who rescued you from Ewell Endicott's house in the first place?"

"Well, dammit, Beau," Tyler said. "Then we just had to turn around and rescue *you* from it."

Beauregard gave Tyler a furious look and menacingly waved his shotgun.

From downstairs came a loud pounding on the front door.

"Yes, it's definitely Ewell's carriage," Vallen reported, gazing out the window again. "And every one of the six men with him has both a rifle and a pistol."

"What are they doing?" Tyler demanded. Maybe, if none of them went around the back, there was still a chance of escaping.

"They're all just sitting on their horses," Vallen said. "And they're all looking at the front door. I can't see for the veranda pillars, but it must be Ewell who's knocking."

As if to confirm her assumption, Ewell began shouting through the door.

"Beauregard! Beauregard Booker, I know you're in there. And I know you have my wife with you."

Beauregard didn't say a word, just kept that damned shotgun aimed straight at Tyler.

"Send Ella-Jane out," Ewell ordered.

"Never!" Beauregard hollered down the stairs, still not moving the gun.

"Ella-Jane is my wife!" Ewell shouted. "If I weren't a reasonable man, I'd smash this door down right this second. But since I *am* reasonable, I'm giving you fifteen minutes to send her out. After that, I won't be responsible for what happens here."

"Papa?" Sarah said.

For an instant, Beauregard's gaze left Tyler.

He made the most of it, lunging forward and mentally thanking the powers that be. With all the uproar back in 1993, the police hadn't remembered to take his stun gun.

He caught Beauregard squarely in the chest. Beau slumped to the floor.

Tyler wheeled around, shoving the stun gun into his pocket. "Are those six riders all still out front?" he asked Vallen.

She stared at her unconscious father for a moment, then glanced out the window and nodded.

"Let's go, then," Tyler said, grabbing both Sarah and Ella-Jane by a hand.

"You paralyzed my father," Sarah said, digging her heels into the floor, her voice trembling.

"What the hell was I supposed to do?" he snapped.

"Well...I don't know *what* you were supposed to do. But you heard Ewell. He only gave Papa fifteen minutes, and now Papa is paralyzed for at least twenty. I guess...I guess we'll have to take him with us."

"What?" Tyler hollered.

"It's the only way," Sarah said. "We can't leave him here. Ewell might kill him."

"What about me?" Vallen demanded.

"You'll have to come, too," Sarah said.

"What?" Tyler hollered again. The last thing in the world he intended to do was take Beauregard and Vallen along. Then he looked at Sarah once more. Her dark eyes were pleading with him.

"But I don't want to go to the future," Vallen was saying. "Even if it *does* exist, I don't like anything anyone has said about it." She stamped her foot for emphasis.

"Fine," Tyler told her. "You don't have to go."

"Do you want to stay here all by yourself?" Ella-Jane asked her. "And maybe have Ewell kill you?"

"Well...no, I guess not."

"Tyler, it's the only way," Sarah repeated quietly.

"Oh, hell," he muttered, letting go of her hand.

"You stay right at that window," he ordered Vallen. "If any of those guys move away from the front of the house, yell and tell me. I'll come back for you in a couple of minutes. And you two," he went on, looking at Sarah and Ella-Jane. "Each of you take one of your father's legs."

Swearing beneath his breath, Tyler grabbed Beauregard under the arms, and the three of them started down the stairs with him.

"Don't you forget about *me*," Vallen called anxiously after them.

They practically dropped Beau several times, but at last managed to get him to the main floor and through the kitchen.

Cautiously, Tyler opened the back door a crack. One of Ewell's damned men had stationed himself right on the back porch, rifle at the ready. So much for Vallen's warning them.

He closed the door again and whispered, "Ella-Jane. One of them's out here. Get him to come over to the door."

"How?" she squeaked.

"I don't know! But if he sees me, he'll shoot. So do it!" He pulled Sarah out of sight.

Ella-Jane swallowed hard, then opened the door a tiny bit. "Sir?" she called quietly. "Sir, I'm Mrs. Endicott. I'd like to speak to you for a moment. I have a message I need you to relay to my husband."

Tyler watched through the crack door as the man walked toward Ella-Jane. When he reached her, Tyler flung himself around the door, stun gun extended, and zapped the guy.

"Good work, Ella-Jane," he said, dragging the latest victim into the kitchen. "Now come on."

He raced along the porch and pulled up the cellar door. "Get down there," he whispered to Sarah and Ella-Jane. "I'll be back in a minute."

While they started down into the cellar, Tyler ran back inside to collect Vallen.

"Hurry up," he snapped at her, on the way downstairs. "I want you to get into the root cellar just as fast as you can. I'll have to hand your father down and you can help Sarah and Ella-Jane catch him."

"Oooowwwhhh," Vallen whined. "I hate root cellars. They're so cold and dirty."

Tyler did his best to ignore the urge to kill her, and waved her ahead of him through the kitchen.

BY THE TIME TYLER had dragged Beauregard along the back porch, all three sisters were waiting in the cellar.

Tyler heaved Beau's limp legs over the edge, then grabbed him under the arms again and began to slide his portly body down the stairs. God, the man had to weigh a ton.

Just as Tyler's arms were about to give out, Sarah and her sisters began supporting Beau's weight. Then a dull thud said he was on the cellar floor.

Quickly, Tyler started down the shaky stairs, pausing only long enough to pull the door closed, plunging them into total darkness.

"Oooowwwhhh," Vallen whined.

"Be quiet," Sarah told her.

"What happens now?" Ella-Jane said anxiously.

"Now we wait," Tyler said as calmly as he could. "And don't worry, we'll be fine." Of course they would. He'd managed the trip on his own once, so surely he could handle it again. Of course, last time he'd been heading for 1850. He hadn't tried making the *return* trip without Clayton.

In the darkness, Sarah found his hand with hers.

He squeezed it and she moved closer to him, pressing the warm softness of her body against him. The meadow-fresh scent of her hair replaced the earthy smell of the cellar.

He wrapped his arms around her and drew her even more tightly to him. He wanted to spend the rest of his life holding Sarah. He just *had* to manage this trip without a hitch.

Otherwise, he could be stuck out of time and place forever, with the entire Booker crew. And *forever,* with Beauregard and Vallen along, would be his own personal version of hell.

"Are we there yet?" Vallen demanded.

"Hush," Ella-Jane said.

Tyler closed his eyes, trying to concentrate the way he'd done earlier. He focused his mind on 1993 and waited.

"Are we there yet?" Vallen demanded again, entirely destroying his concentration.

"Vallen," he snarled, "you say one more word, just one, and I swear I'll use my stun gun on *you.*"

Deathly silence prevailed. He closed his eyes and tried again. He concentrated so fiercely his brain began hurting, but nothing happened.

Oh, God, maybe there were too many of them. He hadn't considered that, but maybe one person couldn't concentrate hard enough to transport five.

And then he heard a noise above them. Either his imagination was running wild, or one of Ewell's men was walking along the back porch toward the cellar door.

"Are those footsteps?" Ella-Jane said softly in a frightened voice.

"Sarah," he whispered against her ear. "Sarah, I need your help. Think of everything I've told you about 1993. Concentrate—as hard as you can."

He clung to her and began concentrating again himself.

Suddenly it happened. The psychic jolt seized him— and the others as well, given their startled cries.

"What in tarnation," Beauregard muttered, his words slurring. "Where am I? Why's it so black? Where's a lamp? What's going on? Oh, Lord, Almighty, my entire body is aching."

"Oh, Papa," Vallen cried, "they've taken us to the future."

"What?" Beauregard shouted.

Tyler could hear Beau clambering to his feet, muttering away to himself.

"We're in the root cellar," Vallen said. "They've taken us to the future."

"Balderdash!" Beauregard snapped. "Hogwash! People can't go to the future. What really happened? Last thing I remember, Ewell was outside yelling."

"Tyler Adams paralyzed you with his stun gun and dragged you down to the root cellar," Vallen explained. "We've been here for a while now and—"

"Never mind," Beau interrupted. "I'll see what's going on for myself."

Tyler stood listening to Beau's feet scraping on the rickety stairs. He nuzzled the top of Sarah's head with his chin, hoping to hell they'd ended up where he'd intended. Otherwise . . .

Above, Beauregard flung open the cellar door.

Sunlight streamed in and Beau clambered up the final few steps, then paused, peering around him.

"Lord Almighty!" he roared.

"What, Papa?" Vallen said. "What is it?"

"Lord Almighty!" Beau exclaimed again, climbing completely out of the cellar. "You know what that damned Ewell Endicott's done? He's burned the house down around us. There's nothing out here but a charred ruin."

Tyler climbed to the top of the stairs with Sarah right behind him, holding tightly to his hand. They stepped out of the cellar and he breathed a huge sigh of relief.

Over at the side of the field, right where he'd left it, sat Clayton's red Ferrari.

"Welcome to the future," he murmured, wrapping his arms around Sarah.

EPILOGUE

SARAH RAN TO THE DOOR, threw herself into Tyler's arms and kissed him. Every day, all day long, he found himself looking forward to this reception.

His friends' wives had decided they liked the woman he'd married down in Georgia, and they'd taken it upon themselves to show her every square inch of Manhattan. But Sarah always made a point of being home before him.

"Mmm," he murmured, giving the air an exaggerated sniff. As usual, there were wonderful cooking smells coming from the kitchen.

"Come on," Sarah said, taking his hand, "I have news." She led him through the living room to the solarium. She loved its view of Central Park.

He lagged a little behind her. He loved *that* view. Short straight skirts had immensely more to be said for them than floor-length dresses over petticoats.

"So? What's the news?" he asked, sinking onto the solarium couch.

Sarah curled into his lap, giving him another kiss, then said, "Ella-Jane called this afternoon."

"Even though we'll be at Booker's Knoll in two days?"

"Well, she couldn't remember the exact recipe for syllabub, and she intends to have a traditional Old South Christmas dinner."

Tyler nodded. He didn't know what syllabub was, but if Ella-Jane cooked like Sarah, it was bound to be delicious.

"The new house is almost finished," she went on. "And Ella-Jane says it's even more beautiful than the original. Imagine going to all the effort of having that burned-out old ruin rebuilt for Papa and Vallen to live in. And Clayton even put in that pond Vallen always wanted. He's been so very nice, hasn't he?"

"Extremely nice," Tyler agreed, unable to keep from smiling. Clayton and he were on the phone at least once a week, discussing Clayton's commodity trades, and he knew perfectly well why his new brother-in-law was being so nice. He couldn't stand having Beauregard and Vallen living with him and Ella-Jane.

It was a lucky thing for Clayton that he had, as Vallen would put it, as much money as the South has cotton.

And as far as Vallen's pond was concerned, Clayton had been only too happy to fill in the root cellar. Just in case old Ewell ever figured out about it and tried to come after Ella-Jane.

"And what's your father been up to?" Tyler asked. Beauregard had been the biggest surprise in all of this. Instead of insisting on being taken back to the past, he'd fallen instantly in love with the future.

"Oh, Papa's met even more men who play poker. And he's learning to drive a car."

"Not Clayton's Ferrari."

"No, a driving school car. But how did you know it wasn't Clayton's Ferrari?"

"Just a lucky guess." Tyler tangled his fingers in Sarah's long hair. He was thinking about taking this conversation to the bedroom when she pressed her lips together, a sign that she was anxious, and began fiddling with his tie.

"What else did Ella-Jane have to say?" he asked.

"Nothing important. It...well, there *is* something else I want to talk to you about. Not about my family, but...well, something's been bothering me for the past few weeks."

"Oh?" he said uneasily. As far as he was concerned, everything was perfect. Sarah had adjusted to life in the future far better than he'd ever dreamed.

After Christmas, she'd even be taking two university courses. She was talking about eventually becoming a psychologist, and they'd gotten her enrolled as a mature student, so the lack of a high-school transcript hadn't mattered.

"Tyler...oh, this is most difficult for me to say."

"Put it plainly, Sarah," he said, brushing back a wisp of her hair.

"Well...it's about the way you keep saying how happy you are with our life. That you wouldn't want to change a single thing about it."

"And I wouldn't. You can't improve on perfection. Has it been bothering you that I'm happy?"

"No, that's not it. It's that..." She buried her face in his suit jacket and murmured something so garbled he couldn't understand it.

"Sarah? I didn't hear you. What's the matter?"

"Oh, Tyler," she whispered a touch more clearly. "I said that I can't keep everything exactly as it is. Not for much longer. For the past few weeks I've been thinking I might be...and I went to the doctor this morning and I am."

Tyler's heart began racing. "Sarah?" He tried to turn her face toward him.

She simply pressed it harder against his chest.

"Sarah?" he said again. "Are you telling me you're pregnant?"

She nodded.

"But that's wonderful! That's the most wonderful news in the world!"

"It is?" she said, daring to look at him.

"Of course it is. But why on earth was it hard to tell me? You didn't think I might not want a baby, did you?"

She nodded once more. "Tyler, it's going to mean our life won't be anywhere near *exactly* the way it is. All kinds of things will change."

"Oh, Sarah," he murmured, hugging her close, "a baby will make things even better. And I'll bet I was wrong about not being able to improve on perfection. And you know what else I'll bet?"

"What?" she whispered, giving him an adorable smile.

"I'll bet improving on perfection is exactly what you and I are going to do. For the rest of our life."

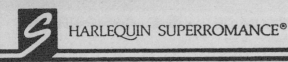

HARLEQUIN SUPERROMANCE®

HARLEQUIN SUPERROMANCE WANTS TO INTRODUCE YOU TO A DARING NEW CONCEPT IN ROMANCE...

WOMEN WHO DARE!
Bright, bold, beautiful...
Brave and caring, strong and passionate...
They're women who know their own minds
and will dare anything...for love!

One title per month in 1993, written by popular Superromance authors, will highlight our special heroines as they face unusual, challenging and sometimes dangerous situations.

**The lady doctor and the sheriff are
heading for a showdown in
#574 DOC WYOMING by Sharon Brondos**

Available in December wherever Harlequin Superromance novels are sold.

If you missed any of the Women Who Dare titles and would like to order them, send your name, address, zip or postal code, along with a check or money order for $3.39 for #533, #537, #541, #545 and #549, or $3.50 for #553, #554, #558, #562, #566 and #570, for each book ordered, plus 75¢ ($1.00 in Canada) for postage and handling, payable to Harlequin Reader Service, to:

In the U.S.	In Canada
3010 Walden Ave.	P. O. Box 613
P. O. Box 9047	Fort Erie, Ontario
Buffalo, NY 14269-9047	L2A 5X3

Please specify book title(s) with order.
Canadian residents add applicable federal and provincial taxes.

WWD-DR

When the only time you have for yourself is...

Christmas is such a busy time—with shopping, decorating, writing
cards, trimming trees, wrapping gifts....

When you do have a few *stolen moments* to call your own, treat yourself
to a brand-new *short* novel. Relax with one of our Stocking Stuffers—
or with all six!

Each STOLEN MOMENTS title
is a complete and original contemporary romance that's the perfect
length for the busy woman of the nineties! Especially at Christmas...

And they make perfect **stocking stuffers**, too! (For your mother,
grandmother, daughters, friends, co-workers, neighbors, aunts,
cousins—all the other women in your life!)

Look for the STOLEN MOMENTS display in December

STOCKING STUFFERS:

HIS MISTRESS Carrie Alexander
DANIEL'S DECEPTION Marie DeWitt
SNOW ANGEL Isolde Evans
THE FAMILY MAN Danielle Kelly
THE LONE WOLF Ellen Rogers
MONTANA CHRISTMAS Lynn Russell

HSM2

 **WORLDWIDE LIBRARY**

HARLEQUIN®
INTRIGUE®

The mystique of mummies and Egyptian jewels comes to life in Dawn Stewardson's Harlequin Intrigue duet:

You're in for a surprise when an ancient sarcophagus is opened—and the occupant is *not* a centuries-old mummy but a murdered young woman.

Don't miss these Intrigues:

THE MUMMY CASE
January 1994

&

THE MUMMY BEADS
February 1994

Relive the romance...
Harlequin and Silhouette
are proud to present

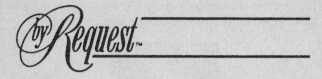

by Request™

A program of collections of three complete novels by the most-requested
authors with the most-requested themes. Be sure to look for one volume each
month with three complete novels by top-name authors.

In September: **BAD BOYS**   Dixie Browning
                                      Ann Major
                                      Ginna Gray

No heart is safe when these hot-blooded hunks are in town!

In October: **DREAMSCAPE**   Jayne Ann Krentz
                                      Anne Stuart
                                      Bobby Hutchinson

Something's happening! But is it love or magic?

In December: **SOLUTION: MARRIAGE**   Debbie Macomber
                                      Annette Broadrick
                                      Heather Graham Pozzessere

Marriages in name only have a way of leading to love....

Available at your favorite retail outlet.

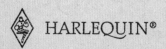 HARLEQUIN®   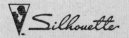 *Silhouette*

1993 Keepsake

Stories

Capture the spirit and romance of Christmas with KEEPSAKE CHRISTMAS STORIES, a collection of three stories by favorite historical authors. The perfect Christmas gift!

Don't miss these heartwarming stories, available in November wherever Harlequin books are sold:

ONCE UPON A CHRISTMAS by Curtiss Ann Matlock
A FAIRYTALE SEASON by Marianne Willman
TIDINGS OF JOY by Victoria Pade

ADD A TOUCH OF ROMANCE TO YOUR HOLIDAY SEASON WITH KEEPSAKE CHRISTMAS STORIES!

HX93

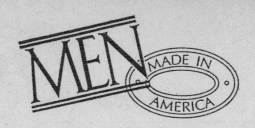

MEN *MADE IN AMERICA*

Fifty red-blooded, white-hot, true-blue hunks
from every State in the Union!

Look for MEN MADE IN AMERICA! Written by some
of our most poplar authors, these stories feature fifty of
the strongest, sexiest men, each from a different state in
the union!

Two titles available every other month at your favorite
retail outlet.

In November, look for:

STRAIGHT FROM THE HEART by Barbara Delinsky
(Connecticut)
AUTHOR'S CHOICE by Elizabeth August (Delaware)

In January, look for:

DREAM COME TRUE by Ann Major (Florida)
WAY OF THE WILLOW by Linda Shaw (Georgia)

You won't be able to resist MEN MADE IN AMERICA!